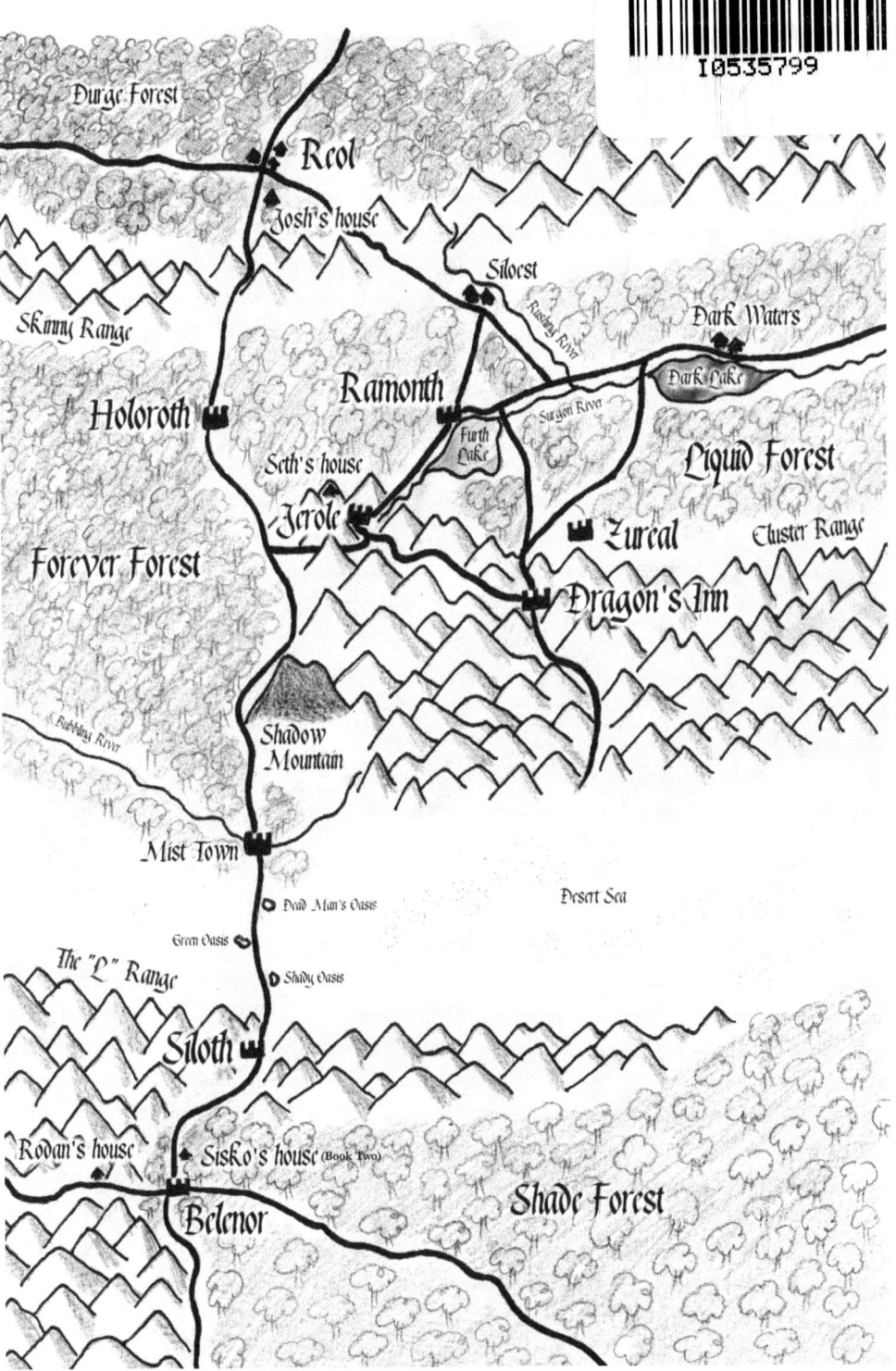

Durge Forest

Reol

Josh's house

Siloest

Skinny Range

Dark Waters

Rushing River

Dark Lake

Ramonth

Holoroth

Liquid Forest

Furth Lake

Sturgon River

Seth's house

Jerole

Zureal

Cluster Range

Forever Forest

Dragon's Inn

Bubbling River

Shadow Mountain

Mist Town

Dead Man's Oasis

Desert Sea

Green Oasis

The "L" Range

Shady Oasis

Siloth

Rodan's house

Sisko's house (Book Two)

Shade Forest

Belenor

Reality's Dawn

R. L. COPPLE

ISBN: 978-0-9864517-7-5
Splashdown Books, New Zealand
http://www.splashdownbooks.com

Acknowledgments

These stories started with a simple challenge at an on-line critique group I frequent: Notebored (www.notebored.com). From that "duel," as they called them, I wrote the first story, then called "Steamy Realities," in response to the trigger: hot. Subsequently, a contest at The Sword Review (www.theswordreview.com) started me thinking of sequels, and the next thing you know, I'd written a series. After some rewrites, the series was picked up by The Sword Review to run at the end of 2007 and published into the book *Infinite Realities* by Double-Edged Publishing. Without the inspiration and guidance from the people at these places, this book would never have become a reality. I also greatly appreciate the many suggestions and proofing done by several, notably Selena Thompson, Bill Snodgrass, the whole Notebored community, The Sword Review editorial staff, and probably some I'm not even aware of.

Naturally, my first critique group is my wife and kids. They not only put up with reading my work, but also often give constructive feedback about what is and isn't working. My thirteen-year-old son, Jeremy, gets special kudos for catching a plot hole that none of the other numerous reviewers caught. Without their support, help, and letting me sit in my room writing, this would not have been possible.

And last, but not least, I would like to thank God from whom all good stories flow, and hope this in some small way glorifies God's work and mercy in our lives. May we acknowledge God's realities.

Reality's Dawn Acknowledgments

One of the most frequent things people mentioned concerning the original publication, *Infinite Realities*, is the novella size of the book. Everyone wanted more. And after that book went out, I always had it in the back of my mind to return to it and fill in the holes with additional short stories. In this new volume, *Reality's Dawn*, I have done just that. The original book contained five short stories. This one adds ten more for a total of fifteen stories about Sisko, his friends, and his travels.

The fun of doing this was two-fold. One, I had the chance to feature characters that didn't get as much page time in the original volume so the reader can get to know them better, like Sisko's best friend, Josh. And new characters are introduced as well.

Two, it gave me the chance to fill in some back-story on characters that come into play in the later novels. So in this volume the reader discovers how Joel, a key figure in *Reality's Ascent* (previously *Transforming Realities*), became involved with Sisko's family.

Thanks goes to Sherry Thompson for doing the initial critique of the new stories, and Grace Bridges and critiquers from Splashdown Books for suggestions and edits that have helped it to shine. And thanks goes to God for whatever benefit and enjoyment the reader finds in these pages.

R. L. Copple
January 24, 2011

Reality's Dawn

Prologue

"Are you Sisko?"

Sisko turned toward the voice. A white-haired man leaned forward in his saddle. Sisko laid down the sanding pad next to the wooden table he'd worked on with the help of his two teenage children, Kaylee and Nathan.

Sisko nodded. "I go by that name, yes. And yours?"

Kaylee brushed the sawdust off her hands against the rough britches she wore. She pushed her golden hair back as she slid nearer to her sword propped against a tree stump.

Nathan stopped his polishing but remained squatted on the ground. His blue-green eyes stared at the man on the horse while sweat dripped from sandy hair.

The man rubbed his chin. "I understand you can do miracles with a ring of yours. I have need of such a ring."

Sisko sighed. He'd thought the stream of miracle seekers had ended.

"If you wish, I'll pray. What is the need?"

Sisko felt a pulling at his ring. He flexed his fingers, but a magical force pulled his hand up. Sisko gritted his teeth as the ring, stuck firmly to his finger, threatened to pull the digit from his limb.

Nathan flung a rock as he leapt to his feet. The rock smashed into the man's fingers cupped toward Sisko, resting against the neck of the horse.

The wizard grimaced and shook his hand. He clenched his teeth and thrust forth his other hand at Nathan. Sisko leaped between the two; a ball of fire raced from the wizard's fingertips and planted itself into Sisko's gut. Sisko slammed against the ground and rolled a couple of feet backwards. Pain vibrated through his body, erupting into a scream.

Kaylee pulled her sword and dashed after the intruder. He cursed and jabbed his heels into the horse's sides. In response, the beast lurched forward and quickly accelerated to a gallop, kicking up a cloud of dust. Horse and rider rounded a corner and disappeared behind a cluster of trees.

Nathan knelt beside Sisko. "What can I do?"

Sisko sucked in a deep breath before pushing himself upright. "Nothing. I just had the air knocked out of me."

Kaylee shook her head as she sheathed her sword. "Come on, Dad. That fireball should have done more damage. Why, you're not scorched at all."

Sisko smiled. "Comes from living right." *And God's protection through the ring.* "Why don't we finish for today? The sun is getting low and your mother will return from town soon. Let's rest a bit, clean up, and be ready to help her with supper."

They nodded and helped Sisko to his feet, then filed into the house. The main room contained a fireplace, a table with chairs, and an indented space where cabinets and a countertop propped up dirty dishes. Darkly stained walls surrounded them.

Sisko slid into a chair; his aching body thanked him with a wave of relief.

Nathan held up a pot of hot water. "Tea?"

"Please."

Kaylee shuffled papers on a desk. "Don't forget me." She extracted some leaves of paper and a quill pen from the mess, then sat at the table with Sisko. She dipped the quill into the inkwell. "Dad, tell me all your stories about the ring from the time you were first given it."

Sisko raised an eyebrow. "Why?"

She frowned. "I want to preserve them. What if you'd been killed today? Nathan and I would recall bits and pieces, but we'd forget too much."

Nathan slapped Sisko on the back. "Yes, I agree. Tell us the stories as best as you can recall. They make good bedtime adventures."

Sisko glanced from one face to the other. He shrugged. "Sure, why not?"

Kaylee smiled. "Good. I'll take notes."

Nathan set cups of hot tea on the table, pulled up a chair, and leaned on his elbows.

Sisko closed his eyes. "In Reol, where I grew up, there stood a very unique steam house…"

Reality's Advent

"Sir?" I looked up at the muscular man entering the steam house. "I don't think you want to go in there. Why don't you use one of the other steam houses in town?"

"What? Am I not good enough for your steam house? And who's gonna stop me? You?"

"Whatever. Don't say I didn't warn you."

He slung a towel over his shoulder, another already securely wrapped around his chiseled waist. He stared at me for a brief moment, as if deciding whether he should waste his time on me. He turned and walked into the wood frame building. A cloud of steam puffed from the doorway into the freezing air; the solid oak door slammed shut behind him.

The pungent smell of pride wafted in his wake. I'd seen his kind often. He wouldn't like the results.

The steam house had developed a reputation as a house of miracles. The sign over the door read, "Steamy Realities Steam House: Sweats out both body and soul. Warning: Only the pure of soul should enter. We are not liable for negative results." Despite that warning, most believed purity flowed from their soul and expected a miracle. They would enter anyway, often leaving with the opposite results.

The church and villagers of Reol viewed the steam house differently: as a rite of passage to adulthood. Young ones both longed for and feared entering the steam house. Everyone took it seriously, everyone except for those not familiar with the steam house's attempts to reveal and correct flaws of the soul.

My father said since I was fourteen, my time had arrived. I had prayed and prepared at the temple. Was I ready? I hoped so, but to tell the truth, I wasn't sure what I would find. I hadn't discovered my place in life, so if this steam revealed anything to me, so much the better. My only fear was in what it would reveal. Would I like it?

My own skinny waist wrapped in a towel, I glanced back at my family standing by a store entrance across the dirt road. My younger brother Jake waved and smiled, standing on his one leg and crutches. Father had talked about someday getting him a fake leg, so he could walk. We all knew our poverty prevented such a dream coming true. Not unless God performed a miracle.

I opened the door and paused on the edge, both fear and excitement holding me in place. I forced myself to take the step inside.

In contrast to the freezing weather outside, the heat hit me in the face. I took deep breaths, but a few moments passed before I adjusted to the hot, moist air. Wooden benches lined the octagonal interior. In the center of the dirt floor, a roaring fire beneath a mound of volcanic rocks heated the air. Fresh steam rose like a cloud; apparently someone had just poured water on the rocks. I moved to an empty spot next to a rather chubby man.

He, also adjusting, breathed hard and purposefully. He looked over at me. "Hi, boy." He paused to catch another breath. "My name's George." He didn't bother to shake hands.

"I'm Sisko," I responded. "You don't look like you're from here. Traveling through?"

"Yes, indeed I am." He relaxed and then stretched as if he lay on a sunny beach. "Right nice steam house you have here. I'm feeling more energy than I've felt in a long time." He had already adjusted to the heated air.

I smiled but said nothing. I could already see his body losing weight and shifting to muscle. He would be happy with his stay here, unless something worse hid inside. You never really knew. People hide lots of stuff where they think no one can see. The steam and heat had a way of bubbling that to the surface and dealing with it.

Yet, while in the steam house, people couldn't see the reality they transformed into, not until they exited the building. Others could see, but they themselves could not.

I scanned the room and spotted the muscular man I had met at the entrance. Already, his body displayed less muscle. If he stayed much longer, he wouldn't be able to lift twenty pounds. He lay back, eyes shut, half asleep as the steam heated his pores and soul.

4

Just four feet down the bench sat an odd man. In addition to his towel, he wore lots of jewelry: necklaces, rings, bracelets. As he chatted with the man next to him, he swung his arms in big gestures, the ornaments ringing with every jerk. I shook my head. This steam bath would likely cost him a lot.

Farther down the bench, a man held a steam-soaked book. He sat immersed in another world, oblivious to his surroundings. I saw in him what my father and priest had warned me about: depression. Shadows grew long over his face, as they do when the sun sets. The longer the shadows stretched, the more he focused on his book.

I moved over to him. He needed help. "Sir, do you mind telling me what you're reading?" People liked to display their knowledge.

He stared over his book at me. His eyes widened. Surprised, it seemed, that anyone would talk to him. Then his eyes narrowed, and he said with irritation in his voice, "Paradise Lost."

"Oh, I've read that. It gets better toward the end."

His eyes froze in place; one eye opened a little wider than the other. "I've never been able to get very far. Once paradise is lost, the story's over."

"Not really."

"Yes, it is!"

I jumped back, surprised by the force.

He continued, "You're all alone, no help, you're doomed. Might as well give up." He looked back into his book as if to say, "Go away."

I thought about trying again. He needed help, but the shadows grew longer. Soon he would exist as darkness. Depression sucked out every joy and ounce of life. Not a pretty sight. He had sunk too far; I couldn't help him.

Sweat freely poured down my face. One man arose and poured more water on heated rocks. Fresh steam sizzled and rose like a cloud seeking souls to squeeze.

One man walked out the door. I noticed the jackass tail that had formed on his backside. I heard him release a series of cries, receding as he ran away, his hooves clopping on the dirt street. Though he probably deserved it, I felt sorry for him.

I spotted three men conversing in a corner. I decided to listen while I waited, so I walked over. I wished I hadn't.

A man with a mustache exposed his sexual exploits to the other two. A real Don Juan, based on his stories. While he certainly exaggerated, I

5

believe he told some truth. Already his feet had turned into roots. His listeners also stared as his skin transformed into a more bark-like substance.

"Sir," I broke in, "you might want to leave now. If you take root here, it could damage the steam house."

The man looked at me with a smirk; his mustache bristled. "Boy, what are you talking about? Taking root?"

One of the men said, "Yes, he's right. You're turning into a tree. I would get out while you're not totally changed." They backed away.

"I don't see anything?" the man said, staring at his body. No one said anything. He looked back at our shocked expressions and then ran out the door, leaving a trail of leaves in his path. He gasped as he left the building, and then a cry of anguish rolled down the street. It would get worse. If he stood in one place for too long, he would take root. I hoped he wouldn't take root in a horrible place like a toilet. There would be no more wandering and girls for him. The steam seemed to have a sense of humor sometimes.

One of the other men looked at me. "Boy, am I changing?"

"Not yet."

"I thought one received miracles here?" The other man shook his head.

"Some do, it all depends on the character of your soul. Didn't you read the sign over the door when you entered?"

The two men glanced at one another and gathered up their things to leave. The previous man's condition apparently gave them pause concerning the risk they took.

"Of course, if you have a good soul, good things also come to the surface," I added by way of consolation.

Their eyes widened, and then they moved with hurried steps to the door. As they left, my gaze landed on the previously well-built man who now snored away. His massive body, I would guess around three hundred pounds, looked precariously perched on the bench.

Maybe I should wake him? I thought about it for a moment and decided it wouldn't do any good. *Hope he has enough muscle left to walk out the door.* I laughed despite myself, but then I pulled myself up short. Such an attitude could cost a person in this place. I walked over to him. Falling asleep in a steam house risked staying too long. He might not wake up in this life.

"Sir." I shook him until his eyes popped open.

"Oh…" He blinked a few times. "Must have fallen asleep. I don't know why, but I'm feeling heavy and sleepy."

"To be honest, Sir, you do have a great weight."

"Yeah, I know! With muscles like these…" He lifted an arm and arched it to pop up his muscle. "I've worked many hours to get my body into this shape."

Instead, I saw three inches of dangling skin wobbling under his arm. "No, not like a wonderful weight, but like a whole lot of weight."

He looked at me with a smile, "Sure, kid." He tried to get up, but fell back. He strained to rise a couple more times without success. Finally he said, "Uh, this is embarrassing, but it seems this steam has drained my energy. Could you help me up, kid?"

I gave him my hand. With a grunt, I helped leverage him to his feet.

He grabbed his towel, which had loosened with the widening of his girth. "I need to get out of here. I think this steam is causing an adverse reaction."

I nodded. Hopefully we could get him out the door before he hit four hundred pounds. He took each step in plodding fashion, pausing to work up the energy for the next step and to keep his balance. He eventually lumbered out the door.

For a while, I heard nothing. Then, a soft and solemn cry floated into the building. No doubt one of the few times the proud man had shed tears in his life.

I checked back with the jewelry man. He now wore necklaces, rings and bracelets crafted of flowers, moving soundlessly as he continued to wave his arms back and forth. His listener appeared more attentive to his flower-laden wrist than to what he said. If the steam held true, it could also mean much of his wealth had turned to grass and flowers. Here today, gone tomorrow.

"Sisko, wasn't it?" A man stood beside me. He appeared ready to leave. "This was great, I'll have to visit more often when I come through."

Then I recognized him. "George?" The overweight man I first met, yet now he sported a muscle set any bodybuilder would be proud of.

"Ah, good! Not everyone has a knack for remembering names. Thanks." He shook my hand with gusto. Then he skipped out the door. I soon heard a "Wow!" and a loud laugh with a few shouts of joy.

I delayed leaving, though I had stayed long enough. I feared to go out. What would I find? Would I finally learn my direction in life, or would I be horrified? I stared at the door, gathering the courage to walk through it. I knew my family would be outside, eager to discover how I'd fared.

There was no reason to put it off. Whatever the steam house had done to me, I'd have to deal with it for the rest of my life. Staying longer would only worsen a bad reality.

I arose and with gathering determination stepped to the door. I opened it and paused at the threshold. I could see my family waiting. *They don't seem to be reacting yet. Maybe I'm okay.*

"Hey kid, shut the door. You're letting out the heat!" someone said from inside.

I stepped out. The cold wind, reacting to the steam rolling off my body, tingled my skin. I examined myself. I looked normal enough, though older, like I'd aged. A good sign, meant I harbored a mature heart. But what else? Surely there must be more.

"My, you've grown in there, Sisko." Mother held me in her arms and then squeezed me in a hug. My father patted me on the back. He seemed satisfied nothing horrible had revealed itself, but I expected more.

While Mother hugged me, and my hand lay on her shoulder, I noticed what had changed. On the third finger of my left hand, a ring of solid gold glimmered in the sunlight. Intricate engravings of an ancient language decorated its otherwise plain surface.

"Am I married?" I pulled away from Mother and displayed the ring on my finger. I tried pulling it off, but it wouldn't budge.

A voice behind me spoke, "Yes you are, but not as you are thinking."

I spun around. The priest stood smiling at me. I lifted the ring on my hand for his inspection.

He continued as he examined it, "Not married to a woman, but to God's service."

"I've not heard of this order, Father. What service is this?"

He moved his eyes to meet mine without turning his head. "The steam revealed you have a heart for helping people. So He gave you the means to do so in greater ways." The priest straightened. "The inscription God wrote in Hebrew says, 'It is more blessed to give than to receive.' If you use the ring to help others, it will be a blessing to you. But if you use it for your own benefit, it will be a curse. So don't use it without careful thought, or you will wish you had never been in the steam house."

I held my hand at eye level in wonder. "How do I use it?"

"Through your prayers. It isn't so much a magic ring in itself as it is a reminder of the commitment between you and God. He will give you whatever you need to help someone. Sort of like Samson's hair gave him

8

strength."

"Me? Like Samson?" I stared at the ring. A weight settled over my heart. What if I misused it like Samson? What if I failed to be a keeper? I sucked in a big breath and let it out slowly.

"Thank you, Father." I turned to my brother Jake and lifted him into my chest. "You won't need those crutches any more." I placed him down on two solid feet.

He smiled, then laughed and ran along the dusty street. Mother and Father stood wide-eyed and mouths open, but joy etched their faces.

I discovered my purpose for existing after all. I didn't find it in the steam house; it already existed inside me. I simply couldn't see the truth until the steam revealed it. The reality each of us should know: we are one another's keeper.

Desire's Trap

There she stood at the edge of the forest. A cute girl, about four years old, grinned at me and then dashed back into the woods. I didn't recognize her but couldn't imagine anyone in the village who would let a young one play in the forest alone. She didn't realize the danger she flirted with. I sped after her.

Underbrush gave way as I pushed into clearing after clearing. I would catch a glimpse of her and race to catch her. Yet I couldn't seem to gain on her. How she could outrun a fifteen-year-old boy, I had no idea. But I couldn't leave her out here.

I stumbled into a large clearing and paused on the edge of it, trying to catch my breath. I scanned the area for a sign of where she had gone. She jumped out from the opposite side of the meadow, giggled, and flew back into the forest. I sighed and pumped my legs after her.

One third of the way across, the ground moved under me. I swayed against the sudden, sideways movement. I turned to go back. The earth bucked, yet I stayed on my feet and wobbled forward. The edge of the dirt whirlpool drew near. I would make it.

The ground dropped into a spinning cone. I crashed upon the vortex and slid toward the bottom. I glanced behind me. The churning funnel dragged me toward a black hole at its base.

I clawed at the dirt, but the more desperate my attempts to climb out, the faster I careened toward the hole. I drove my fingers into the hungry ground, hoping to at least stay my descent, but to no avail. The gold ring on my left hand, resting over the dirt, sparkled in the sunlight.

As I gazed up toward the receding trees, there stood the little, cute girl. Then she changed. A chill flowed down my body. The girl morphed into my best friend, Josh. A thin smile creased his lips. This had been a trap; he had intentionally done this. But how and why? No answers came as the black hole swallowed me into its darkness.

I fell for I don't know how long. Pitch blackness surrounded me. No sense of space or time penetrated this void, only a sense of doom and hopelessness. After an eternity, I floated to a stop upon a cold, stone floor. My arms shook as I felt around and discovered four walls of rough stone enclosing me in a cell. I could find no door. My voice echoed when I cried out. An ever so slight smell of sulfur hung in the air. Utter nothingness seeped into my pores.

Then I heard a scream. Very faint at first, but growing in volume until I realized someone had fallen into my cell. He seemed to calm down once he landed, but grumbled under his breath.

"Josh, is that you?"

He sighed. "Yes." His tone rang with bitterness.

"Let me guess, you fell in."

"Yes, I slipped. Are you happy?"

"No, but how and why did you do this?"

"It's your accursed ring, Sisko. Why you and not me? Why didn't the steam house grant me such a power as you possess?"

"What have you done, Josh? How did you do this?"

"Since the steam house had not granted me the same power, I decided to take it myself. I've been under the instruction of an old wizard in the forest. I've learned magic, and now I have power." He snickered. "The power to lock you in this cell forever, in the netherworld."

Time spent together over the past year had drifted to darker topics since he had entered the steam house. Often the ring entered these discussions. "You may not have left the steam house with a physical difference, my friend, but with a curse nonetheless. Self-delusion."

"Sure, condemn me to the pit of hell with all your righteousness. Why do you think I've gone to all this trouble? Because you acted like a god, dispensing miracles at merely a prayer. Everyone loves and praises you."

"No, not everyone. Having such a gift means having few friends. I had hoped you could be one, but I guess my own pride kept me from seeing your resentment. Yet, you're deluded on one point."

"Oh? What sin do you convict me of, Almighty Sisko?"

"I don't control this power. I ask and He grants. And truth be told, it is the same for the wizard and you, whether you acknowledge it or not."

"Right! That's why you're here, eh? No, I accomplished this, without a fancy ring!" He laughed, as if finding delight in my predicament.

A light cracked through the darkness, and a glow emanated around us. As it faded, details of benches and people formed into view. Heat blasted upon my skin, and humidity drenched my forehead. Steam billowing from hot rocks sharpened into focus. The people in the steam house reacted to our appearance, but turned back to their discussions. Odd things happened in here all the time.

I glanced at Josh. He screamed, and as he did, his face contorted into a hideous half-bulldog, half-goat beast. A growl erupted from his snout.

I jumped back. "Josh, get out now!"

He fled to the door. I followed. Miracle or no miracle, he needed a friend. Josh raced out of the steam house and down the dirt road of the village. I followed him.

"Josh, wait!"

I caught up to him as he squatted by the edge of the pond, weeping and growling at the same time. His jowls hung loose and low, his nose sat on the end of a short snout, and horns protruded from his head.

He swung his eyes around and stared at me. "See what you've done!"

"This isn't my doing. You know that, but I can help."

"Help! This is the help I've received so far from you. No, there's only one who's helped me. Maybe he can fix me."

Josh leaped into the air and dashed to the forest toward the wizard's house.

"Here we go again." I raced after him.

The old wizard kept to himself, and few bothered him. I had not seen the man before, at least that I knew. But conversations I had heard spoke of him as evil. People always left his house in a worse state than when they entered. If Josh had been with him for a year, no wonder he had turned so bad.

My parents had warned me to stay away from the wizard and his house. Their warnings echoed in my mind as I hurried through the forest. But my concern for my best friend shoved those aside. Yet, I knew if it came down to doing battle with the wizard, I could not fight. Not to save myself with a miracle from the ring. Some would consider that a handicap, but so far it had turned out for the good. So far. Maybe this would be the exception.

Josh had outrun me, but in his haste he left a clear trail to follow. He definitely sought out the wizard. His path led straight to where the house should be. Though the sun set low in the sky, I continued through the brush until a large cabin revealed itself in a clearing among the trees.

The house appeared black, even against the dusk sky. The windows displayed curtains backlit by an eerie, orange glow. A chimney shot clouds of smoke into the gray clouds hovering over us. Drizzle peppered my face as I moved forward into the clearing.

I drew close to a window and stared in. Before I could take in the sight, I heard a growl behind me.

"Josh?" I turned. Two wolves bared their teeth at me. I didn't dare move.

A light appeared in the center of the clearing and a man materialized before me. He wore white robes that matched his white beard. But oddly, his eyebrows grew as black as his house.

"Sisko, the miracle worker. I've been expecting you." He hovered in my direction.

Expecting me? Had Josh been bait? No doubt Josh had told him of our friendship. I heard the door to the house open, and saw Josh exit.

"Josh, whatever this wizard has done to enchant you, resist it. We can work through this."

A laugh that chilled my bones echoed from the wizard.

"Enchant? Me? No, I merely give people what they want. Any enchanting comes from themselves." He waved the wolves away and moved to my face. "What is it you want, Sisko?" A smile curled on the ends of his lips.

My legs shook. I took a deep breath to steady myself. "I want to free Josh from his curse."

"He's cursed himself." He stroked his beard as he stared at the house. "However, there is a way."

"What way is that?" I didn't trust him, but if this wizard held him, it would be through him that Josh would be released.

His eyes grew weary, and his smile faded. "Through the Ball of Desires. If you can survive it, and he with you, he will be released from his curse."

"The Ball of Desires? You mean it's real?" I had heard stories, but that's all I thought they were.

"Oh yes, real. Very real indeed, and it sits on my table."

"But I don't need your magic. God's given me the gift to do miracles.

I can save him."

His smile returned and he chuckled. "Ah yes, the ring. Why don't you try then?"

Now I felt on solid ground. This battle I knew I could win. "Just watch." I approached Josh. He had said nothing, as if in a trance.

I placed my hand upon his head. "Father, return Josh to his former appearance."

Crickets chirped. Josh stood there, motionless, staring off into the night sky. No change occurred as his snout breathed out a puff of smoke in the cool night air. Why didn't this work? I knew it would. Could it be an illusion of some kind?

The wizard drew near and placed his hand on my shoulder. His touch felt icy, and shivers sank into my body. I pulled away.

"You're forgetting, my boy, his own desires brought out this physical change in the steam house. The outside will not change without changing him."

The wizard did make sense. Or had he already bewitched me as well? I stared into his deep-set eyes covered in black eyebrows.

The wizard continued, "He must desire to change. You can help him only by changing his mind in the Ball of Desires." He opened the door and waved a hand inside.

I had no choice if I wanted to help Josh. I had to risk facing my own desires. I stepped inside and approached the table. Josh followed me like the walking dead.

The wizard sat at the table and pulled a cloth off what appeared to be a crystal ball. Little mountains and valleys, lakes and meadows could be seen inside it. He held his hand over it and mumbled a spell, and the glass radiated a bright light.

His eyes locked onto mine. His lips curled into an exaggerated smile. "You're a fool, Sisko. No one comes out of the Ball of Desires unscathed. How do you think Josh became as he is?"

He laughed, and then yelled, "Enter in!"

The ball flashed beams of light around us. Brightness blinded me. Once it dimmed, I stood inside the ball. I gazed up to see the giant eyes of the wizard, distorted by the sphere, staring down upon us.

Josh stood next to me, but he no longer had the form of the beast. He had returned to his sandy-haired self.

"Sisko, what are we doing here?"

"Don't you recall anything?"

"Like a dream." He rubbed his eyes as if waking. "No, more like a nightmare."

"It's a living nightmare that I'm trying to save you from."

"Save me? But don't you realize? The Ball of Desires is what sent me into that nightmare. You've brought me back to relive it all over again."

I scanned the area. It appeared as if we stood in any valley on the outside, except the giant wizard watching over us with glee filled the sky. "You're back to normal, nothing has happened to me. I don't see a problem. This Ball of Desires isn't what it's cracked up to be."

I laughed. "Get it? Cracked up?" The laughs grew stronger. "I can't believe I'm so funny!" I sat on the ground, laughing so hard I teared up.

"Stop laughing!" Josh's face grew red.

His tomato face appeared so comical; my laughter grew stronger. "Watch out, you're going to pop!" Now heaves left my throat. I could hardly breathe in. I would soon suffocate with laughter.

His fist fell across my face, and a biting sting broke me out of the desire for humor. Instead, anger filled the void.

I leaped to my feet and swung my fist across Josh's face. Blood dripped from his nose as he staggered back. He screamed and threw himself upon me, knocking us both to the ground. We rolled and hit upon each other until welts covered us. Blood reddened our faces.

Josh pinned me down. "Sisko, we have to stop before we kill each other. This is what the Ball of Desires does. It takes what you want and magnifies it at any given moment until it becomes a single-minded desire."

"But God protects me. I won't fall into this wizard's trap. I can save you." I pushed him aside and stood.

"No, Sisko. It's happening to you. Like it did to me. I admit, when I left the steam house, I was disappointed I didn't get a ring like yours, have the power you had. I had hoped, wished we could be partners, spend our days having people beg us for miracles."

Josh shook his head. "See, talking about that is drawing me back into it."

"But I don't have to wish for that, I have it. People do crawl to me with their pleadings for miracles. They know I'm the only one who can give it to them. I alone wield the power to heal them!" I felt it too. The immense energy of God at my fingertips. All I had to do was speak the word, and it would be done.

15

I watched as Josh groveled on the ground before me. "You too, beg for healing. I've come into this Ball of Desires because only I can defeat it. Can you worship me as I should be worshiped? Then maybe I'll grant your request."

Josh curled at my feet as if in pain. "Sisko, listen to yourself. It's taking you."

Something in my words did sound wrong. Yet, they seemed right. Oh, so right. I only fulfilled my destiny, after all. The calling of God to be equal to Him. Surely that's what it meant to be wed to Him. He gave it to me. I simply had to take it and use it as any god would.

I smiled upon Josh. "I've healed you. Now I can go into the world and take my rightful place in it."

"No! Don't leave yet, or this will be your fate. Remember what you told me? You don't have this power, you ask and He grants it."

The words triggered such a memory. I lifted my hand and watched the lights dance across the ring's surface. I must have been deceived when I said that. Certainly I must have.

Or, maybe now I stood deceived?

I gazed into the sky. The wizard's wide eyes and giant grin caused him to appear as a wicked jester. Expectation of my defeat rolled off him like sweat. I wanted out, but not on his terms.

I breathed deep and forced myself to focus. "You're right, Josh. I'm sorry." I lifted him to his feet and laid a hand on his shoulder. "You've saved me instead."

"But how do we get out without getting trapped into some untamed desire?"

I watched above as eyes, widened unnaturally by the globe, blinked from outside.

"That's it. I tried to change the wrong person."

"What?"

"I asked God to change you back, and He didn't. But you're not the key to all this." I craned my neck to the sky and held my hands toward the eyes that now narrowed in confusion.

"Father, bestow upon this wizard a desire for contentment."

The enormous eyes flew open, and his mouth dropped. A vibrating thunder penetrated the globe. We covered our ears as we collapsed to the ground, and the wizard fell backwards. Cracks shot along the glass enclosure, fracturing it into tiny pieces until it reached the top.

16

An explosion ripped the fabric of reality, throwing me into the air. I crashed into pots and pans. We had left the ball and returned to the wizard's house.

My body, bruised and aching, recoiled at the idea of moving, but I pushed myself up anyway. Pans rattled as they fell off me. The Ball of Desires lay in pieces over the table, and fragments had scattered upon the floor. The ball fed off a person's desires. Giving the wizard contentment must have caused a reaction it couldn't handle. No one would be trapped in it again.

But did we come out in good shape? The thought of being equal with God sounded abhorrent to my ears. I couldn't believe I had said that. But the ball magnified what was buried inside. The idea that such an idea lurked deep within scared me. I would have to stay on guard against it.

I located Josh groaning under blankets from a cabinet. I hobbled over and uncovered him. He smiled back. I pulled him up and hugged him.

"Thank you, Sisko," he said. "You did save me."

"No, not I. I only asked."

"But you did ask, and for that I'm eternally grateful."

I couldn't help but smile. "Thanks. But you would have done the same for me if our roles had been reversed."

A weak groan sounded from the other side of the table. I approached the fallen wizard. He stared up at me. A gentle smile rolled over him.

"Sisko, my dear boy. You've freed me from the Ball of Desires."

"You?" I helped him to his feet.

"Yes. I found it in a cave, hidden for good reason. I fell into it and the desire to be the ultimate wizard overtook me. It bound me to its service, to draw others into its snare. Now, I'll be content if I never use magic again." He settled into a chair. He seemed more like a tired, old man now, rather than the menacing wizard he had been just moments before.

"Sir, I understand completely. Believe me." I didn't want to go through that again. Wanting to be the best has its drawbacks when pride motivates the desire.

Josh and I returned to the village. I had one good friend, still. He now understood me more than most. And for that, I was eternally grateful.

I realized that being able to do a miracle isn't what defines you. It's simply a tool in the right hands. Contented hands.

Friendship's Gift

I held out my gift. I hoped Josh would like it.

Josh smiled and lifted the present from my palm, then ripped the wrapping off.

I wished I could have found something prettier than green leaves stitched together, but I had nothing else to wrap it in. I put such thoughts aside. I knew Josh wouldn't mind. Being best friends meant we didn't have to impress each other.

Josh pulled a polished wooden stick out of the wrapping. He smiled. "A wand. Thanks, Sisko."

I nodded. "I carved, sanded, and stained it myself. Should be useful in your wizard training."

Josh waved it around. "I like it. Thanks." He glanced at me and back to his new wand. "Did your ring add anything to it?"

"No, why would it?" The ring I'd received allowed me to do miracles, heal people mostly, help them in general.

"Just wondering." Josh examined the wand close up. "As a matter of fact, this will help me to give you a gift."

I raised an eyebrow. "Josh? What are you thinking?"

He smiled. "That would spoil the surprise." He twirled the wand through the air over his head and mumbled some words.

"Hold on!" I jumped from the porch. I felt a wave of distortion pass over me. Combined with the movement, it caused my stomach to lurch. My front yard vanished and a forest of trees took their place. I stumbled and crashed onto the leaf-covered ground. I rose to my feet, decaying foliage falling from my shirt.

Josh scanned the area as if searching. I followed his eyes to see a house nestled among the trees. Josh pointed at the house. "Does that look familiar?"

I shook my head. "Never seen this place before."

Josh sighed. "I thought I had the transport spell down better."

I frowned. "Where are we?"

Josh stared at the ground. "I don't know."

"But you sent us here."

"I thought I had a better picture of your Uncle Lothem's house."

I slapped my forehead. "So that's why you kept asking me all those questions about my uncle's house."

"Milore said a transport spell worked if you had a clear image of where you needed to transport to."

I leaned against a tree. "So why didn't it work? I think I painted a clear enough picture."

Josh thought for a second. "Milore must have meant I needed to be there. To have a complete visual picture in my mind, I have to experience the place."

"Do me a favor? When you're experimenting with spells, leave me out of it."

Josh hung his head. "Sorry. I only wanted to give you a visit with your uncle for Christmas."

I placed a hand on Josh's shoulder. "You had good intentions. No harm done. Just send us back. You do have a mental image of our village, don't you?"

He smiled. "Of course."

The door to the house swung open and banged against the wall. A young boy flew from it followed by a man wielding an ax chasing after him. "Get back here, you thief!"

My heart leaped within me. I glanced at Josh. "I'm supposed to help someone here."

"Are you serious? Who, that boy?"

I shrugged. "That's the only one I can see in trouble at the moment."

Josh shook his head. "You can't go running between that boy and an ax-wielding man."

I jogged toward them. "Someone has to."

Josh huffed. "And of course it has to be you. Some Christmas present this turned out to be." He ran after me.

19

As I drew closer, the man's features grew clearer. Despite his size, his hunched back, and big warts protruding from his forehead and cheeks, he couldn't run very fast.

The boy, his black, shoulder-length hair flapping behind him, pulled away from the odd man.

"It's an ogre," Josh huffed from behind.

An ogre! I'd never met a live ogre before. The stories I'd heard weren't too flattering either. And this one's face, jaw locked as he chased after the boy, didn't dispel those impressions.

The boy tripped and tumbled to a stop in the grass. The ogre caught up with him and held the ax over his head. "Give it back!"

I drew close enough to attract their attention. They both watched as Josh and I slowed to a stop before them.

The ogre growled. "Stay out. This is none of your business."

I stepped beside the boy. "When I see bullies chasing someone with an ax, it becomes my business."

The ogre pointed at the boy. "He stole from me. I have a right to get it back."

The boy shook his head. "He wants to eat me."

The ogre laughed. "I don't want to eat him."

Josh cleared his throat. "I heard ogres like to eat people."

The ogre shrugged. "Some do." He raised his ax higher. "I don't have to explain myself to you two. Step aside. I have no reason to cut you down, but I will if I have to."

I stared into the eyes of the ogre. "Sorry. You'll have to kill me first."

Josh's eyes widened. "Sisko, what are you doing?"

The ogre nodded. "He's right. Why would you want to die for someone you don't know? Why protect a criminal?"

"Because he's worth as much in God's eyes as you or me. All I know is you're chasing him with an ax."

The ogre sighed. "Have it your way." He pulled the ax back.

Josh flipped his wand out and said some words. Mud flew from the ground and splattered over the ogre's eyes. The ogre dropped the ax and then wiped his eyes. "You idiots!"

The young boy leaped to his feet and fled into the forest.

Josh motioned for us to leave. "You've done your helping thing, now let's go."

I checked my heart. "No, I'm not done here."

Josh groaned. "Why not?" He watched as the ogre splashed water over his eyes from a basin by the side of the house.

"All I know is I still haven't helped the one I'm here for. The boy must not have been it."

Josh stared at the sky. "I would at least recommend we go to a nearby town to find the one you're supposed to help. I'd rather not still be here when the ogre comes back. He's not likely to be too happy with us."

I ran fingers through my hair. "I feel this ogre is the one I'm supposed to help."

"You can't be serious."

I watched the ogre wiping his face with a cloth. "I'm afraid I am." But what did the ogre need help with? I couldn't imagine. Finding out would be the tough part.

The ogre approached us. "You two! Why did you interfere?"

I glanced at Josh before facing the ogre. "Like I said, it appeared you intended to hurt the boy."

"I wouldn't have hurt him. I only wanted to scare him." The ogre sat on a stump. "He has stolen from me before. It's become a game with them. See who can steal from the fat, slow ogre." He stared into the forest.

Josh glanced toward me, and then back to the ogre. "What did you do to deserve that?"

The ogre jerked his head up and glared at Josh. "Why do you think I deserve it? Because I'm an ogre!"

Josh stared at the ground. "Uh, no, that's not what I meant."

"Of course it's what you meant. Everyone assumes because I'm an ugly and lumbering hulk that I must be mean, dangerous, and deserve every bad treatment." He bared his teeth. "What are you two still doing here anyway? You've done your humiliate-the-ogre bit. Begone and leave me in peace."

I wondered if the poor ogre's problems would be changed if he appeared more handsome, trim, and winsome. I could change that with one prayer and the power of my ring. I reached out a hand, but stopped. No, it didn't feel right. The creature had been created an ogre, and I shouldn't mess with it. But then what should I do with my miracle-producing ring to help this ogre?

Josh met my eyes. He motioned with his head to leave as the ogre suggested.

The ogre stood. "Go away. I've no patience with troublemakers." He stepped toward the house.

Go away? The words resounded in my mind. How lonely must this ogre be? I froze. Ogre. That's all he was to the boy, to those who lived in this area. To even Josh and myself.

I stepped forward. "My name is Sisko, and this is Josh. What's yours?"

The ogre stopped and paused. A few seconds passed; then he turned. "What did you say?"

"I asked, what's your name?"

The ogre's eyes softened and his mouth relaxed. "No one's ever asked me that before." For the first time, a hint of a smile creased his lips. "My name's Xilner. Glad to meet your acquaintance, Sisko and Josh."

I bowed. "The honor is all mine, Xilner."

He sat back on the stump. "So tell me, how come you stayed?"

I grinned. "Because God told me I needed to help you."

"Help me?" He shook his head. "That's a first. No one has ever helped me. Call me names, scream at me, beat on me, steal from me, yes. But help me? No."

An idea popped into my head. I'd likely get in big trouble for this. "Xilner, do you have any plans for Christmas?"

"Plans? What I do every year. Sit in my house, munch on food, and watch the world drift by oblivious to me."

I nodded. "Not this year. This year, I'm inviting you to my house for Christmas."

Josh's mouth fell open. "Your mother isn't going to like this."

I smiled. "Probably not. But I have a feeling Xilner will grow on her pretty quick."

Xilner grinned. "I wouldn't be too much of a problem, would I?"

I waved a hand. "No, no. You're my personal guest."

"And your mother isn't going to like it." Josh glanced at me. "Just sayin'."

I stared into the sky and nodded my head.

Xilner rose and headed toward his house. "I'll get ready. I need to change clothes." He stopped and turned around. "Sisko, thank you."

"For the invite?"

"Well, yes, for the invite. But mostly for treating me as a person." He grinned big before heading back to the house.

"What do you know, Josh. I didn't need to use my ring to fix this one.

He's just lonely. He needs someone to care about him." I slapped Josh on the back. "You gave me the greatest Christmas present ever."

Josh watched me from the corner of his eye. "Really? You're helping him. What are you getting out of it?"

"The satisfaction of being my brother's keeper. And for finding that brother in the most unlikely of beings."

Josh crossed his arms. "Well, glad I could help. I had this planned from the beginning. Just wanted it to be a surprise."

"Right. Now how about getting that transport spell tuned up. And please, please, get a good image in your mind of Reol before you do the spell. I don't want to end up in some strange place for Christmas."

He blew air from his mouth. "No problem. I'm ready." He watched as Xilner stepped through the door, a bundle under his hands. "But I know your mother isn't going to like this."

Josh and I strolled down the street in Reol. Xilner, our newly befriended ogre, followed close on our footsteps. Citizens of the town stared at the ogre as he walked by. One man in a horse drawn cart nearly ran over a child as his eyes followed the bulky creature.

Josh turned down a street. "See you later. Have a good Nativity feast." He smiled at Xilner. "And you too, my friend."

"Thank you." Xilner bowed.

"And Sisko…" Josh drummed his fingers on his jaw. "Good luck with your mother."

I smiled. "Have a great one yourself. I'm sure my mother will be fine, eventually."

Josh turned and proceeded to his own house. I resumed my trek toward my own.

Xilner stepped up beside me. "You sure your mother will be all right with this?"

I sighed. "It'll be a shock to her, I'm sure. But you are my guest, and I think she'll come around. She's a very loving woman."

"Is there anything I can do?"

"Just be your loving self."

Xilner grunted. "An ogre? Loving isn't usually associated with us."

"You'll be fine. Don't worry." I considered the best way to break this to her now that the time had arrived. Ideas floated through my head, but no good ones lingered. We arrived in front of the white fence to my house.

I turned to Xilner. "Stay out here for a moment."

Xilner nodded.

I walked up the steps and entered the house.

"Sisko, is that you?" My mother's voice rang from the kitchen.

"Yes, Mother." I stepped into the room.

"It's about time. I'm busy getting ready for the Nativity service and you're out playing around. Probably with Josh no doubt."

"I wouldn't say playing around. Josh and I were exchanging presents." I sat at the table.

"Oh, well that's nice. What did he get you?"

I rubbed my chin. "Well, ah...a new friend."

She turned from her dough kneading to stare into my eyes. "Josh gave you a friend for Christmas?"

"Yes, and a friend who didn't have anywhere to go for Christmas. I hope it's all right, but I invited him to spend Christmas with us."

She kneaded the dough two more times, slammed her hand into it, and folded it over onto a wooden slab, covering it with a cloth. She wiped her hands as she gazed into my eyes.

"You could have asked me before you invited him."

"Well..." I bit my lip. "That would have been nearly impossible since we were miles away."

She put her hands on her hips. "Miles away? Did Josh do something crazy again?"

I shrugged. "I tried to stop him, but he used a transport spell before I could react. Next thing I know, I'm in another land, who knows where. I met my new friend there. When I found out he would be alone for Christmas, I was sure you would agree I had to invite him."

She stared at the ceiling for a moment before resting her eyes on me. "You have a big heart, son. I can appreciate that. It certainly is in the spirit of Christmas to help those without family. I'll set another place at the table tomorrow and increase the size of the meal."

I jumped from my chair and hugged her. "You're the best." I released her. "He's outside waiting. Would you like to meet him?"

She strolled toward the door. "Of course. Why wouldn't I want to meet your new friend. We can't leave him outside." She reached for the doorknob.

I put a hand on hers. "Hold on, first you should know…"

"Yes?"

I breathed deep. "His name is Xilner."

"You could have told me that when you introduced me." She reached for the knob again.

"Wait!" I pulled her hand back.

"Sisko, do you want me to meet him or not?"

"There's one other thing you should know about him."

She stared at me.

I tried to think of a way to break this gently, but nothing came to mind. This was as gentle as it would get.

"My friend, he's an ogre."

She continued staring at me as if my words failed to register. She appeared frozen, but then she sucked in a breath and let it out slowly.

"Are you sure this is a good idea, son? We're as likely to be eaten by him as to eat with him." She peered out the window and stopped breathing again.

"Mother, he's really nice. If he wanted us for Christmas dinner, he had plenty of opportunity with Josh and me. I doubt I would be here right now."

She shook her head. "I don't know. He's so big."

"He's my friend. I promised him he wouldn't be alone this Christmas. If I need to, I'll spend it with him out of the house."

She pulled away from the window and faced me. "I'd better send your father out to kill another calf."

I smiled. "Thank you, Mother."

She straightened her dress. "Now can we meet him?" She put on a smile and swung the door open. "Xilner! How wonderful to meet you."

The time neared for the Nativity service. Xilner sat on the floor, not finding a chair big enough for his rear. "I've never been to a Nativity service before. What's it like?"

I pulled on a fresh pair of socks. "Very joyful and reverent. Just what you'd expect at the birth of a king."

"You'll have to tell me more about this king sometime."

Screams echoed from the street outside. Then loud, deep voices gruffly arced through the night air.

Xilner's jaw dropped open. "Not now. Not here!"

I leaped up and raced toward the door.

Xilner scrambled to his feet. "Wait, Sisko! Don't go out there."

I swung the door open and stumbled outside. If anything bad was to happen, I couldn't allow it to happen inside the house. I didn't want to put my family in danger.

I gulped as I examined four ogres holding torches in hands. Xilner exited the house and stopped on the porch.

One of the ogres spun his head toward us and saw Xilner. "There you are. We followed your smell from your house."

Xilner clenched his fists. "Can't you allow me this one luxury?"

"We told you not to leave your house. We warned you what would happen if any should help you." He turned to me. "Men, we have our Christmas dinner."

Xilner leaped into the yard beside me. "I will not let you take him."

The ogre threw his head back and laughed. "As if you could do anything to stop me. Have you not learned anything?"

Xilner growled. "I've learned more from this human than I ever have from you."

I whispered toward Xilner. "Is he serious about eating me?"

Xilner nodded. "I did say some ogres do eat people." Xilner met my eyes. "Problem is, he's a wizard too."

I groaned. "Naturally. Why wouldn't an ogre be a wizard? Especially one who wants to eat me."

Xilner stepped toward the group. "Leave us alone."

The ogre grinned. "Good idea. Why don't you leave us alone!" He cast his hand out and mumbled some words. A bluish light emanated from his hand and enveloped Xilner. Xilner froze, grew bright, then dimmed until he disappeared.

I felt my gut wrench. "Where did you send him?"

"Back where he belongs. Alone, in his house."

I stepped toward them. "What gives you the right! He's my friend."

"Not anymore. You're our dinner." He spoke more words I couldn't hear and flung his hand out. Bands of silver whipped themselves around my body, immobilizing me. I fell onto the ground with a thud.

The world dimmed. I fought against it, but the spell pressed in upon me, overran my thoughts, numbed my fingers and toes, and then darkness rolled over me, drowning me in frightening thoughts and dreams.

I heard gruff voices and felt rocks jabbing me in the back. I cracked my eyes open and attempted to wiggle into a more comfortable position. Trees lined a clearing. In the center of the clearing, a cast iron pot sat on a fire, filled with a bubbling liquid. Several ogres sat on logs around the fire, some in conversation, some napping.

I found the moon in the night sky. The Nativity service would be in progress now, and my mother would be worried sick. Probably blame Xilner for carrying me away, never to be heard from again.

A foot jabbed me in the back. I rolled over.

An ogre knelt beside me. "You're a bit scrawny, but the bones are the tastiest part anyway. I think we're about ready to chop you up and add you to the soup. Any last words before you provide us with enjoyment?"

I thought about the character-revealing properties of the steam house. "Yes. If I get a last request, I would that you cook me in the main steam house in Reol."

The ogre laughed and shook his head. "You think ogres are dumb, don't you. You think we don't know about your steam house? When's the last time you saw an ogre enter there?"

I sighed. I knew it was a long shot. "Never."

"Exactly. And for good reason. We know what would happen to us in there. Now, do you have any last words at all? Any message you want us to convey to your parents?"

I didn't want these creatures going anywhere near my family. "No, but we have some calves you can have for your dinner. No need to eat me."

The ogre grinned. "We eat cattle all the time. Humans, on the other hand, are a delicacy. Only for special occasions, like Christmas."

I shook my head. "How can you celebrate a birth with a death?"

The ogre drew out a long knife. "Who says we're celebrating a birth?

Christmas for an ogre only means two things. Giving gifts and eating good. You're the eating good part." He turned to the ogre manning the pot. "Is the broth ready for the meat?"

It nodded. "Good and ready."

The ogre flipped the knife around so that the blade pointed down. "Nothing personal, you understand."

My mind raced. What could I do? "My name's Sisko. What's yours?"

The ogre sputtered. "I don't need to know my food's name, nor do I give mine to a meal. Hold still, I'll make this painless." He pulled the knife back.

That didn't work. I closed my eyes and gritted my teeth.

"Stop!" Another ogre entered the clearing. I flung my eyes open to see Xilner moving toward us.

The other ogres all stopped talking and stared. The ogre over me ground his teeth. "How did you get here?"

"I've had a lot of time to study in my house. Some of my time I spent on learning spells."

The ogre curled his lips. "If so, why haven't you used them before?"

"I didn't have a reason before. Now I do." He stared at me and smiled.

The ogre threw a hand out and said something under his breath. A flash of light blasted toward Xilner, but Xilner cast his arms up and it landed short of its target, as if hitting an invisible wall.

Xilner raced toward us. The other ogres launched from their seats.

The ogre over me pulled his knife back and plunged it toward my neck. A hand grabbed the knife's hilt and shoved it back up, the tip barely missing my neck.

The other ogres watched as if it were entertainment for them. And I figured it probably was. They jeered, clapped, and cheered.

The two ogres rolled onto the ground. Xilner ended up under the other ogre. The knife pressed toward Xilner, the tip of the blade inching downward.

I prayed for God to do something. I could barely move my arms and feet.

But my gut wretched when Xilner's grip gave way, and the knife plunged into his heart. "No! Xilner!" I felt my eyes tearing up.

The ogre lifted himself to his knees, and then pulled the knife from Xilner's chest. Xilner breathed twice before his chest rose once more, fell, and then remained still.

I wiggled, but my bonds remained strong. The ogre knelt beside me once more. "Now his blood will be mingled with your own. We'll still gnaw on your bones." He raised the blade. "Time to finish this."

He thrust the blade once more toward me. But he stopped in midair as another blade shoved its way through the ogre's chest. He exhaled a gasp, his eyes wide. Then he fell over onto the ground, revealing a bright, angel-like being holding a red sword.

The rest of the ogres scattered like cockroaches when a lamp is lit, leaving me alone with my savior. The bright being waved his hands and the silver bands snapped one by one until I could lift myself to my feet.

I gazed at my rescuer. "Who are you?"

"You don't recognize me?" He cast his arms out as if allowing me to get a better look.

"Sorry, not at all."

"I'm Xilner."

I gasped. "Xilner! How? You don't look anything like him."

"This ogre put a curse on me, turning me into one of them. I denied them a meal before, and this ogre cast a spell on me that locked me into an ogre's body and required me to stay in the house where you found me.

"But there was one condition he didn't know about. An angel told me if I were to ever give my life for another, the curse would be broken, for no greater love can one show than to give his life for another. By dying for you, I've been freed from that corruption and have been glorified."

I smiled. "So when he killed you in your attempt to defend me, the curse died and this is the real you."

"As God created me. Yes."

I nodded. "I always knew you were beautiful inside."

"Thank you for being a friend. Without you, I couldn't have been saved. I had to have someone to die for."

I grinned. "You're welcome."

"Have a blessed Nativity celebration. You'll find Reol about a mile to the east." Xilner vanished.

I didn't waste any time grabbing a torch and jogging back home before the ogres decided to show up again. I dodged trees and brush until the village of Reol broke into view. I kicked up dirt until the steps of the church fell under my feet.

I put out the torch in my hand and laid it by the entrance, then entered the service to hear the singing of the Nativity hymn. I slid in by my mother.

She jerked and saw me beside her. She bent down and whispered, "Where were you? I thought that ogre had dragged you away."

I smiled at her. "Helping a friend to give birth, actually."

About that time the priest raised his hand and said, "Christ is born!"

The congregation responded in unison, "Glorify Him."

I felt a warmth settle upon me. I mumbled under my breath, "Yes, it is glorious."

Captivity's Faces

I slammed the ax into the wood, and chips flew onto the forest floor. The horizon nibbled at the sun. "It'll be dark soon."

Josh chopped away at the felled tree trunk a few feet down. He stopped and wiped his brow. "Good thing we're nearly finished here."

"Nearly finished?" I shook my head. "We've at least another hour."

Josh smiled. "Only if we do this by hand." He laid the ax on the tree truck and pulled out his wand.

I backed away. "Are you sure that's a good idea? You might hurt yourself."

"No problem. Just a simple levitation spell. What could possibly go wrong?"

I slapped my forehead. Did he really have to say that? Now we were doomed. I retreated behind an oak and prayed that Josh didn't kill himself.

Josh whipped his wand into the air and mumbled a spell. The ax lurched upward and hovered over the trunk. Another spell rolled off Josh's lips and the ax whacked at the tree. Then it swung again, and again, and each time the speed increased until the ax blurred as it ate into the wood.

Josh held out his hand, glancing back at me. "See, perfect." He rubbed his chin. "As a matter of fact, we could chop it up faster if we had eight axes. A simple multiplying spell should do the trick."

"Josh! Don't you dare. That's tempting fate."

Josh ignored me and said a spell as he swooshed the wand over the ax. The ax split in two, then divided again, and again. Eight axes chopped into the tree trunk.

Josh stepped in my direction. "See, we'll be done in minutes instead of an hour. And be back home before our parents worry about us."

I jerked my finger to point behind him. "Josh! Look out!"

The first ax had finished cutting through the trunk and sought another object to chop. Josh saw it flying his way and dropped to the ground. The ax brushed his hair as it flew past him, headed toward the tree I hid behind.

I ducked behind the trunk, then heard the ax digging into the tree. I dashed to another tree. "Don't you think you should stop them?"

Josh rose to his feet and dusted himself off. "The others aren't finished yet."

"It almost chopped off your head." I winced when another ax finished cutting and shot to another tree.

"They've got less than a minute." Josh watched the other six axes hitting the wood so fast it reminded me of giant woodpeckers with large, flat beaks. Three of them finished and flew to a tree away from us. The other three completed their cuts and raced to a third tree.

I cupped my hands. "Now stop them!"

Josh nodded and raised his wand. A loud cracking sound echoed through the forest. The first ax had finished cutting through its trunk, and the tree fell toward Josh. He jumped to the side, but the trunk smashed his legs into the ground. Josh wailed as he put a hand against the tree in an attempt to move it off.

"Josh! Stop them now!" I watched as the axes on the other trees left them and raced to cut up the fallen trunk.

Josh pointed his wand toward them, and for the first time, I heard Josh yell out a spell. "Erase the spell, axes desist!"

Axes further away fell to the ground, but three of the axes careened toward Josh and the tree. One plunged into the wood three feet from Josh, another glanced off the other side and thudded onto the leafy dirt, but the third smashed into Josh's head. His body fell limp.

"Josh!" I raced to his side. The ax lay on the ground next to him. A large gash on the side of his head pooled blood underneath it.

Shock immobilized me, watching my best friend lying dead before me. The distant rays of sunlight, diving behind the mountains, glinted off the ring on my left hand. Using the ring, I often healed people. But could it heal this? I had to try.

I placed my hand on Josh's head. "Father, heal Josh's injuries. Please."

Josh's body jerked. His eyes rolled back in his head, then I saw the blood-matted hair pulling together, and the gash sealing. Josh's eyes rolled back down and he blinked a few times before color returned to his face. He grimaced and pointed to his feet, still crushed under the tree trunk.

I started to grab the trunk when Josh yelled out, "Duck!"

Whatever Josh saw, I didn't react in time. A sharp pain raced over my head before darkness overtook me.

Voices echoed through my mind as throbbing pain broke through the black world. I eased my eyes open, but fought to focus them enough to see my surroundings. But I caught enough to spot vertical lines around me. I rubbed my head and blinked back the fogginess. The voices sounded like men. I didn't recognize them.

I lifted my body up, despite the complaining pain, and realized I sat inside a cage. Next to mine, another cage rested on wheels. I noticed Josh lying unconscious. Other cages formed a line in front and behind mine, mostly filled with animals of various kinds. *A circus! I've been shanghaied into a circus!*

I followed the sound of the voices to find three men sitting by a campfire. The moon hung high in the night sky. One of the men glanced my way. I watched the black-haired and bearded man as he stumbled to my cage.

He leaned against the bars. "It's about time ya came to, young one. How old er ya anyway?"

I smelled alcohol heavy on his breath. "Sixteen, sir. May I ask why you've kidnapped me and my friend?"

His friends at the fire laughed along with him. "Hey, Duke. Tell him it's a beauty pageant."

Duke wagged a finger at me. "Boy, it should be obvious."

I knew probably why, but didn't want to give away our abilities if I could avoid it. "My name is Sisko. And I fail to see why two guys sitting inside cages would entertain anyone."

The man shook his head while smiling. "You take us for fools, boy? We saw your friend there conducting an ax dance. That would be entertaining, but when he lost control we didn't like the idea of our customers getting hacked to death. Not good for business."

So they might suspect Josh was a wizard, but didn't know. However, that meant they most likely saw—

"But when you healed your friend from the grips of death, well, there's something you don't see everyday. People'll pay good money for that."

I bowed my head. "It doesn't work that way. I can't use it for such purposes."

"You'll use it all right." He pointed to Josh. "Or your friend will be the one who suffers."

I crawled closer to him. "You don't understand. I don't have full control over it. I can't guarantee that I'll be able to heal anyone."

"Tsk, tsk. That would be bad. For your friend's sake, you'd better make sure you perform." He returned to the campfire.

I studied Josh now that my eyes could focus better. Once he woke up, he'd be able to break us out. I hoped. He moved slightly, but he acted groggy, as if in a deep sleep and unable to pull out of it. Then I noticed several stones placed in a circle around him. They appeared pink in the moonlight. Either those rocks emitted some type of gas, or these circus folk knew a few magic spells of their own. Whatever the case, it appeared Josh wouldn't wake up.

I sank back into the hay and rested. At least my body rested. My mind raced with thoughts of what I could do. I prayed and searched out my heart. The answer arrived. I closed my eyes and asked, *Someone needs my help? Here, Father?*

"I want to go home," I whispered to God. Yet I knew until I helped the person or persons God intended, I would stay.

I watched the tall, leafy-green trees crawl past us on the road. With nothing to do, and very little given to eat, my entertainment consisted of watching birds fluttering between the branches and counting the different colors of flowers gracing the forest floor. At least the forest provided more interesting scenery than the trip over the Skinny Mountains.

The horse's hooves clopped against the road's packed dirt as the wagon bounced back and forth. Josh remained asleep in the wagon ahead of mine. When they fed him, they pulled him from the circle enough that he would swallow a thin soup, but put him back before he regained consciousness. I continued to wonder who might need my help.

The caravan rolled to a stop, and shortly a small man pushed a bowl of soup through a horizontal slot in the bars. Usually he continued on, but this time he stared at me.

He grabbed the bars with both hands. "Is it true, that you can heal people?"

Could this be the person? "I don't, but God can. He works through me."

The man ducked down, then held up a small child, around three years old. "She has some disease that prevents her from thinking right."

I raised an eyebrow. "Thinking right?"

"Yes. Can't hardly talk at all, still acts a lot like a baby. She should be running and playing with the other children, but she don't. Can you do anything?"

I drew close to the bars. Yes, God wanted me to help her. Maybe this would be it. I stretched out my hand and laid it on the matted brown hair of the child. "Father, heal this child of yours to think clearly."

The foggy eyes abruptly focused on me and blinked. A smile spread across the girl's face; she reached up arms to hug me.

The small man turned the girl toward him, and he cried out, "You did it! You healed her. I can see it in her eyes."

I smiled. "What's her name?"

He reached a hand through the bars and grabbed mine. "April. And mine's Tulo. Thank you so much! I don't know what to say."

I held his hand firmly in mine. "There's nothing to say to me. I only did what I was told. Thank God instead."

He hugged his daughter. "We must go tell Nina. Oh, thank you." He dashed off to another wagon.

I checked my heart. No, I still needed to help another here. He would lead me to them in due time.

Whips cracked ahead, and the wagons jerked from their sleep. Creaking of wooden wheels bounced over the rough ground. A tall, thin man headed toward the rear and yelled out as he passed, "We'll reach Holoroth in an hour."

I slurped my cold soup. I could hardly wait, but feared what the man would do with us. And, would I "perform" as he wanted?

The caravan of wagons rolled into Holoroth about mid-afternoon. The town boasted a market. Many traveled from surrounding villages and farms to shop or sell here; a perfect place for a circus to stop.

And the children, racing along with the wagons, gave me the distinct impression the crowd would be large tonight. Duke didn't waste the opportunity of an attentive audience. He swaggered down the line of wagons, teasing the audience with the shows to come later that evening.

He matched the speed of my wagon. "And here we have two normal looking folk. But tonight you'll see the most amazing miracle of healing by Sisko the Great. You've never seen the likes of it before. Don't miss it!" He stepped on down the line.

I watched the children and adults staring at me as I passed by them. I could tell curiosity had grabbed hold of their minds. "Well, Father, I couldn't think of a better way to help a lot of people at one time, if that's what Duke has in mind. But I don't like the idea of someone making money off it."

The circus set up outside the edge of town. Tents rose into the air, workers scrubbed down the elephants, fed the lions, and a few practiced their routines.

Amidst the commotion, Tulo approached my cage, a wide smile graced his face. "April's picking up words quickly, and there's a sparkle in her eyes where confusion used to be. I can't thank you enough."

I grinned. "Your happiness is thanks enough. And thank God, he's the one that did it."

He nodded. "And I know you'll do great tonight. You'll like it once you get a taste of it. It's not a bad life." He jumped down and scampered away before I could respond.

I didn't know whether I wanted to "do good" tonight. I didn't have a clue what God intended to do, much less myself. I'd find out soon enough.

Night fell, workers lit torches, and the people poured into the circus. I could hear them laugh, ooh and aah, and clap at whatever spell-binding acts they viewed. An hour hadn't passed before four workers arrived at my wagon. Two of them entered Josh's cage and pulled him out. One slung him over his shoulder while the other grabbed one of the rocks and kept it close to his nose.

I smiled. So the rocks did emit a gas keeping Josh unconscious.

"Come on, son." One of the men pulled me out and kept a firm grip on my right arm. The other clamped down on the left, and they guided me toward the tent. Upon entering, I saw the vast crowd all around in staggered seating rising up high against the tent walls. The two men leading me followed the other two carrying Josh until we stopped in the middle of the tent.

Duke, dressed in black and holding a top hat, announced through a megaphone, "Tonight, we will amaze and dazzle with a miracle the likes of which has never before been seen in any circus." He waved a palm at Josh being laid on his back, his left arm extended over the wooden stage. "Before your very eyes, we will cut this man's arm off, and the Great Sisko will heal him anew!"

I leaped forward, but the men's arms held firm. "No! You can't do that!"

Duke's megaphone swallowed my voice. "Observe, and keep your eye on this man. The amount of blood will confirm this is no hoax!"

Another man entered the ring holding an ax. Josh lay groggily on the floor; two men held him down.

I jerked against their grips to no avail. What could I do? I needed a miracle of a different kind, for Josh's sake. Would God hear that? "Father, don't let them cut his arm off."

The man raised the ax into the air. Drummers rolled a cadence. Duke raised his arm over his head and paused to allow the drama to build. All eyes in the audience froze onto the scene. Silence reigned as the ax wavered over the man's head.

"Please do something," I whispered. I couldn't think of anything to stop this. God would have to do it.

Duke dropped his arm, and the ax swooshed down. The sound of smashing wood echoed over my ears. Josh jerked and groaned. Gasps and screams rose among the people. I felt sick as Duke picked up Josh's arm, blood draining from the freshly cut end.

"A real arm, real blood and bones." He waved it before the audience as if they might see the detail. Duke swung the arm and pointed it toward me, slinging blood across the stage. "And now, the Great Sisko will heal his friend, right before your very eyes!" He nodded toward the two holding me in place.

They released their grip and I fled to Josh's side. The pool of red grew large about him. Duke handed me the arm, now cold and clammy. I hated the whole thing, but I had to try. Josh shouldn't be punished for the greed of this man.

I placed the arm against the bleeding stub as best as I could match it. "Father, please heal Josh of this severed limb!" The blood continued to flow. Nothing happened. Tears formed in my eyes. "Please, Father. Don't punish Josh."

A small group in the upper reaches of the seating booed. The chorus grew louder. Duke scowled at me and drew close. "Do it, now! Or we'll have a riot on our hands."

I ground my teeth together. "I told you, I don't control it like that. It's up to God. All I can do is ask."

"Ask more then. Or we may both be hung from a tree."

I stared at Josh's severed limb. What more could I do? What else could I ask for? I searched my mind, delved into my heart, searching for God's answer. A thought emerged from the confusion of the moment. Josh needed more than the healing of his severed limb. He needed blood restored, he needed nerves reconnected, he needed... I froze. He needed to wake up! My prayer had been too narrow.

The booing grew louder, and some moved to the aisles to leave. I placed one hand on Josh's arm and another on his head. "Father, restore the arm, restore the legs, restore the blood, restore the energy, restore the consciousness. Make Josh whole."

Bone, sinew, skin, and muscle reached out to greet each other, merge, and pull each other into one. The skin reformed, color returned to Josh's arm.

Duke flung his hands into the air. "He did it!" He reached down and grabbed Josh's arm and flapped it around. The boos turned to cheers and clapping. Many stared at me in awe. Duke continued to address the crowds, "The Great Sisko will be available in the fairway to heal all who need it, for a small price of two pounds, right after the show."

Josh flicked his eyes open. I shook my head and pretended to shut my eyes. He cracked a bare smile and slightly nodded, then closed his eyes. I didn't want them catching on that I'd immunized him to their gas.

The two men grabbed me by the arms again and led me out the tent. A hallway of smaller tents, stages, and various games lined the grounds for about one hundred yards. They guided me to one such stage, upon which sat a chair, painted gold and lined with red. A black cape, decorated with sliver stars, lay over the back of the chair. A tall, cone-shaped hat rested in the seat, the point on top slightly bent.

One of the men pointed at me. "Put those on." They both took positions on either side of the chair, as if they were my personal body guards. No easy escape from these two.

I grabbed the cape and tossed it over my shoulders. "You know, this is all wrong. How can you be party to a kidnapping and forced labor?"

Neither moved or gave a hint they heard me. I finished tying the cape and stuck the hat on my head. I felt ridiculous. I wondered what they would do if I refused to cooperate? Duke had cut off Josh's arm because he thought I would heal him, and thankfully God enabled me to do so. But would he kill Josh or me? Would he stoop to murder?

After another hour, people filed out of the big tent and filled the fairway. A small group gathered around my stage. One of Duke's workers sat with a money box, preparing to receive people's meager wages, feeding upon their hope.

Duke worked his way through the crowd until he stopped in front of me. He leaned over and whispered, "I forgot to tell you, twenty-five percent of the proceeds we earn is yours. I feared for your life in the ring, but luckily you came through. I knew you could do it!"

I frowned. "Sir, I don't appreciate you risking my friend's life. I nearly didn't heal him. Next time, I may not be able to. "

He scratched his beard. "You have a point there. You did give me a bit of fright, but it turned out well enough. But one failure would ruin a good thing. So we'll figure out something else. Yet that did jumpstart your career as a circus performer. People will be talking about this up and down the countryside. All you need to do now is heal those you can, and we'll both be rich."

I stared into his coal-black eyes. "Why do you want the money so bad?"

Duke grinned. "My innocent lad. Sisko, correct?"

I nodded.

"Let me fill you in on the business side of life. Money, you see, equals power. The more money you have, the more power you obtain. The more you can control your own destiny rather than others controlling you. It is freedom to do and be what you want."

I raised an eyebrow. "So working this circus is what you want to do with your life?"

"Humph." Duke put his right palm against his cheek. "Not that I hate it, mind you, but no."

"When will you get enough to do what you want? You know, freedom?"

He frowned. "I'll know when I get there. And I won't get there if you aren't seeing people. A line is waiting for you. Don't disappoint me." He turned and stepped off the stage.

Don't disappoint him? He was not the one I worried about disappointing.

A mother carrying her baby approached. Seeing the tears in her eyes as she held her baby out melted my resolve. She nodded at the child. "My baby is deathly ill from the flu. Please, heal him."

The child did appear near death; no color graced his cheeks. I couldn't deny this woman simply because someone made money off her. I nodded and held the baby in my arms. "Father, release him from the bonds of sickness and revive his life." The child lurched, a peach color flooded the baby's body, and it started crying.

"It is a miracle!" The woman received her baby and examined it, then met my eyes. "Thank you so much for this miracle."

"Thank God."

The worker at the money box yelled, "Next."

The lady left, and I could see her chatting with several about what happened. As God healed another three through the ring, the crowd grew and the line snaked farther back. Word spread and everyone with the slightest problem flocked to be healed by "the Great Sisko."

As the evening merged into early morning, the money box bulged with cash. I'd never seen so much money. Duke's reminder that twenty-five percent of it would be mine hit me. Naturally I wouldn't use it for myself, but my parents struggled to get by. Father needed to repair the house but couldn't buy the materials. Now he could. Maybe that's why God had led me here, to help out my family financially?

I smiled as the next one stepped up to be healed.

Crickets chirped in the forest darkness; the moon hung low in the star-filled sky. Josh stirred in his cage, stretched his arms and yawned.

I tossed a small stone and it hit him on the back of the head.

"Hey, what's that for?"

"Sleeping so long."

"What else am I going to do while pretending to be knocked out cold." He rubbed the back of his head. "So, I assume you're ready for me to transport us back home?"

I shook my head. "Not a good idea."

Josh threw up his hands. "Let me guess. You need to help someone here."

I pulled myself to the bars in order to speak softer. "There is that, but also I'm not finished helping as well."

Josh raised an eyebrow. "What do you mean by that?"

I stared into the forest darkness. "Well, I'm helping my parents by staying for a while longer."

"Your parents? How?"

"I'm earning money."

"Really? Doing what?"

I cleared my throat. "Ah, doing miracles."

Josh stared silently at me for a moment before drawing close to the bars himself. "All right, where's Sisko? Who is this?"

I stared into the night sky. "He's going to make money off of me, but he promised to give me twenty-five percent. I can use it to help my parents. God's healing people despite Duke profiting off of me. I'm not doing it for myself, so I'm not risking the curse of the ring."

Josh shook his head. "There are more curses than abusing your ring."

I breathed deep. "Besides, I do feel I'm needed here. I don't know for sure who yet. What's the harm of earning a little extra for my parents while waiting for God's direction?"

"The harm is I'll have to continue to play the part of unconscious boy during the day. You know how boring that is?"

"One more night, then we'll get out of here, unless God won't let me. Then you can vanish if you want."

"I'm not leaving you." He lay down.

I stared at him. "All right. I'll give you a cut of the money."

He jerked up. "Sisko! I thought I knew you better."

I wrinkled my forehead. "You don't want any of the money?"

41

Josh threw his hands up. "Of course not! You should know better." He shook his head and laid back down.

I listened to the crickets and watched the stars marching across the sky.

I didn't sell it; Duke did. And I helped people at the same time. As long as I remained here, seeking who God wanted me to help, I couldn't prevent Duke from using me. I might as well get some of what he made off me and use it to help others.

As promised, Duke bypassed chopping off Josh's arm again, thank goodness. Especially since Josh would feel it, he wouldn't be able to pretend unconsciousness through that. And as Duke predicted, the word of my healings spread around surrounding towns and the countryside, and drew in bigger crowds. A long line led from my stage down the fairway.

I caught some unhappy glances from the other fairway vendors. The sin of jealousy floated thickly through the air. Their problem, not mine. And nothing they could do about it either, as long as Duke remained happy with me.

After several healings, one man approached using a cane. I smiled. "I guess you need your leg healed?"

He nodded to the side. "Yes, but I have a further need." He pulled a hand out of his pocket and held out some coins. "I want to buy a further miracle. Pray that my house turns into a mansion."

I sat in the chair, and stared at the man. I realized my jaw had dropped and closed my mouth. "I can't do that, sir."

He frowned. "Why not? You're taking money to heal people, why not other miracles? This is three times the price for a healing." He waved the money before my face. "Please. I have a family that needs something more than a leaking roof and biting cold."

I stared at the coins. I had justified taking Duke's money because I had no choice in the matter. But this, this was different. Or was it? Whether accepting Duke's money or straight from someone in line, the gift was sold all the same? The only difference being I allowed Duke to sell it for me.

I breathed deep. "I need to ask God." I closed my eyes. *I'm sorry,*

Father, for rationalizing the selling of your gift. But how do I help the one before me now?

I dove deep into my heart before the answer arrived. I opened my eyes and met the man's gaze. "I can heal you, but can take no money. And once I heal you, you'll have the physical ability to fix your house." I placed my hand on his head. "Father, heal him of his broken leg."

He squeezed his eyes shut, then opened them again. He put some pressure on the leg, then more, then bounded on it. A grin spread across his face. "You really did it! Thank you so much!"

Then I said in a voice everyone could hear, "Father, return all the money into the pockets of those who have paid to be healed."

The man at the cash table yelled, then cursed as he checked under the table and those nearby. "Who took the money?" Then someone yelled from the fairway, "Look, the money I spent has returned to my pocket!" The man I'd just healed pulled out cash from his pocket and stared at me with wide eyes. Others checked and spoke the same.

Duke plowed his way through the crowd and stared into the money box. His gaze shifted toward me as his jaw muscles tightened, no doubt hearing the story of what I said and did from the money handler. He moved my way.

I jumped from my chair and dove into the crowds. I dashed behind the tents and pumped my legs toward the cages. Now Josh could get us out of here, and quick. But I heard the sounds of footsteps following behind me. I pushed my legs, but I couldn't squeeze out any extra speed.

"Stop, please," a voice called out from behind me.

The voice didn't sound like Duke's. Maybe one of his workers? But it sounded familiar. My cage lay a few feet ahead, but I stopped and turned to meet the person chasing me.

The small man, Tulo, pulled to a stop in front of me. "Don't run away."

"I'm afraid Duke isn't going to deal with me nicely if I don't get out of here."

Duke's voice rang from behind me. "No, you aren't going to like how I deal with you."

I spun around; Duke held a knife in his hands.

I backed up. "Sir, I warned you that I can't sell this gift to the highest bidder. Anyone who takes it as you have done runs the risk of losing what little they have. So this is as much for you as for me."

He growled and stepped closer. "I've not lost anything but the money you gave away tonight."

Tulo jumped from behind me and stood between Duke and myself. "Sir, he tells the truth. Did not your own keeper of the books say that the other vendors lost money because so many spent it at Sisko's booth? If that keeps up, the others will have to leave, and you'll be left with one vendor on the fairway. Your sales will go down."

Duke lowered his knife and his face relaxed. "I hadn't thought of that, but you're right."

I breathed in some air. But I sensed in my heart that I'd not finished. I stared into the sky. What now?

Tulo held my arm. "So, what you do is have him heal for free, you see. That will draw the crowds and they'll still have money to spend on the other vendors. They can all offer a percentage of their proceeds to give Sisko some income."

Duke patted the flat of his blade against his cheek. "Not a bad idea."

I raised my hand. "One problem, sir. Our parents are most likely worried sick about us. We can't stay here."

Duke shook his head. "Tulo's right. You stay and be the draw. Once here, they'll spend their money on other shows and goods as well. A win-win for both of us."

The argument sounded good, but I realized it differed little from my previous rationalizations. Duke would still earn money because of my gift, and in the end, for myself as well. I wouldn't fall for that again.

"No, sir. It is a lose-lose. Any money you make from my gift will be devoured, and spread to the other vendors."

He laughed. "If that were true, boy, I would've heard about it by now."

A man flew from behind a tent and skidded to a halt. "There you are, sir. I'm afraid we have a problem."

Duke's face fell and he slowly turned toward the man. "What is it?"

He caught his breath. "Several of the vendors gave us money, but we found it half eaten. By what we don't know. But it's as if someone has taken bites out of the coins."

Duke jerked back around and pointed his knife at me. "It's your fault!" He dove toward me.

I jumped to the side and fell to the ground. He hovered over me, the knife raised into the air. "How dare you try and take all my money! You're a thief. And you'll die a thief." He thrust his blade toward me.

As the weapon raced toward my heart, the image of Duke vanished, and Josh appeared over me. His hand thumped against my chest. He smiled. "How was my timing?"

I breathed deep. "A little too close, if you ask me." I held up my hand and Josh lifted me to my feet.

He shrugged. "Never satisfied." He stared at his cage, which now contained Duke.

Duke shook the cage. "Let me out of here, thieves!"

Josh waved his wand and an ax lying by a stump floated over to stare Duke down. Duke's face fell and he backed away from the bars. "No! Please, don't make the ax start going. I'm fine in here!"

Josh smiled. "Are you sure? It's just a simple levitation spell. What could go wrong?"

Duke shook his head as his legs trembled. "I'm fine in here. Please, don't use the ax. Go and leave me alone. Someone will let me out." He fell prostrate on the cage floor. "Please!"

Josh shrugged. "Have it your way." The ax fell to the ground. He turned toward me. "Can we go now?"

I checked, and my heart gave the all clear. "Yes, I can leave. God's done here what He wanted to do."

"And what about you? Are you still money hungry?"

I glanced back at Tulo waving at me. I waved back. "Thanks to a friend and someone who brought me to my senses, I'm fine with what I have. God can come up with his own miracles well enough."

He patted me on the back. "Good. I was starting to think maybe you didn't have any sense left to return to." Josh mumbled the transport spell, and we vanished back to Reol.

Magic's Curse

I yawned as I sat up in bed. Sunlight poured through my window as birds sang their songs. The smell of bacon wafted by my nose. I smiled. It wasn't every day we ate bacon for breakfast. I wondered what the occasion might be. Whatever the case, I couldn't wait.

"Sisko! Are you up?"

I cupped my hand around my mouth. "Yes, Mother. I'll be right out." I threw on my clothes, straightened my hair, and darted into the main room.

I sat at the table. "So, what's the occasion? Are we going anywhere?"

She nodded as she heaped scrambled eggs upon my plate while I grabbed three strips of bacon. "Have you forgotten so soon?"

I shrugged as I scooped up some eggs with a piece of flat bread. "I guess so." I stuffed the delicious morsel into my mouth and chewed. Long forgotten flavors rolled over my tongue and soaked down my throat.

"The dentist."

I gagged, but stopped short of spewing my food over the table. I swallowed. "Uh, yes. I did forget. But my teeth are fine."

She glanced over her shoulder. Her eyes glared at me from under furrowed eyebrows. "If you call a mouthful of cavities fine."

Vivid memories of the last time I sat in the torture chair raced through my mind. I had nearly passed out from the pain. I stared at the wall as I contemplated my fate.

"Eat up. No telling how long before you'll be able to chew again. Enjoy it now."

"I don't feel much like eating now."

She turned, hands on her hips. "Sisko!"

I grabbed another piece of bread and a helping of eggs. "Yes, ma'am."

Breakfast ended way too soon. Mother guided me out the door and pushed me down the street, since my feet rebelled at approaching my impending doom.

The cross on top of the dome caught my eye. "Can't we stop at the Church?"

She raised an eyebrow. "Why?"

"I want the priest to read me my last rites."

She shook her head. "Oh for crying out loud, Sisko! You're not going to die."

I glanced at her. "When's the last time you've been to the dentist?"

She laughed. "When they pulled all my teeth out and gave me my false ones."

I groaned. "Do you think the dentist could pull all my--"

"No, son. You're teeth aren't that bad."

I sighed. "They will be once he's through with them."

We opened the door to the office. Wooden benches lined a small waiting area. A lady sat behind a desk. "Sign here, please," she said as she shoved a pen, ink, and paper toward us.

Mom did as the lady asked. Then we turned to sit down, and that's when I noticed Josh and his mother sitting against the wall. We sat beside them.

I leaned over. "So, what are you in for?"

He leaned back. "Tooth needs pulling."

"Can't you whip up some magic spell to take care of it?"

He nodded to the side, and one end of his mouth curled up. "I think there is a spell for it. Milnore refuses to teach it to me, though. Says I need to endure the pain for myself."

I stared at the door behind which I could expect Hell's gates to open up and swallow me whole. "I think if you did know a spell for it, I would risk having you do it. Almost anything is better than this."

He smiled. "I said, Milnore wouldn't teach it to me. I found someone who would, though."

"Really? Can you zap me with it quickly?"

"One note. It doesn't fix the teeth..." He tapped his cheek. "It removes any pain."

"I'll take it."

47

The door flung open and an assistant poked her head out. "Josh?"

Josh rose and headed to the door, glancing back and mouthing, "Sorry," as he slipped into the room.

The lady poked her head out again. "Sisko, you're next too. Come on."

Mother shoved me to my feet, and I dragged them across the floor. Sweat broke out upon my forehead. The lady guided me to a chair and leaned me back.

"Mr. Cav will be here in a couple of minutes." She wheeled around and headed out.

At least ten minutes passed before the lady entered along with a man. He positioned some mirrors, which directed sunlight into my mouth.

He peered in. "Ah yes. We have a cavity on three, another on six, a baseline on ten." He peered around some more. "And one on fifteen. That should take up twenty minutes."

He pulled out a sharp, pointed tool and a mallet. "Hold still. This will only hurt a little."

Before I could protest his lie, the assistant grabbed my upper and lower jaws and pulled them back. The dentist picked around for a moment, then positioned the point and whacked the end of the tool with a wallop.

Fiery, piercing pain vibrated through my skull, and I screamed in response.

Mr. Cav laughed. "See, I told you it wouldn't hurt much." He drew back the hammer and nailed it again.

The session lasted forever. Strike after strike. Pulsating agony after pounding pain. I whispered to God that now might be a perfect time to depart this life. But at long last, the dentist laid down his tools of destruction. Then he packed the holes with some type of sticky stuff that would harden. After rinsing they let me go.

My throbbing mouth felt like one giant bruise. I could barely open it to talk, much less eat anything. Josh sat in the lobby.

Mother grabbed my jaw; I winced and pulled away. She drew me closer. "Should take a week or so to heal."

I mumbled, "Can I go with Josh?"

She glanced at Josh, standing by the door with a grin spread across his baby face. She faced me again. "Against my better judgment, yes." She headed through the door. Meeting Josh's eyes, she said, "He's all yours."

I followed Josh outside and grabbed him by the shoulders. "Pain relief. Now!"

Josh snickered. "Do you realize how funny you look?"

"Josh!"

"All right. Hold still. This won't hurt a bit."

I growled and held up a hand. "You said Milnore didn't give you this spell."

He nodded. "I ran into an old wizard passing through. He gave it to me."

"Are you sure you can trust him?"

He shrugged his shoulders. "Like I said, it works. I'm not feeling any pain."

My throbbing head demanded relief. "All right, do it to me."

He pulled out his wand and waved it around my head as he mumbled something. The pain subsided, but before I could offer thanks, everything grew dark.

I yawned as I sat up in bed. Sunlight poured through my window as birds sang their songs. The smell of bacon wafted by my nose. I smiled. It wasn't every day we ate bacon for breakfast. I wondered what the occasion might be. Whatever the case, I couldn't wait to enjoy breakfast.

Dread fell upon me. "It's the dentist." How did I know that?

"Sisko! Are you up?"

I cupped my hand around my mouth. "Yes, Mother. I'll be right out." I dragged myself from the bed. I would much rather stay there than go to the dentist. I draped my clothes over my body and headed for my last meal.

I sat at the table. Not even the bacon and eggs enticing my nose smelled good now. I watched as she placed a plate before me and poured eggs onto it.

"You remember what we're doing today?"

I nodded. "The dentist."

"Well mark up some points for Sisko."

I stuffed eggs into my mouth. Might as well eat. It might be a week or more before I could down a meal this good.

Mother smiled. "Glad to see you're taking a positive attitude about this."

I groaned inside. "I wouldn't label this a positive attitude. I'm thinking that if I can make myself sick enough, we'll have to cancel."

Her hands shot down and pulled the plate off the table. "You've had your fill, young man. Now let's be off."

"Mother!"

She pulled me from the table. "Let's go."

She pushed me out the door and down the street.

The cross on top of the dome caught my eye. "Can we stop at the church?"

She glanced at me. "Why?"

"Because…" I knew what her answer would be. Of course, I said it partly in jest, so I knew she wouldn't take me seriously. But I knew what she would say, word for word.

I decided to test it. "I want the priest to read me my last rites."

She shook her head. "Oh for crying out loud, Sisko! You're not going to die."

Yes, she said exactly what I knew she'd say. Am I becoming psychic on top of having a miracle-producing ring?

We entered the office. As Mother signed us in, I turned, fully expecting to see Josh. He sat on the bench, grinning at me, his mother sitting beside him.

My eyes grew wide. He knew a spell. A spell to keep me from feeling pain. And I had limited time to get it from him.

I raced to him and planted my hands on his shoulders. "Now, Josh. Do the pain erasing spell, now!"

He jerked back. "How did you know I had a pain erasing spell?"

"Never mind that. Just do it! Now!"

His eyes darted up and down me. "All right. Give me some room."

I backed up and waited for him. He waved his wand around me and mumbled some words. Tension drained knowing I wouldn't have to go through that pain again. Again? What did I mean "again"?

Before I could think further, blackness overtook my mind.

I yawned as I sat up in bed. Sunlight poured through my window as birds sang their songs. The smell of bacon wafted by my nose. I...

Wait a minute. I'd done this before. My mother would soon call for me.

"Sisko! Are you up?"

"Yes, Mother. I'll be right there."

Memories flooded my mind. I'm going to the dentist today. I'll meet Josh there, and he'll put the spell on me to relieve my pain. And..., yes. He said he retrieved that spell from a strange wizard.

I jumped from bed and tossed on my clothes. I needed to catch Josh. I couldn't let him use that spell.

I dashed across the living room.

Mother's head jutted out. "Where are you going? Your food will get cold."

"I have to meet Josh." I reached for the door.

"But you have an appointment."

I stopped at the threshold and turned to her. "I know, but this is extremely important. I've got to reach Josh."

She frowned but nodded. I closed the door and fled down the street. I skidded to a halt at the town crossroads. I scanned the area for a minute. People milled around the steam house; one man exited with a nose about a foot long. I wondered for a moment what his character flaw might have been for the steam house to have caused that reaction. But such thoughts distracted me from my mission.

A few more seconds passed before I spotted Josh and his mother approaching the walkway leading to the dentist office. I sped along the dirt road toward them until I halted in front of the pair.

"Ma'am, I need to talk with Josh. It's very important."

She twisted her lips. "Hurry it up. He has an appointment."

I nodded, and pulled Josh to the side. "Josh, about that pain spell you have from the strange wizard—"

His eyes widened. "How did you know about that?"

"That's not important right now. Have you used it on yourself?"

He wrinkled his forehead. "I was about to."

"Whatever you do, do not use that spell. I don't know why, but it appears to send you back in time."

He ran his fingers through his hair. "That might explain why everything feels so familiar."

51

I nodded. "It may be the ring allows me to perceive the effect more than you. But I've been through this at least twice before."

Josh sighed. "That means I can't avoid the pain."

"Me neither. But, I might as well go with you since I have an appointment as well. Bad thing is, I've been through the pain once. I hate to do it again." I rubbed my chin. "If you told me the spell, would you activate it?"

"Well, no. There's a series of actions you use to activate any spell you speak. We're not allowed to tell that to anyone unless they've agreed to be trained."

"But you can tell me the spell?"

He sighed. "Not supposed to, but considering the circumstances, you might be able to spot what's wrong with it."

Josh stared at the sky. "As the stranger gave it to me, it says, 'Bodily pain disappear, its source erased and rolled back.'"

The sky grew dark with black clouds. I glanced at Josh. "I thought you said it wouldn't do anything."

The wind whipped up and blew Josh's hair into his eyes. "It shouldn't have."

The clouds funneled down toward us and engulfed everything. Josh and I sank to the ground as darkness obscured any signs of Reol. I held onto Josh, my eyes tightly shut against the storm.

The wind died off, the clouds vanished, but the buildings of Reol didn't return. Instead, walls of bricks surrounded us, mold growing heavily over their surfaces, giving the room a dank smell. On one end of the room, bars covered an opening leading into a hallway. A torch burned, casting flickering shadows against the far walls.

I let go of Josh. "Any idea what just happened and where we are?"

Josh, his eyes staring blankly around the room, shook his head. "I don't have a clue."

A man slid in front of the bars. I tapped Josh on the shoulder. "I'll bet he does."

Josh turned and his eyes widened. "It's him!"

The man's white hair and beard on a thin face contrasted with the black cloak he wore, as firelight danced upon his form. The man frowned. "Boy, where's Milnore?"

Josh's forehead wrinkled. "Milnore? I didn't expect to be here, why would he be here?"

"You're his apprentice, are you not?"

Josh hesitated, apparently afraid to confirm the man's assumption. "What does that..." Josh's eyebrows raised. "Oh no. I'm so stupid!"

The man threw his hands into the air. "I've already confirmed that. Not only are you naïve, but you broke one of the cardinal rules of wizards! Never tell a non-wizard your spells! You can both rot in here for all I care. Maybe Milnore will come for you." He stomped down the hallway; a door shut with an echoing clang.

Josh dropped to a bench by the wall and cradled his head in his hands. "How could I have been so dumb!"

I placed a hand on his shoulder. "Mind telling me what's happened?"

Josh raised his head and met my eyes. "The spell he gave me was a carrier spell. A carrier spell appears and acts like a normal spell, but if said without the actions to start a spell, it activates a different spell encoded within it.

"He expected me to tell the spell to Milnore and transport both of us into this magic prison." Josh buried his head again. "Milnore warned me of such things, and I completely forgot."

I sat next to Josh. "So, we've been transported to who knows where, into some wizard's dungeon."

"That about sums it up." He turned to me. "I'm sorry I got you into this. I should have never told you that spell."

I chuckled, which sounded odd in the dungeon. "I asked for it."

Josh smiled for a moment, but it quickly faded. He rose and strolled toward the bars. "I'm beginning to think I'm not cut out for this wizard stuff."

"Why do you say that?"

He stared down the hallway. "Just like this wizard, most all of them I've met have been bad. Having such power tends to foster self-fulfillment, greed, control over others. So many wizards use it purely for that, with no thought for what good they could do with it."

I stared at my ring, recalling the curse I would face if I ever used its miracle-producing power for myself. "I know the feeling."

Josh shook his head. "Not like this. I don't have any dire warning attached to how I use my spells. When I get good at this wizard thing, how do I know I won't be tempted to use that power for myself? How do I know I won't turn out like this wizard—revenge and power over others becoming my life's purpose?"

He turned to face me. "I can't guarantee that I won't be like him. It scares me."

I rose and moved beside him. "There's your curse. Didn't you tell me not too long ago, trapped in the circus cages, that there are more curses than what my ring had? I'd say the fact you're worried about it is the best sign you'll do it differently."

He allowed his head to fall against the bars. "I wish I could be sure of that."

I patted him on the back. "Maybe we could talk more about this later. Right now, I'd rather focus on getting out of this place. Can you transport us out?"

He breathed deep. "I can try, but something tells me it won't work. Chances are, he cast a magic-prohibiting spell over this cell." He pulled out his wand and waved it as he mumbled a spell. Nothing happened. He shrugged. "See, told you."

I snapped my fingers. "Of course, he designed this to trap wizards. He has no clue what I can do."

"But you can't use the ring to break us out. That would be using it for selfish reasons."

I nodded. "Yes, but what I need to do is figure out what will 'help' this wizard."

Josh smiled. "Oh, I see."

I tapped my chin. "What does this wizard need? Humility? Yes."

Josh gazed into the walls. "A spanking is what he needs."

I smiled. "Of course. He needs a good lesson in humility. We'll give him what he asked for."

Josh raised an eyebrow. "Which is?"

"He wanted Milnore. But having him trapped in here with us wouldn't do this man any good. Milnore needs to be out there, where he can help him."

Josh grinned. "Perfect. Do it."

I closed my eyes. "Father, bring Milnore to us, outside our cell."

A second passed, then Milnore's form appeared before them on the other side of the bars. He jerked back before he caught sight of us. "My words, Josh. Did you do that?"

Josh shook his head and pointed at me.

Milnore stood straighter. "Well, that's some most powerful magic you have there, Sisko. It's not just anyone who can yank me away to meet them."

I smiled. "God can."

Milnore laughed. "Yes, I suppose He can." His laughing died off. "Now, what have you two gotten yourselves into this time?" His eyes focused on Josh.

Josh bowed his head. "I messed up, Master. I told a spell to Sisko that was a carrier spell for one that sent us here. I believe it was meant for you and me."

Milnore nodded. "I warned you about those. And we'll have to have a talk about telling others your spells."

I raised my hand. "That's the only one he's ever mentioned, sir. And he only told me it in the hope we could figure out why the stranger's spell kept repeating time for us."

Milnore huffed at Josh. "You received this spell from a stranger? And you didn't think to be suspicious?"

Josh nodded. "Yes, Master. I'm a lousy wizard."

Milnore shook his head. "Naïve, yes. Lousy, no. You're better than most."

Josh lifted his head. "Really?"

"Your heart is in the right place. Not too many wizards can say that."

Josh stood taller. "But what if I don't keep it in the right place? Wouldn't it be better to not be a wizard if that were to happen?"

Milnore opened his mouth, but the door down the hallway burst open. Milnore turned to face the wizard. "Droik. I should have known you were behind this."

"There's a lot you should have known, like how a spell could affect a sick woman."

"I am truly sorry, Droik. I committed a mistake, yes. One I regret deeply. But you shouldn't spend your life in hatred."

He growled. "Easy for you to say!" He flipped a wand out and said a spell. A flood of flames raced toward Milnore.

Milnore responded by sending a strong wind to push back the fire. Droik stopped when the flames blew back toward him.

Then Milnore countered with a string of rope spinning around Droik. A sword appeared out of thin air and cut through the strands.

A row of knives materialized, hovering in the air before Droik. He flung his hands out and they raced toward Milnore. Milnore swung his wand in a huge circle, and a large piece of wood appeared before him. The knives stabbed harmlessly into it. Milnore cast the wooden slab back toward Droik, who tried to duck. The plank whacked him in the head and fell over him.

Nothing moved. Milnore took a deep breath and turned back to us. "Hold still." He mumbled off some words under his breath as he pointed the wand at various sections of the bars. After a minute, a series of sparks flashed across the iron. The door unlatched and then swung open.

Milnore chuckled. "Droik has learned a few twists. Took me longer to find the combination than usual."

We stepped out of the prison. Milnore stared at Josh. "Now, can you get us home?"

Josh nodded. "After you answer my question. How can I know that I won't misuse my ability and become evil like Droik?"

"Oh." Milnore scratched under his beard. "What about me? Am I using magic for evil?"

Josh shook his head. "Of course not, Master."

He leaned over. "Magic is one ability that some have. Every gift, ability, and power we control can be used for good or evil. If it isn't magic, it will be something else. The most important thing is to learn to invest whatever you have to help others and not for selfish purposes. Once you have that down, you could be the most powerful wizard in the world and not be corrupted by it."

Josh smiled. "Well, when you put it that way, I'll keep working at it."

Milnore nodded and smiled. "Now, you think you could take us home?"

Josh opened his mouth, but then Milnore gasped, and grabbed his side. He turned to reveal a knife plunged into his back. The wizard collapsed onto the floor.

Josh dropped beside him. "Master!"

The wooden plank shifted, and hovered in the air. Droik slipped out from under it, smiling. "Old fool."

I fell beside Josh. "Deal with Droik, I'll heal Milnore." I watched Josh as I pulled out the knife and placed my hands to pray.

Droik smiled. "You don't want to challenge me, boy. You're no match for my power."

Josh held his wand at his side; it trembled. "I'm not challenging you. I'm here to help you."

Droik laughed. He flipped his wand forward. Josh spun his wand through the air and flung it toward the cell. Droik vanished, then appeared in the prison. Before Droik could re-orient himself, Josh pointed his wand at the four corners of the cell. The door locked shut.

Droik spun his wand around, but nothing happened. "You can't keep me in here!"

Josh smiled. "I don't have to. You'll be in here long enough to consider the fact that you were trapped by a mere apprentice."

Droik's teeth ground against each other. "And when I get out, then you'll be sorry! Both you and Milnore!"

Josh drew close to the bars. "No problem, because I know the most powerful spell of all."

Droik's eyebrows shot up. "What is it? Tell me and I may not come after you."

Josh stared at the wizard, his mouth straight. "Forgiveness."

Droik opened his mouth to say something, but then he paused. I could see the thoughts bouncing around in his head.

I helped Milnore to his feet. The wounds had sealed and breath had returned to his body. Milnore patted Josh on the back. "See, I knew you had it in you. Let's go."

Josh grinned. With a flip of his wand and a mumbled spell, we returned to Reol.

History's Perspective

I placed my card on the table. "Ah ha! My king trumps your joker."

Jake, my sandy-haired, ten-year-old brother, stared at his cards. A smile grew on his face. "But not this." He slapped a card on the table.

An ace. An ace added to any card above ten created a combo, but alone meant nothing.

He put his remaining cards on the table. "Blow up. I win."

I fingered my cards for a moment. "I don't think I have any other card to counter with." I sat the cards down. "You win." I shook his hand. "Congratulations, brother. Ready for another?"

He started to speak but a knock echoed from the door.

"Sisko, would you get that?" my mom yelled from the kitchen.

"Yes ma'am." I rose and opened the door.

A clean-shaven man carrying a five-year-old girl stood before me. "Is this the home of Sisko?"

I glanced back at Jake sitting at the table before nodding. "Can I help you?"

He held out the girl. Her short, brown hair swung under his hands. "This is my daughter. She is crippled and can't work. She'll live in poverty her whole life. Can you help her?"

I recalled Jake used to be crippled before I entered the steam house. It granted me the ring by which I could help others. I checked and felt God wanted me to help her.

I placed my hand on the girl's legs. "Father, please make these legs whole and strong."

The feet that dangled from his arms straightened. The man slipped her feet first to the porch and gingerly let her put weight on them. A grin grew on the girl's face as she bounced on her toes, and then took a step.

She flung herself upon me and hugged tight. "Thank you, Sisko."

The man couldn't hide his joy. "If I could, I would give you all I possess."

I smiled at the rejoicing, my favorite part of using this gift. "I couldn't accept any gifts if you did offer them. But can you tell me something?"

The man fixed his eyes upon me. "Anything."

"Where are you from and how did you hear about me?"

"We're from Siloth, and I heard about you from a circus that passed through town a few months ago. Upon confirming the reports, I decided to seek you out. And am I glad I did." He held his daughter close as she stood by his side.

"Do you have a place to stay? And food?"

"Yes. We've been living on the road for the last month traveling here. We don't want to be a burden to anyone. You've done enough. Thank you so much."

I smiled. "You're most welcome. Have a good trip back."

They hugged me again, then turned and left, his daughter skipping down the road ahead of him.

My mother entered the room, wiping her hands on a towel as I shut the door. "Who was that?"

"Another person who needed healing."

She stared at the door. "They're the third ones this week. As many as came in a whole year before. You're getting known, son. The number will grow, I dare say."

"This one was from Siloth. About a month's journey to get here, he said."

"At this rate, we'll need to rent an office for you."

I laughed. "I've already heard rumors that I'm putting the doctor out of business."

She gave me a half smile. "What I really need from the great Sisko, the healer, is to go to the market and get me some fresh tomatoes. You think you can handle that with your busy schedule?"

I shook my head. "Mom. I'm not that famous."

"But you will be." She held out her hand. "Here's the money to buy them."

I pocketed the coins. "I'll be right back."

She nodded and returned to the kitchen. I told Jake I'd return soon for the next hand and then headed out the door.

I strolled into the center of town and circled the church as I dodged people and the occasional wagon. I entered Reol's small market. Mostly they sold produce, as many took the non-perishable items to Holoroth across the mountains.

I spotted Josh staring at some cucumbers and sneaked up behind him. "Looking for a fat wand you can eat?"

He jumped before turning around. "Sisko. It's never smart to sneak up on a wizard, you know. I could have turned you into something horrible."

"You're more dangerous when you think you know what you're doing."

He bopped me on the head. "Not funny."

I patted him on the back. "Only for you. So did your mom send you here to get something?"

"My mom? No way."

"Let me guess. You grew bored of casting spells and decided to entertain yourself with vegetables."

He grunted. "Not even close. I'm filling Milore's shopping list."

"Oh, I see. My mom sent me for some tomatoes." I spotted some. "And there they are. I'll see you later."

"Very well. But don't bother running to me next time you need some magical help. You obviously don't appreciate it." Josh thrust his nose into the air.

I laughed then headed to the tomatoes. I purchased three ripe ones and returned to the house. As I opened the door, I felt an unsettling knot in my gut grow.

"Mom? Jake?" No one answered. I entered the kitchen and placed the tomatoes on the counter. Then I noticed a note. I picked it up and read.

Sisko, if you wish to see your father, mother, and brother alive again, come one mile down the road leading to Siloest and leave your ring on the stump you find there. Come alone, or they die. You have til sundown.

I fell into the chair and stared at the note. Seconds ticked by as the reality of the news sunk in. What could I do? The ring wouldn't come off; I couldn't leave it anywhere. My parents and Jake would die.

But I had to do something. Maybe I could talk to them. But what would they do once they realized I couldn't give them the ring?

The sun sank in the afternoon sky. It would take me at least half an hour to get there. That left a couple hours at the most to figure out what I could do.

A knock thudded from the front door. Dare I answer it? I tiptoed to the porch window and glanced out. I relaxed; Josh stood outside. I opened the door.

Josh entered. "I was thinking, Sisko," He caught my eyes. "What if we…what's wrong?"

I handed him the note. He studied it for a moment. I watched his mouth drop open.

He met my eyes. "Sisko, I'm so sorry. What are you going to do?"

I shrugged. "I wish I knew. The only thing I can do is go and try to talk them out of this. Maybe whoever this is will understand."

Josh sat his basket of vegetables on the floor and leaned against a wall. "More likely they'll kill you and your family once they learn the truth."

We stood there in silence for a few minutes. I continued to examine the situation, hoping to find a solution. It appeared Josh did the same.

Josh snapped his fingers. "I can do a duplicating spell on your ring, create another that looks just like it. Maybe they'll take that and run."

I ran my fingers through my hair. "I don't know. Once they find out it doesn't do any miracles, they'll come back with a vengeance."

"Sure, but by then, Milore and I will be ready for them. We'll make sure they're taken care of." Josh watched me. "Can you think of a better plan?"

I mulled it over. "Not really. But if they find out, we're all dead for sure. It's risky, but less risky than what I proposed. The question is, however, can you duplicate it? The magic of the ring is stronger than any of your spells. It may not let you."

Josh pulled out his wand. "It would be a fake duplicate, not an identical one. I can duplicate the object, not any inherent magic attached to it. Hold your palm out."

I stretched out my hand; Josh grabbed my wrist and waved the wand over my palm. A few mumbled words later, and a ring materialized onto my finger next to the real one.

I pulled on it and it slid off. I held it up between my thumb and finger. It appeared identical enough, though I doubt they would have seen the real one to know any different. Even the Hebrew letters which spelled out, "It is more blessed to give than to receive," appeared the same.

I put the ring in my pocket. "Guess I had better get this over with. No sense waiting until the last minute." I pointed a finger at Josh. "Remember, they said alone. Don't jeopardize my family's lives by following me. Promise?"

He bowed his head. "I promise." He reached out and hugged me for a second. He stared at the floor. "That's in case next time I see you is in Paradise."

I breathed deep. "I'll be back. God can work this out." I hoped.

"Good luck. May God be with you." Josh picked up his basket and left.

I stared at his receding figure. "He'd better be, or we're all lost."

I closed the door and worked my way down the road, praying. I hardly noticed the trees of the forest as I left town, or the birds singing in their branches. My focus rested on saving my family.

I came to the clearing by the road where the old stump stood alone. I scanned the area, but saw no one. I kept my fingers closed to hide my real ring, and pulled the fake one from my pocket. I crept into the clearing; the wind blew in gusts, causing the tree branches to sway.

I placed the ring on the stump and backed away. Nothing happened. Perhaps they had not arrived, not expecting me so early. I turned and nearly jumped.

Blocking my access to the road stood four men, clothed in leather jackets and pants. Each held a sword and grinned. I heard noise to my left and behind. I turned to find more men emerging from the trees.

A thin-faced man, his chin covered with a black beard, stepped forward to the stump, picked up the ring, and held it in his hands. "Looks like a ring, but how do I know this is the one? How does it work?"

I stared at the stump. "You ask God for something."

The man waved his hands toward the edge of the clearing, and two of the men pulled off branches to unveil my father, mother, and brother tied to three tree trunks, their mouths gagged.

I jumped watching them struggle against their bonds, but the swords rising up in defense caused me to hold my ground.

The leader pointed the ring at Jake. "So, if I stab him, I should be able to heal him with this ring? Yes?"

I stared into his eyes. Any answer I gave would give away the truth. I hoped he wouldn't test it.

He sighed. "I thought so." He nodded toward one of his gang.

The one by Jake drew his sword back.

"No!" I screamed.

The blade plunged into Jake's chest. He gasped and stared into the sky, then slumped against the ropes.

I ran to him, and surprisingly none of the gang stopped me. I felt the faintest of breaths on his lips. "Father, heal Jake of this wound."

Jake's body jerked, the blood stopped flowing, and Jake flickered his eyes open.

I felt hands wrap around my arms and pull me back.

The leader stood before me. "Just as I suspected. This one is a fake." He tossed the ring into the forest. "Now, how about giving me the real one?"

"I can't."

"If you don't, I'll force you to watch as each of your family dies a slow death. I know a few techniques that are quite entertaining."

"No, what I mean is I can't give it to anyone. I can't take it off my finger."

He nodded to one of his gang again, and the man lifted his sword.

I reached out my hand. "No, please. I'm telling the truth."

The thief placed the blade tip on Jake's neck. Jake squirmed. Father and Mother stared wide-eyed at the sword against their son's throat.

The leader stepped toward me and handed me a knife. "You have two options, Sisko. You can do nothing, and watch us kill each of them slowly and painfully. Or you can get the ring off, cut it off if you have to, and give me the ring. I'll throw in healing your finger for you if you're good about it."

My breathing grew shallow. "I…I…"

The man ripped Jake's tunic off, and slid the edge of his blade down Jake's chest, eliciting a scream muffled from under the gag and leaving a beading trail of blood in its wake.

"All right, stop!" I gulped. "I'll try and get it off."

I felt wetness drip over my cheeks as I lifted the blade to my finger. *Father, forgive me.*

No! echoed from my heart.

But I can't watch them die before me. I don't have the stomach for it. It'll kill me. Tell me what to do!

The leader grunted. "Come on, boy. I was young once. Do you want your brother to live to old age or not? It's only a finger."

Then a prayer came to my mind. "Father, help this man to examine his life and repent."

The leader shook his head. "If that's the way you want it." He started to signal the torturer to continue, but before he could, the colors of the forest swirled about us, blurring into a white cloud before slowing, reforming, until he and I stood on a schoolyard play area.

He jerked his head about. "What happened?"

"You tell me. Does this look familiar?"

Kids danced in a circle, holding hands, singing, "Once upon a time, I was a wee little boy, and everyone grew up—like Cody. One became a baker, one a butcher, and another a candlestick maker. But you grew up into nobody!"

They giggled and scattered. One boy sat in the middle, crying.

The leader stared at the scene. "Why, that's me, when I was a kid. How can this be?"

I glanced at him. "You're lonely."

He grunted. "Not lonely, just…independent is all."

I walked over to the child. He acted as if we weren't there. "It's a very sad independence."

He waved his hand. "I got over it. Made me into the man I am today. Strong. Tough."

A teacher poked her head out of the door. "Everyone, recess is over. Come in." She noticed the child sitting before us. "You too, Clark."

The kid rose slowly and dragged his feet as he pushed himself to the schoolhouse.

I grinned. God was forcing Clark to review his life. Before I could say another word, the colors blurred again, spinning like a cyclone about us. Once they reformed, we stood on a street before a wood frame building. A sign on the front read "Clark's Investments."

A man approached the door of the building from the busy street of people rushing to and fro. Another man stopped by him, holding a cup out. "Please give for my starving family."

The man grunted and pushed the cup aside. "Begone, scum." He entered the building and slammed the door shut.

The man with the cup shook his head and stepped away.

Clark next to me laughed. "Those guys use that money to buy booze and drugs. It's a big scam."

I stepped to follow the beggar. "Let's find out."

Clark placed a hand on my shoulder. "No. I'm not falling for this trip down memory lane. Take me back to the clearing or I'll choke you where you stand.

I shrugged. "Have it your way."

He smiled. "That's better."

"Go ahead. Choke me."

His eyes grew big, then he reached for my neck and squeezed. I felt nothing. I blinked at him and smiled.

"Why, your neck feels like iron." He pulled back and swung at my face.

"Ouch!" He cradled his fist in his gut, covered with his other hand.

"It's as I suspected. We're inside the ring's influence now. It protects me. You have no choice but to follow this out. Now, do I have to force you to follow, or will you come willingly?"

He grumbled. "All right, let's get this over with. But as soon as we're back, you'll be dead by my hands."

I smiled. "Fair enough."

We caught up to the beggar and followed him as he asked for money from several more before he headed to his house. Few gave, but with what had been given, he stopped at the market and bought some bread.

He led us outside of town and to a lean-to. Four kids and a wife hovered inside over a small table, and blankets were spread on the ground for beds.

The beggar slipped inside. "I had enough to get some bread today."

A smile spread across the woman's lips. "Oh, that's wonderful, Clive. At least we'll have something to eat today." She broke the bread up, giving the biggest chunks to the children.

Clark nudged me. "All right. So he is poor and not using it to buy drugs. What difference does it make to me?"

"All our lives are intertwined." I kept watching the family eating the bread so fast you'd think they feared it would disappear.

The beggar slammed his fist on the table. "This begging is getting me nowhere. People don't give. I'll have to take if we're to get ahead."

"Oh, honey." The woman covered his hands. "Don't talk like that. We'll make it somehow."

Clive rose to his feet. "I'm going to check on something."

She followed him out of the lean-to. "Don't do anything you'll regret."

He stared into her eyes. "I'll do what I have to." He pushed past her and slipped between us as he passed into the street. Lines of worry plowed over his face, his eyes spoke of desperation.

"I know that man."

I turned to Clark. "This beggar?"

Clark's head sank. "Yes, he's a member of my gang."

I blinked. "What happened to him and his family?"

"He told me once. He joined the gang I eventually joined. During his first robbery with them, a drunkard attacked his wife and children. He returned to find them dead."

"How horrible."

"Next to me, he has the coldest heart of the group." Clark breathed deep. "That's the way it is. The world is a cruel place."

I stared at the family, hoping God would change the scene before the drunk attacked. "So we should add to the cruelty instead of countering it?"

He grunted. "I don't expect you to know about life yet, young as you are. You'll find out soon enough if you want to survive, you have to look out for yourself before anyone else."

"I read by someone who should know, that if you seek to save your life, you will lose it. And if you give your life away, you'll find it."

He laughed. "Riddles. Why should I expect anything else from a vision?"

The trees and lean-to stretched and spun into a blur. Once the scene materialized again, we stood in a wooden room. From the desks, papers, and fireplace, I gathered it was Clark's office. The young Clark sat hunched over a desk, transcribing numbers.

The door swung open, and another man entered followed by two muscle-bound men. The first man pulled a cigar from his mouth and lifted a clump of papers into the air. "I've bought you out, Clark, and I'm taking over. Leave now."

The young Clark rose from his desk. "You can't do this to me!"

"I did. Done. Gone. Out." He motioned for the two bodyguards.

They grabbed Clark by the arms and pulled him toward the door.

"What did I do wrong? We're profitable!"

He waved his hand. "Bye. Have a great life."

The two men threw Clark onto the street and slammed the door shut.

Clark pointed. "See what I mean? Life sucks."

"How do you know that wasn't an opportunity? A call to change your life for the better?"

He shook his head. "I lived a comfortable life. I expected to marry her in the near future. Then I lost it all. Everything."

"You're still thinking of it from your perspective."

He shrugged. "What other perspective is there?"

I nodded toward the building. "So what became of him? How did he fare?"

Clark stared at the sign as someone came out and changed the name to "Henry's Investments." "He gained the money to buy me out from a woman who entered his life. She pushed him, but apparently didn't have to push hard. A few months later, she divorced him and took it all. I heard he killed himself."

"Doesn't sound like keeping it helped him much. How come you didn't kill yourself?"

"I probably would have." He shifted his feet. "But that's when I found the gang. I discovered a home there, people that would watch out for me, better than anyone else I knew. Better than my parents."

The swirling began again. Spinning lights slowed until we found ourselves viewing the scene we'd originally left. Except now I watched myself kneeling on the ground, a bloody finger held by my other hand. Clark held the ring in the air, watching the sunlight sparkling off it.

Clark grinned next to me. "See, I'll succeed."

Two of the gang standing behind Clark lifted their swords. As Clark pushed the ring toward his finger, the two blades plunged into Clark's back. He breathed one last breath as his eyes widened, and he collapsed onto the ground, limp.

Clark next to me shook his head. "No, they wouldn't do this. This can't be real."

"Well, I certainly hope not. But I guess that's up to you. Actions have consequences, for the better or worse."

He shrugged. "Then again, I would die anyway. So my life sucked. I don't think I could have done anything to change that."

I shook my head. "I wish you hadn't said that."

Once again the colors swirled about us until we stood among a great crowd by a fiery sea. A brilliant light poured from one end of the sea and reflected off many around its shores. The light conveyed peace, contentment, joy, pure and glorious.

But among the throng, some also writhed on the ground, as if in an eternal fire. I turned toward Clark and found him squirming on the ground, crying for relief.

He spotted me. "Please, please, let's leave this place! Why aren't you in agony here?"

I gazed over the crowd, observing those who rejoiced and those who screamed in pain. "They would cry out for the rocks to fall on them and hide them from the presence of the one who sits on the throne. We're standing before God."

A brilliant flash shot from the throne, covering everything in white. Clark screamed at the top of his lungs.

The light receded, and we stood once again in the clearing. I held a knife next to my finger while Clark's scream died off into the swaying forest.

One of the gang asked, "Is something wrong?"

Clark breathed hard and glanced around at each of his men, before landing his eyes on me. "Unbind them and let them go."

"But we've planned this for so long. We can't stop at the point of success."

Clark gritted his teeth, pulled a knife from his belt, and then slung it under the gang member's neck. "I've seen a vision. This ring would destroy us, not save us. For us, it would be a curse."

The gang glanced at each other.

Clark removed the knife from his throat. "You've trusted me before. Trust me now. We've been together too long to have all we've worked for torn down in a moment of greed. Let them go."

They wordlessly conversed through eye contact, then nodded. Two of the gang cut Father, Mother, and Jake down, then removed their gags. We stepped onto the road and headed back to town. I glanced back toward Clark. He stared at me with a frown on his face but wonder in his eyes.

As we followed the road back home, I healed Jake's wounds and thought about my own life. I watched Mother, with her eyes still wet from the event. Father's legs shook as he walked. Jake leaned against me, one arm wrapped around my waist.

"Mother, Father."

They focused on me. Mother said, "Yes?"

"I think it's time I traveled to find those God wants me to help. I can no longer stay in one place."

She wiped her eyes. "Travel? Are you sure?"

"He is nineteen, dear. If he's not going to marry and settle down, maybe he should get some traveling in." Father kept his eyes fixed ahead.

"I'm sure, Mother. The longer I stay here, the more of a circus our house will become, and the more danger I'll put you in."

Jake pulled my arm. "But who will I play Blow Up with?"

I patted him on the back. "I'm sure you can find one of the other kids."

"I don't want another kid. I want you."

I breathed deep, trying to keep the tears from surfacing. "I'll miss you too, little brother."

Upon returning home, I found Josh waiting for me. He bounded from the porch and hugged me, overjoyed to see not only me, but the whole family in good shape. Naturally he demanded a full account of all that happened.

Then I told him my plans. His face fell, but he nodded in agreement. "Come and see me at Milore's before you go."

I agreed and he left. I ate dinner with my family, wondering if I'd ever do so again. I knew I wouldn't be returning for a long, long, time. Maybe never. The less anyone thought I resided here still, the safer my family would be. I couldn't put them through another incident like this one. I'd never forgive myself.

I tossed and turned that night, finding it hard to sleep. I rose early at dawn and stuffed what I could carry in a pack. I ate breakfast, then rose and slung the pack onto my back.

"I've got to go. Tell anyone who comes searching for me that you're sorry, but I'm no longer here."

Mother wiped her eyes with a handkerchief and hugged me. "Take good care of yourself, Sisko. I dreamed last night I would see you again, but not alive."

I rubbed her back. "Don't say things like that, Mother. I'm sure I'll return someday."

"You promise?"

I hesitated. "I wish I could, but that will be up to God. But if at all possible, I will."

Jake hugged me. I would miss seeing him grow up. Father shook my hand, but then gave in and hugged me as well.

I pushed my feet to move through the yard. I opened the gate and stepped into the road. I shut it and stared at my family. They waved and I waved back. I smiled as best I could, despite the urge to retreat back to my comfortable room.

But I couldn't do that. I took a deep breath and forced my feet to step away. The scene felt surreal as I passed familiar houses, gazed upon the church and the cross lifted high upon its dome. Then once out of town, strolled the familiar path to Milore's house, recalling the first time I'd run to his house, in the dark, chasing Josh.

I entered the clearing and spotted Josh chopping wood beside the cottage. He stopped and wiped the sweat from his brow and chest.

I pointed at the ax. "What? No levitation and multiplying spells to speed up the work?"

He laughed. "I'd only do that if you were around to heal me when the axes go haywire."

I grinned. "So, why did you want me to come by, other than to say goodbye?"

His mouth lost its smile. "I've learned a spell that I want to use on you."

I slapped my forehead. "No, Josh, not another spell!"

He shook his head. "No, you don't understand. This is serious. I've spent hours studying it to make sure I can do it right the first time. I can't get this one wrong."

So this was to be my going away present. Figured. "What does this spell do?"

He smiled. "It will create a mental link between us. No matter the distance, we will be linked together and can communicate at will."

I rubbed my chin. "Sounds interesting. That could be helpful."

"Yes. I could find out what's happening with you and relate that to your family, and I could tell you anything you need to know about what is going on here."

I tilted my head to one side. "That sounds good. Any downsides?"

Josh half-smiled. "It can only be broken by agreement of both parties when they are physically present. So until you return or I come and find you, we'll be able to contact each other, whenever."

I stepped closer to him. "You are my best friend. One promise you'll need to make."

"Go ahead."

"Now this is serious. However long this link exists, that's how long this promise will last."

Josh nodded. "I understand."

"I want you to watch out for my family and keep them safe. There may be others who come here, thinking they can get to me through them.

70

Eventually word will get around that I'm no longer here, but some will not realize that until it's too late. Promise you'll do that for as long as you live or this link between us exists."

He opened his mouth. I interrupted. "And that means to protect them, you have to promise never tell any living soul that we have this link. If people knew about it, they would continue to affect me through them. Never a word to anyone. It will be our secret, until we're dead or unlinked."

The corner of his lips lifted slightly. "It will be so." He reached out a hand to me. I grasped it and pulled him to me in a hug.

"All right, now you can do it."

Josh stood back and pulled out his wand. He took a deep breath and closed his eyes. He twirled the wand between us and recited a spell. Sparkles appeared in the air and grew in density and length, until they reached our heads. Then the lines sharpened and brightened. The line grew into an electrical shock which threw me back to the ground.

I shook my head. That was some strong magic. But it gave me a headache.

Can you hear me?

Josh? Is that you?

He laughed out loud. *Yes! It worked!*

I sat up. "You weren't sure it would?"

He rose to his feet. "I figured it would, but you know, it's exciting when it does work."

I huffed. "I'd better not find out about any strange side effects in a few days."

He laughed. "Out of this world, isn't it?" *I bet no one ever invents anything like this, eh?*

I smiled. "Probably not." I stared down the road. This would never be easy, and I dreaded the parting. "But I need to go."

He nodded and his smile faded. "I knew this day would come. That's why I've worked on preparing that spell. I didn't want to lose contact with the one best friend I've ever had."

I pulled him into my arms. "Likewise, my friend. Thank you for everything." I released him and he blinked back tears. "Keep that promise."

"I'll do all in my power to protect them. May God go with you."

I waved. "And with you." He barely smiled. I turned and headed toward the road going south out of Reol. Now God would lead me to the people I should help. No more waiting for people to come to me. It felt

71

more like a real ministry now. A mission God had called me to fulfill.

I turned onto the road to Holoroth. The Skinny Mountain range loomed over the tree tops. The sun rose high into the sky. I breathed in the fresh air. Something about it all rejuvenated me. Who knew what adventures God had planned, or how many years I would travel before settling down somewhere?

Sisko, can you hear me now?

Yes, Josh, I can hear you just fine.

How frequently should I check in?

I sighed. *When you have something to tell me, I would guess.*

He paused. *Well, so far, everything's going as planned.*

Josh, I've only been gone for thirty minutes.

I'm sorry. I already miss you.

I chuckled. *I miss you too. I'll chat with you tonight once I bed down.*

All right. Signing off, for now.

Bye. I shook my head. Until the novelty wore off, I might regret having agreed to this link. But I knew it could prove to be the only contact with my family for some time to come. Maybe for the rest of my life.

"Thank you, Josh."

Anger's Spell

Sweat stung my eyes as I wiped my brow. The wide, dusty forest road and the blazing sun didn't make for good traveling weather. My dry throat forced me to the shade by the side of the road. I sat on a rock and poured cool water down my throat.

Tall green trees bordered the well-used route. Birds sang in the background. It should have lightened my spirits, but it didn't.

I lifted the ring and examined the ancient language engraved upon it. Hebrew, the priest had said, and translated it as "It is more blessed to give than to receive." Through the ring God had called me onto the road, to unknown places and people, to fulfill the task bestowed upon me: to be my brother's keeper.

The ring and the calling had come at fourteen. Now nineteen years of age, I still didn't feel ready to venture alone on paths in the middle of a forest. Despite my desire for their safety, it seemed a great folly to leave my family. What hope did I have to make a difference?

Then I realized the birds had stopped singing. Quietness pervaded the forest save the wind gusting, swirling dust down the road. Uneasiness settled into my heart.

What am I doing out here? I'm not ready for this; I'm going back home.

I arose, placed the water back into my pack, and proceeded home with quickened pace.

I had barely gone ten feet when five young men jumped onto the road, brandishing swords.

I froze. My heartbeat pounded in my ears, and my leg muscles tightened like a coiled viper ready to spring.

"Give me your valuables, boy," a chunky young man snarled at me. His muscles bulged under his plain white shirt and leather vest. His wavy, blond hair contrasted with his steel gaze. I could tell his confidence masked a deep hurt. The need to control often hid out-of-control lives.

"My name's Sisko, and I don't have much of worth, Sir."

"I don't recall asking for your name." He swung the sword under my neck. "If you've nothing of worth, then you won't mind if we take an inventory." He motioned, and one of the thieves pulled off my pack. Another joined him in rummaging through it.

"Nothing in here worth anything, Dragon Breath."

Dragon Breath sheathed his sword and drew close. He grabbed the pack and slammed it onto my back.

I stumbled with the force but kept my feet under me as the pack fell off and crashed on the ground. My back throbbed, but I picked it up and put it on.

His eyes grew big. He grabbed my hand and yanked it up. "This ring should fetch us a tidy sum." He attempted to pull it off, but it wouldn't move.

"It won't come off." Pain shot through my finger as he strained and yanked.

Dragon Breath whipped out a knife. A grin creased his face. "That's easily solved."

"Father, change…" I wanted to change the knife into a feather. But I could only use the power to help others, not myself, lest I be cursed instead of blessed.

What would help this thug?

Sweat dribbled down my face as Dragon Breath placed the knife under my finger.

"Father, take Dragon Breath home."

What else could be better? I wished I could be home, so surely this man needed to be home as well.

The colors of the forest spun until they blended. Because Dragon Breath held my hand, I traveled with him.

As if someone had brought a spinning ride to a sudden halt, the colors formed themselves into an unknown place. I stood at the top of a mountain. A log cabin rested in a clearing among tall trees.

The world continued to move as if we had spun round and round. The knife thudded against a rock, fresh blood on the blade. We both collapsed onto the ground. My pack rattled as it rolled down a slight incline.

Once the ground stayed in one place, we both stood up. A teenage girl, about fifteen, rounded the corner. A breeze flowed through her blond hair. Her blue eyes widened, and she covered her mouth with her hands.

"Who is it?" a deep voice sounded from around the corner.

"No one, Father." The doubt in her voice betrayed her.

Her father appeared from behind the cabin. Tall and brawny, he held an ax in his hand. His jaw set, and his eyes narrowed. "I thought I told you never to come back here again. I disowned you as my son."

"It wasn't my doing, Father."

"Father? What did I just say? It's sir to you." His father dropped the ax onto the porch and grabbed a sword leaning against the cabin. He held it ready to strike and stepped toward us.

Dragon Breath drew his sword and raced toward his father. Metal rang as the blades flashed in the sunlight.

Maybe sending him home wasn't such a good idea after all.

I examined the cut on my ring finger. The blood had almost crusted over. It would heal.

I felt like an uninvited guest as the family feud progressed. The two men parried, thrust, swung, and dodged. Sweat beaded on their necks and dripped from their noses. One would attack from one side, then another.

Then their father swung his weapon and followed with his fist, landing a blow to Dragon Breath's face. Dragon Breath grunted and staggered back.

The father swung down onto his sword arm. Dragon Breath's weapon fell to the ground, still held by his severed hand.

Dragon Breath let out a cry and fell to the ground. Pain etched his face. His eyes conveyed not only physical pain but the pain of death approaching and being helpless to stop it.

The father lifted his sword to run his son through.

"Sir," I called out, "do not kill him on my account. I'm responsible for bringing him here. I didn't know."

The father sneered. "You're doing us all a favor today, boy. Now stay out of this, or you'll be next."

Now I knew where Dragon Breath had inherited his pleasant disposition.

The father lifted his sword again, but before he could bring it down, the girl ran in front of him.

"Father, he may not be your son anymore, but he is still my brother.

Do not kill him." Tears rolled down her cheeks as she stared unblinking at him.

The sword wavered, and then he brought it to his side.

She ripped a strip of cloth from her dress, grabbed a stick, and tightened the cloth around his stub to stop the bleeding. Dragon Breath's eyes had glazed over from the loss of blood.

The father turned and left. The girl stood and glared at me. "Well, if you're responsible for bringing him here, the least you could do is help me get him into bed."

I worked to overcome my shock. My family had always been so warm and loving. I'd heard stories, but experiencing the reality impressed the horror upon me.

"Sure." I wondered if I should heal him, but my heart checked that thought. Not yet, later. God must have something to teach him.

I stumbled over to help. "He'll live."

Her face relaxed. "I'm sorry for being so snippy. My name's Gabrielle, and this is my brother, Seth."

"Gabrielle. What a nice name." I noticed her face flushing. "My name's Sisko." I stuck out a hand.

She placed hers in mine. As if I had tapped into an unused nerve, her thoughts rushed toward me. Her soul lay bare before my mind's eye, and what I saw scared me: an image of us embraced in a kiss.

I jerked my hand back. Confusion fought against joy, and confusion won. I had never experienced another's thoughts. Why now? Why her? Yet, her slight smile disappearing into her own confusion revealed she experienced it too. "Hum, yes. We had better get Seth into bed."

Then she raised one corner of her lip as she focused on Seth. "Yes. On the count of three."

She knew. Knew that I had felt something too. I wondered if she had seen into my soul as well, and what she saw in me.

I entered the cabin after a few hours in the forest. Seth lay groaning and tossing in his bed. It felt uncomfortable knowing I could heal him. Had I judged correctly? At least it had given me time to think and pray without fear of an attack.

Their father had left to hunt after making it clear to keep my hands to myself. The two-room cabin had a fireplace on one end. A pot full of soup simmered over the fire, spreading a savory aroma through the room.

Sitting by Seth's side, his sister Gabrielle tended to him, changing the bandages on his stub. Her soft eyes met mine and brightened.

Seth turned his head and frowned. "What's he still doing here?"

"Because I want him here." She smiled at me.

She radiated joy and warmth, a striking contrast from the other two. Like a single star shining in a pitch-black night sky.

"Just look at me." Seth stuck his stub into the air. "I commanded men, and now I'm useless. You've taken away my life!"

"You were in charge of a gang of thugs," Gabrielle said. "He may have saved your life."

"I tried to help," I said.

"You were trying to keep from getting your finger cut off." Seth dropped his arm to his side. "Besides, Sis, this guy's a wizard. He'll bring nothing but evil." He glared at me. "Where does your power come from?"

I fingered the ring. Probably not a good idea to tell him everything. No telling what ideas he might get. "God has given me the ability and responsibility to aid others."

Seth grunted. "You're not very good at it. Maybe God should give you an easier job, like shoveling horse—."

"Seth, stop!" Gabrielle scowled at him.

I lowered my head. If God hadn't called me, I would agree. I pulled on the ring, just in case He had changed his mind. It remained firmly in place.

Gabrielle motioned to me and grabbed two jars. "Pick up two and come with me to draw water from the stream."

We followed a forest path as we talked.

"I apologize for my brother. I'm afraid he's too much like Father. Both are very proud and stubborn."

"If I had known they would try to kill each other, I wouldn't have asked God to bring him here." My eyes remained focused on the path.

"That's probably why God didn't tell you, because He had other ideas." She sighed. "Though, I admit, there doesn't seem to be much hope for either of them. They are both afflicted with a mental sickness that comes and goes. They'll go into a rage over the smallest things."

"If you don't mind my asking, why are they so at odds with each other?"

"Long story, but Father caught him stealing from a neighbor. Ever since then, just seeing him can send my father into a rage, and that triggers Seth's. They can't be together long before they are swinging swords or fists at each other."

I shook my head. "A mental sickness?"

"That's what I call it. Others say it's the demonic spell an old wizard placed on our family generations ago. And it would seem to be true. All the men since then have raged."

"A wizard, huh? That means there's hope for a cure."

"Hope?" She stopped and faced me. "I often feel hope has failed."

I gazed into her blue eyes. They flickered like a wavering light, barely holding on. "I don't think you can lose hope. But people can give up on it, usually before they should, when things seem blackest."

She stared back as if searching my soul. "You haven't lived as I have, have you?"

I closed my eyes. "No, I haven't."

"Then what do you know of holding onto hope?"

I opened my eyes and saw tears falling down her cheeks. "You haven't lived as I have either. If so, you would know."

She held my gaze for what seemed minutes. Then she continued to the stream. I followed in silence. When we arrived, I helped her fill the jars. Once done, she sat on the root of an old tree by the bank. I sat next to her. Her hand grabbed mine, and a surge of tingles ran up my arm as her thoughts flooded in again.

"If it were not for duty, I would fly away with you. I would experience your life and see this hope you speak of." Her longing eyes stared at me. Her soul lay bare through her touch. Sadness, pain, and despair crowded around a spark of love and hope—in me.

I pulled my hand away, but the feeling of her soft skin and desire for me remained. I didn't want to lead her on, not when she couldn't come. I didn't want to desire what I couldn't have.

"Hope is within each of us. It is in you, I can feel it. My path is to wander, to seek those God wants me to help. You would not find hope there any faster than you would here."

She dropped her head. "You could give it to me."

I lifted her chin to see her eyes. "No, I cannot. I could for a moment.

Maybe a day, but it would fade if it doesn't come from within and above."

She stood. "Well, Sisko, if you'll not help me with hope, at least help carry these jars of water to the cabin." She scooped two into her arms and proceeded down the path.

I shook my head, picked up the other two, and followed after her. Did she just ask me to propose marriage? Did I want to? No, I couldn't. It didn't matter what I wanted.

We arrived at the cabin, but she stopped before entering the clearing and turned to me. "Kiss me."

"What?" I blinked.

"I said kiss me. It will confirm the truth of your words." She set her jars on a stump.

"I…I can't. I mean, I shouldn't."

She stepped closer to me. "Then I think you do love me. Kiss me to prove it isn't true."

This seemed a silly way to prove it. But her touch had revealed much. I could only imagine what a kiss might reveal. I doubted I wanted to find out.

I sighed. "Fine." I put the jars on the ground.

She leaned to me, and I to her. Images of silky hair flowing with the wind imprinted upon my mind. Eyes, searching my face, watched as I drew near. I paused, my lips almost touching. *Should I?*

"What did I say, you miserable leech! Keep away from her!"

I jerked back and saw the father striding toward me, sword unsheathed. "But Sir, I…, I mean, she…" What could I say that he would believe? And would it matter if he now raged?

Gabrielle shoved me. "Run, he means you harm. Get away."

Run I did. She probably thought I could disappear at will as I had appeared. But I couldn't, not to save my life. The father ran after me. Where could I go? What could I do?

He gained on me as I shot across the grass. Into the forest? He knew it better than I did. He hunted in those woods, and I would be another kill among many. But where?

I could hear his footsteps behind me. Stealing a glance, I saw him draw his sword back. I ran around a tree as his blade headed for my neck. It embedded into the tree instead.

I dashed for the house while he worked to pull his sword from the trunk. I swung open the back door and rushed to the center of the main room. I searched for anything I could use.

My eyes fell on Seth. He glared at me. No time for him, I had to find something. I spotted swords hanging on the mantle. Impulsively I grabbed one and ran for the front door.

The father charged in. "He attempted to kiss Gabrielle," he said to Seth.

I saw Seth rising from his bed. I sped out the door and into the yard.

What am I doing? I don't know how to sword fight. Yet, there seemed no other way to defend myself. I had nowhere to hide. Best to face him.

I stopped and turned. The father slowed as he approached, his sword lifted high. Behind him followed Seth, holding his sword in his left hand.

"Run, Sisko!" Gabrielle's voice rang with hopeless desperation.

The father brought down his sword. I blocked it, but the force nearly knocked it from my hand. He swung again fast. I strained as my sword barely kept his next strike from my chest. I wouldn't be able to keep this up much longer. He pulled from underneath. I attempted to block, but he pushed my blade into the air.

Their movements slowed to a third of what it had been, while I moved at a normal speed. His sword swung from the left. I fell backwards as it glided over my dropping body. I landed on my hands and back-flipped away from his reach.

On my feet again, my back settled against an old elm. The father and Seth glided toward me, swords ready to strike a blow.

I had to heal them of this rage. But how could I reverse a wizard's spell? An answer settled into my heart. To undo the spell, I had to take on the sickness. Within, I could defeat it.

I dropped to the ground as their swords passed over me and into the tree. I rolled between their legs and sprang to my feet behind them as they slowly searched me out. To them, I probably seemed to disappear.

I placed my hands on their shoulders. "Father, heal their rage though me."

A light shone around the three of us. I stiffened as I felt a creeping sensation filling my soul. Muddied thoughts clouded my thinking. My rational mind disengaged, and left my body. I watched myself from the outside as well as inside. My eyes glared in anger, and I felt helpless to stop it. The light dimmed around us.

The father and Seth shook their heads and returned to a normal speed. They lowered their swords, but I raised mine.

I stared on as my other self lunged at the two men. They dodged my stab. I swung around with amazing speed and clanged my metal against theirs. My blade raced from one sword to the other, pushing, probing, seeking a weakness. I handled the sword as if I had trained all my life.

I watched myself, this stranger, fight in a brilliant dance of death. The seething rage, the single-minded desire to kill the source of my hate drove me. I wanted it, yet my mind knew I shouldn't.

Gabrielle raced up from the side. "Stop, stop the killing!"

But it didn't matter what she said. It sounded like babbling sounds. Eradicating these two men so they could never threaten me again reigned as my single concern.

My sword blurred as it leapt between the two blades, then I saw my opportunity. Seth left himself open. In one sweeping move, I sliced my sword across his belly and landed on the father's blade in time to block it. Seth fell back onto the ground, grimacing.

"No!" Gabrielle sobbed.

I felt my heart sink. *How do I stop myself?* Hope, I had been told. I had to defeat this hate with hope. I focused, attempting to break through the mind-numbing rage.

Yet, I couldn't make a dent. Now my sword concentrated on the father. He struggled to parry my blows as they blurred from right and left, up and down. He weakened, I could tell. It wouldn't be long now.

"Sisko, stop!" I felt her hand on my shoulder.

I tried to stop, but I couldn't break the mindless reaction. I watched in horror as I swung the sword around and plunged it into her. I paused, staring at her through clenched teeth and fiery eyes.

Oh God, stop me. I'm killing them all! Inside I wept even as my body and mind focused on extermination.

Hope, the answer came again. Hope kills hate.

The father, having seen me pause, attacked. I pulled the sword from her and swung around to lock with his. His eyes betrayed fear, while mine betrayed hate. I shoved, and he flew back, falling to the ground against a tree.

I knew I could break through. I had to. God said I could, and I had to believe. As my sword paused at the father's neck, I found an opening. My

81

face flushed; I breathed hard through clenched teeth. *I can stop. I must stop. I will stop the hate. It isn't real. I must not allow it to destroy me.*

Will pushed against will. Swords of a different nature clashed in an internal combat. A crack developed in the hate, and hope wedged its way into my numb mind. I felt myself sink back into my body.

"I will not kill you," I said to myself as much as to him. With every movement I struggled to not fall into the hate though it raged hotly throughout me. Reason battled irrationality.

I rose and stared at the spot where Gabrielle lay, blood oozing from her wounds.

Seth had crawled to her and spoke to her in staggered breaths and sobs. "Sis, you're the only one who gave me any hope. I can't live if you leave me. Don't leave me."

I moved closer and heard Gabrielle push the words through the gurgling in her throat. "Brother, I can't give it to you, just don't give up on it." The effort seemed to take all she had. She laid back and waited for death to arrive. Seth joined her in the pool of blood.

Inside, I knew this couldn't be allowed to stand. I killed them. And through God, I could fix it. I pushed my body toward them and knelt beside their dying flesh.

"No you don't—"

I held up a hand to the father. I struggled with all my strength to keep from attacking him again. "I'm going to heal them," I snarled. "They're already dead if I can't, let me try."

He paused and then lowered his sword.

I placed my hands on their bleeding chests. "Father," I growled, "heal their bodies."

Another light fell upon us, but it glowed from within each one rather than without. I cast my head back as rage, fighting to stay, spewed out in one long and loud scream until I collapsed into unconsciousness.

I opened my eyes to a new day. I no longer felt the rage. God had helped me expel it into the abyss. I felt weak, but refreshed.

"Good, you're awake." Gabrielle sank into a seat by the bed. She held a bowl of soup with dry bread in her hands. "Eat this, it will help you regain your strength."

"You're alive. It worked."

"You did it, why act surprised?"

"God did it. I asked." I sat up, and my head spun for a moment. I took the soup from her. As I ate, warmth filled my stomach, and energy flowed through my muscles.

"Wherever the power came from, you healed not only our bodies but rid us of the rage as well." She pointed behind me.

I turned and beheld the father and Seth at a table, talking, smiling, and eating together. The night had given way to day.

I finished my soup, and after talking about the events for a while longer, I decided to move on. I grabbed my pack from the floor. "I'll be going now. I'm finished here."

Seth jumped from the table. "Sisko…" He scratched his head. "I've been doing some thinking. Maybe it's not such a great idea for me to go back with my old gang." He stared at the floor and bit his lip. "Maybe I can join up with you?" His eyes glanced up.

"With me?" I hadn't expected this.

"Yeah, I mean, you'll need protection while you travel. You never know when a gang of thieves will jump you." His eyes gleamed.

"Deal." I extended my hand to grab his newly reformed hand. My prayer had healed both his wound and hand. Then he lunged at me and squeezed with his muscular arms.

I turned to Gabrielle, her face beamed with joy. She motioned for me to draw near, reached out, and pulled my face to hers.

I glanced at the father.

He waved his hand. "Go ahead, she ain't getting any younger."

I smiled, then pulled her lips to mine. Scents of basil rolled into my nose as her lips imparted a sweet energy, cementing us in the moment. Floods of thoughts raced through the connection, so vivid but all loving and happy. And there I was at the center of them. She loved me. And I knew she must have seen the same thing in me. I broke the kiss.

"And remind me again, why I cannot go?" she asked.

"Well, it wouldn't be proper, unless we were…" My mouth hung open in mid-sentence.

"Yes, you were saying?" Her eyes sparkled with expectation.

"It just wouldn't be proper, that's all."

She sighed. "You will return, won't you?"

I held both her hands and clasped them against my chest. I knew she could hear my thoughts and my love for her just as I experienced hers.

I looked at Seth, the father, and then back to Gabrielle. "Well, seeing how my new traveling companion is your brother, I would say that is highly likely."

I stood and saw the father extending his hand to me. A gentleness glowed from his eyes as we shook.

Then the father reached for Seth's hand. "I hope you find what you're looking for." He lowered his gaze to the floor as if he explored unfamiliar territory. "Son."

"Thank you, Father." A tear fell down Seth's cheek as he clasped the outstretched hand.

Once packed, Seth and I walked down the mountain path. Gabrielle waved while standing at the threshold. Her father stood next to her. I waved back and then turned to face the path. I didn't want to leave her, but staying wasn't an option. Nor was going home. God would use me to make a difference.

Maybe someday when the ring had finished with me, I could return and marry her. There's always hope.

Demon's Beast

I shifted the pack on my shoulder and glanced at Seth as the road neared the bottom of the mountain. "I've not camped out much. Haven't spent one night out on the road since leaving home."

Seth grinned. "There's where I'll be of some help to ya. Me and my gang lived out in these woods. I've learned a good bit of hunting and cooking skills."

I nodded. "I'm sure there's much you could teach me in that regard."

As the mountain path skirted around a clump of trees, broken rays of sunlight pierced the forest canopy like needles threaded by God. I wondered about Seth. A few days ago, the young man tried to cut off my finger to get the ring, through which God used me to do miracles, and subsequently tried to kill me. Though my healing of him and his sister Gabrielle from near death had brought about a dramatic change of heart on his part, I didn't know how long it might last or how deep it ran.

My thoughts turned to Gabrielle. She'd captured my heart, no doubt about it. Already I missed her and we'd left only a couple of hours ago. I sighed. It could be many days, months, or years before I'd see her again. Best not to think about it too much.

Birds darted between the trees and into the air as we rounded a corner. The wooden walls of a city rose before us.

Seth stopped. "This is Jerole. I suggest we don't go in there. Let's head to the south."

I stared at the walls, and a faint call echoed in my heart. "I believe I need to go in there."

Seth wrinkled his forehead. "Why?"

"I sense God wants me to help someone in there." I met his eyes. "Why do you want to avoid it?"

He cleared his throat as he turned away to watch the city. "Let's just say, there are some folks in that town who are not too happy with me."

I pointed a finger at him. "That's right. Gabrielle told me about your local crimes."

He shook his head. "It's more than that. After Father kicked me out of the house, that's when I started my gang. We hung out in these woods, stealing from travelers like I tried to do with you. My sister didn't tell you the half of it."

I noted his build. "You don't look like someone who could be bullied about."

He frowned. "No, but I don't have my gang with me, and there's a bunch of them in there. If they know I'm in town, they'd likely form a lynch mob. On top of that, there's the creature."

I lifted an eyebrow. "The creature?"

He nodded. "Some say a myth, others speak of hearing its growls. But under the city is said to live a beast who devours anyone they throw into its caves. I've no desire to test out how real it is."

I shrugged. "I don't have a choice. If God tells me to help someone, then I must do it."

He waved a hand toward the city gate. "Be my guest. But I'll wait out here, however long it takes."

"I'll do my best to be quick about it, but I have no clue how long it will take to find out who I should help."

Seth smiled. "Like I said, I'm used to living in the woods. Take a week if you must. I'll set up a small camp over behind that clump of trees." He pointed into the forest.

I nodded, gave him my pack, turned, and then strolled toward the gate. Once inside, I could see the other side of the wall down the road. A few people scurried about while others worked in their shops. Over by a store, a group chatted. While the town appeared average enough, a sense of evil overshadowed the area. I knew I would deal with that evil before I finished here.

I stood in the street, feeling lost. *How do I go about finding out who to help?* Everyone I saw appeared happy enough. But then, hurting people tended to put on a happy face in public, hiding pain, allowing it to fester.

I closed my eyes and tried to zero in on where I should go. I hoped I could deal with this in an hour or two and get back to Seth. I slowly turned until I felt an internal nudge. I stopped and opened my eyes. I faced a sign that said *Last Leg Tavern*.

I stepped toward it. I'd been in a tavern a couple of times with my father, but otherwise rarely visited. While most people treated them as social centers, and the young drank ale with the old since drinking water risked sickness, I'd had little reason to enter one. I'd heard from travelers that some taverns could be rough places.

I pushed through the doors. The room harbored shadows, but sunlight from windows cut paths across the floor. A polished, deep-red bar ran along the far left side. Behind it scurried a barkeep and rows of glasses and bottles of various liquids. I leaned on the counter.

The barkeep finished wiping a section before dropping the towel and stepping toward me. "You're new to these parts. What's your name?"

I held out a hand. "Sisko, from Reol."

He raised an eyebrow. "Reol, eh? That's a far piece. What brings you here?"

I laughed. "You wouldn't believe me if I told you."

He shook his head. "You should hear some of the tall tales I hear every week! I doubt yours would surprise me."

I didn't want to argue with him. "The story's too long to get into here. But I can tell you I'm here to help someone."

"Really? Who?"

I shrugged. "I'm still trying to figure that part out."

The barkeep filled a mug of ale and put it before me. "Here. If you've traveled all the way from Reol to help someone, and you don't know who, you're going to need this. On the house."

"It'll take more than ale to help me. But thanks." I lifted it and slurped the amber liquid.

I turned around to get a view of the people, hoping God would point out who in here I should help. A couple sat at a table in a corner, holding hands. They couldn't be interrupted. One man ate alone, reading a book. But in another corner, a group of men and a couple of women laughed and chatted around a set of tables.

They appeared to be the most likely candidates for my help. I strolled over and sat at a table close by and listened to their conversation.

"...been that way for a while now. Crops are doing fine, but we could use some more rain," a black-bearded man said.

A thin-faced man held up a finger. "At least we don't have that no-good-for-nothing Seth around lately to steal our stuff."

Another nodded. "It has been a while since we'd heard anything about him. I wonder where he's gone off to?"

A woman dressed in a blue skirt and white blouse placed a hand on the man's shoulder. "As long as he's not around here, who cares."

I grimaced. Seth spoke the truth. Maybe that's who I needed to help: Seth. Get him back in good graces with these people. But what could I do about that?

The black-bearded man laughed. "I'll drink to that."

I gritted my teeth. They shouldn't speak about him like that. "What makes you think a man like him can't change?"

The table full of people all turned to face me, eyes staring at me as if surprised I would dare speak.

The black-bearded one said, "Where you from, boy?"

"I'm Sisko, from Reol."

"I doubt you've heard about these folk on the hill. Mental cases, the whole lot of them. Except that girl. She's the only one with any sense."

"I met them a few days ago. I can vouch that he's changed." I watched uncertain eyes bore into me.

The thin-faced man shook his head. "A caterpillar changes once, then they're done. Seth has already become what he is. Not much is going to change that."

"I—"

"We've got 'im!" rang from the street. Murmurs from a crowd grew. Everyone in the tavern leaped to their feet and headed out the door. I followed them. When the street slid into view, I saw a group of people pulling ropes; Seth, wrapped in the ropes, pulled back against them.

I felt a knot growing in my gut. How did they find and capture him? I had left him less than an hour ago.

The crowd surged down the street as they hauled Seth toward a building displaying a sign, upon which they'd written "Prison."

I decided I would wait for them to lock Seth up, then I would reason with them for his release.

The men pulling Seth yanked him onto the small, wooden porch in front of the door. One of the men, a tan-skinned farmer judging by his clothing, held a hand up and the crowd quieted.

"There's few here who haven't been cheated or stolen from by this man standing before you." He lifted a hand and pointed it at Seth. "His crimes are many and varied. He's given our town and the people here a bad name through the land. A judge and court would be a waste of time, therefore I will pronounce the sentence and execute it immediately unless anyone objects or vouches for this man."

Seth hung his head low. No one spoke.

I sighed, then lifted my hand. "I can vouch for him. He has changed."

Faces all turned toward me. The man on the porch widened his eyes. "And who are you, young one?"

"Sisko, of Reol."

"I'll bet he's one of Seth's gang!" someone from the crowd yelled. Murmurs and nodding of heads surrounded me.

The man pointed at me. "No doubt he is. No one but a gang member would think of vouching for this man. Grab him!"

Hands wrapped around my arms and pulled me to the platform. "No! I tell the truth! He's been healed."

Yells rose from the crowd, drowning out my attempts to defend Seth. They shoved me up next to Seth. I caught Seth's eye. I expected an "are you crazy" look. Instead, I saw wonder.

The man held up his hand and the crowd grew silent. "If there are no more interruptions, I will pronounce their sentence."

A chant grew among the crowd until its roar filled the air. "Creature, creature, creature, creature…"

The leader raised his hand once more. "It will be done!"

Cheers rose from the people. Seth and I stumbled into the building as they yanked him and shoved me. Three men pulled Seth by the ropes across a wooden floor and into another room. In the center of the room, a winding staircase bore into the ground. Hands directed me to follow them down the stairs.

Darkness swallowed us as we sank into the hole. Faint, flickering light danced against walls, creating ghostly images of our shadows. Dripping of water in the distance reached my ears. Caves under the city. Seth's myth may be true after all.

The leader stopped before an iron bar gate. He stared into the cavern on the other side for a few seconds before pushing a key into the lock and opening the door with a rusty screech. Two of the men shoved Seth into the prison. A strong hand pushed me, then a boot jabbed my rear and thrust me forward. I couldn't keep my feet under me; I crashed face-first onto the cold rock. My grunt echoed against the walls.

The gate clanked shut and the lock snapped as they turned the key. The leader of the men stared at us. "This is a great day for Jerole. Two trouble-makers in one day, one being the leader of the bunch. I can't say I'm sorry to see you go."

I pushed myself to my feet. "Sir, I'm afraid you've made a mistake."

He laughed. "Mistake? I don't think so. But in either case, the creature hasn't been fed in a while. I'm sure he's hungry for some warm flesh." A smile spread across his face. "You'll reduce the pain if you go ahead and kill yourself. Bye." They filed out of the room and climbed back up the stairs.

I dusted my hands off and began unwrapping the rope from Seth. "Why didn't you defend yourself?"

"It wouldn't have made any difference. Besides, they're right. I've done all those things they accuse me of. In their eyes I'm guilty, and I can't blame them." He paused. "Why did you try to defend me? You could have walked away, left me to die. I deserve this, but you? You shouldn't be here."

I pulled at a tight knot. "Friends don't let friends die alone. We're too bound for me to run away." The knot came loose.

Seth's hands wiggled out of the bonds; he rubbed his wrists. "My gang wouldn't have done that, and I'd say we're pretty tight."

I pulled on the rope, loosening it, until Seth could push it down, and it coiled into a pile by his feet. "Might be closeness doesn't have as much to do with it as love. Or maybe I didn't want to lose my camping cook."

Seth smiled. "In any case, you're stuck in here with me. And whatever this thing is, myth or not, we're about to find out."

I examined the walls in the flickering light. "These are caves. Perhaps we could find a different exit."

Seth shook his head. "These caves are like a maze. We'd never be able to find it, if there is one. We'd likely get lost and die of starvation assuming there is no creature to eat us."

He was right. How could we hope to find an exit? Maybe this creature didn't exist, and everyone thrown in here died of starvation. Quick death at the hands of a beast didn't sound so bad in comparison.

"All right, God. What do I do now?" I peered into the next cavern.

A few seconds of silence passed before Seth responded. "Well, did He say anything?"

"Not yet."

"Figures. I've never heard anything myself. I doubt God exists."

"I have. And He does."

Seth eyed me. "You've heard God speak?"

I nodded. "In my heart, yes."

He laughed. "Oh, well. Of course. In your heart. But nothing like a voice that I could hear as well?"

"God doesn't work that way, normally. I suppose He could if He wanted to."

"You'd think He would on occasion. Like right now."

I shook my head. "If you heard Him, you'd die. You're not healed yet. He's doing you a favor by not talking directly to you."

Seth waved his hand. "Now you're talking in riddles."

A growl echoed in the caves, and the sound of shuffling feet followed behind it.

Seth froze. "He's coming. He's real!"

"Any ideas?"

"There's two of us, but one of him. If we work together, we can kill him before he kills us."

I hid behind an outcropping of rock, waiting for the beast to appear. Seth did likewise, a few yards away.

I watched the opening. The footsteps grew louder, methodical steps punctuated by a flurry of footfalls. But in my heart I felt an evil growing stronger and stronger. I dawned on me that the evil presence I'd felt earlier was this creature.

The beast slid into the doorway and glanced around the cavern. Hair covered its head and seven-foot frame. Torn pants stretched across his legs, and the remnants of a shirt hung over his shoulders. The face appeared more ape-like than man. Warts on the face distorted the nose and cheeks while evil corrupted the inner man.

The creature spotted me behind the rock and bared his teeth with a rumbling growl. I stepped backwards, moving to the wall, attempting to draw its path close to Seth. The beast leaped toward me and galloped on all fours.

As it passed by Seth's hiding place, Seth leaped out and wrapped his massive forearm around the creature's neck. I attempted to aid Seth, but the creature swung himself around, whipping his head. Seth lost his hold and flew against a cave wall, sliding to the floor limp.

The beast turned its attention back to me. With Seth unconscious, this would be it. He'd eat me, and take care of Seth before he could wake up enough to fight.

As the beast drew near, I saw its eyes. Fiery red, he glared at me with both hunger and indifference. The sense of evil thickened until I thought I could cut a slice and eat it.

I pushed myself up against the cave wall, wanting to run, but where? I could not escape. This would be—

I froze. The creature's eyes. Yes, my heart confirmed it. All I needed to do was—

The creature leaped toward me, his arms outstretched and claw-like nails bearing down toward my throat.

I jerked to the side as his hands hit rock. "Father, cleanse the demon from this man's soul!"

The creature's other hand plunged toward my chest. I started to close my eyes, but then he froze. His eyes grew wide. He jerked back and roared at the ceiling, his arms outstretched. The creature gagged, then fell backwards upon the floor, squirming and growling.

I stepped to the side and backed away, but kept my eyes on the monster. His head expanded, then morphed. Warts disappeared, the nose grew thinner and longer, the mouth pulled in and regular lips replaced the exaggerated ones. Hair receded over his legs, arms, chest.

I gasped. The creature was a demon who had turned this poor guy into the ugliest mess I'd ever seen. Casting out the demon caused his life to return.

The man sat up. His auburn hair, a mangled mess, overshadowed his eyes, now blue. He rubbed his forehead and attempted to view his location. "Anyone here?"

I stepped from the shadows. "I am."

The man jumped at the sound of my voice, then turned to me. "You're the one that freed me."

I nodded. "I may have prayed the prayer, but God did it."

He blinked his eyes. "Where am I?"

"In the caves under the city of Jerole."

"Jerole, Jerole…" He mumbled words while he stared at the floor. "I've heard of that name before—oh yeah! They're the ones who threw me in here. I despaired of getting out. When I lay on the ground, about to die, someone approached me and said he could give me eternal life."

I raised my eyebrows. "Eternal life?"

"Yes. Said I could live forever. Naturally I said yes, considering the predicament I faced. But I didn't realize what the cost would be. Who wants to live eternally in a tormenting prison?"

"How long have you been like this?"

He closed his eyes as if holding back tears. "I don't have a clue. How long have I been gone from my family?"

Seth groaned and squirmed, then placed a hand on his head. "Anyone see the mule that kicked me?"

I sat beside him and placed a hand on his shoulder. "Are you all right?"

"I think so, just dazed. I thought the monster…" Seth saw the man sitting on the floor. "Whose that? Another victim?"

"No. He's your mule."

Seth's eyes widened. "You mean, he's the monster that attacked us?"

The man stood. "My name's Gregory. I vaguely remember throwing you off. I'm sorry for that, but I didn't have much control, being demon possessed and all." He held out a hand to Seth.

Seth reached up and grabbed it; Gregory pulled him to his feet. Seth dusted himself off. "No disrespect, but you don't look like you could throw off a flea, much less me."

"The demon changed me. As if it were a dream, I recall certain actions, but the details are fuzzy."

Seth shook his head. "So you're the mythical monster who ate everyone they threw in here?"

Gregory's mouth hung open and color drained from his face. "Ate people." He blinked. "Yes, there are images." His eyes stared into the distance as his cheeks drooped. "The blood, and their…eyes…" He sank onto a stone and heaved, though nothing came out.

Seth glanced at me. I nodded. "He was the creature. I cast the demon out and the monster changed into him."

Seth found a rock to sit on. "Now what? We may not get eaten by a monster, but we're still likely to starve in here."

Gregory lifted his head; his arms shook. "I recall a light. The demon didn't want to go to it, but I suspect it's a way out."

I watched the man's labored breathing. "Do you know where this light is?"

He frowned. "No. Like I said, everything felt like a dream. There's a lot I don't remember, but I think I would know the place if I saw it."

I sat down as well and thought. No one spoke. *All right, God. You obviously placed me down here to get these two out. Now what?*

A thought surfaced in my heart. I smiled. "Gregory, you're going to drive and I'll be the horse that pulls you."

Both Seth and Gregory stared at me with blank expressions. Seth wrinkled his nose. "What?"

I stood up and held out my arms. "Each one of you grab an arm."

They both glanced at each other before rising and wrapping their hands around my arms.

I nodded. "Now, I don't know what I'll do, but hold me up if need be. But I'll move. Both of your jobs will be to let me pull you in the direction that we need to go."

Gregory cleared his throat. "What do you plan on doing?"

I smiled. "I'm going to enter your memories, and find the way out."

His eyes grew wide. "You can do that?"

I shrugged. "I've not tried it before, but God said do it, so I'm sure I can. Ready?"

Seth nodded, but Gregory winced. "I don't feel good about the idea after being possessed. How do I know you won't do the same thing?"

I slapped myself inside. Of course he'd be sensitive to such an idea right now. "I could say because I freed you, and I want to help us get out. But I guess in the end, you'll have to trust me."

He gulped as he stared at the wall.

"I won't control you, and I'll get out if you ask me to. We'll do this together."

He breathed deep, then faced me. "All right."

I nodded and closed my eyes. "Father, allow me to enter Gregory's mind and find his memory of the light."

A coldness washed over me as if I'd been thrown into water. The disorientation lasted a couple seconds before the darkness gave way to an amber-filtered scene. I stood among rows of bushes. I stepped toward them. As more detail appeared, I realized they weren't bushes, but shriveled trees. The ground lay parched, the limbs of blackened wood protruded from gnarled stumps. Leaves here and there dangled gently from their limbs, as if at any moment they would fall to the ground and die.

As I gazed upon the barren landscape, I noticed movement to my right. Upon focusing on it, a body sat on the ground, its arms wrapped over its head, shaking.

"Gregory?" I approached the man.

His head raised enough that his eyes peered over his knees. "Go away! I don't want to be controlled again. Leave me alone!"

I knelt beside him. "I'm here to help you find the way out of these caves."

"No, you're here to force me. Force me to do nasty things. Stay away."

He flinched when I touched him. "I'm not here to control you. Trust me. I need your help to free all three of us."

He stared at me. "Trust me. You said that once before. Out there."

I nodded and smiled.

Gregory closed his eyes and swallowed. "Please help me. I want to trust you. I want to get out."

I stood and held out my hand. "Take it, and we'll be on our way."

His eyes studied my hand, then he focused on my face. He stopped shaking. Haltingly, he extended his hand, and it met mine. I lifted him onto shaking feet.

I pointed at the rows of charred trees extending into the distance. "I need to find the memory of when you saw the light in the caves. Do you know where it is?"

He nodded and stepped down the row. I followed. He led me to a path that ran perpendicular to the lines of trees, cutting across them. When he reached the sixth one, he turned in between the barren trees and stepped down it for a few feet, examining the branches to his left.

He stopped at one and felt the leaves on it. "This is it." He pointed to a small, dried berry hanging by a small stem.

I reached out and gently touched it. The scene changed, and now I watched through the creature's eyes, as if sitting inside his head, viewing a play. He growled and left the room where Seth and I had been.

The beast loped along the cave floor. I hoped I didn't go too fast for Seth and Gregory to follow. He darted into one cave, turned around, then sped back out. He zigged and zagged among the stalagmites and underwater pools. Then a flash of distant white caught the beast's attention. He stopped, then turned back.

He stared for a moment at the small dot of light, faintly calling from among the cave's darkness. The creature moved toward it, slowly at first, but then faster, until the faint light gave way to a glaring glory. The creature flung his arms over its eyes, and yelped. He scurried away from the light and back into the cave's soft, caressing flames.

I let go of the fruit and my mind returned to the orchard. Already the trees appeared a healthier color. Clusters of berries grew on the stems, and fresh leaves budded from the branches. A scent of fresh basil wafted in the air.

I turned to see Gregory smiling.

"You've done it," Gregory said.

The trees and Gregory dimmed, but then another Gregory filled my vision again. I stood outside, the wind whipping around my face, and the sun warming my skin.

Gregory wrapped me in his arms. "Yes, you've really done it!"

I hugged him back. "Thanks to God. You helped as well."

Seth stood to my left. He stared at me; his eyes filled with wonder. "That was freaky." He smiled. "In a good way, of course."

Gregory stepped back. "You're both welcome to come with me. But I need to find my wife and children. No telling how long I've been gone, and she may think I'm dead."

I smiled. "I'd love to meet your family."

Seth cleared his throat. "That might not be a good idea. If they see me again, they'd throw us both back into the prison."

I groaned. "Seth's right. I went in to help someone, and that someone was you. We'd better be on our way."

He frowned. "I'm sorry to hear it, but I understand. Hopefully they don't throw me back in. I may take my family and move."

Seth patted him on the back. "And I wouldn't blame ya one bit."

Gregory hugged us both one more time before heading back to town. Seth and I tracked back to where we'd left our packs before I had entered the city. I shouldered it and headed south from Jerole.

I glanced at Seth. "So, how did those folks see and capture you?"

He stared at the trees around us as if he hadn't heard me.

"Seth?"

He wagged his head then sighed. "I fell asleep by the road."

I laughed. "Fell asleep?"

"Yep. Next thing I knew, I woke up to ropes being wrapped around me. I could hardly wiggle, much less break free."

I smiled. "So how does it feel being used by God to help that poor guy?"

"God? Use me?" He grunted. "I got in the way more than helped."

96

"If it weren't for you, I would've never gone into that prison and found Gregory. He'd still be down there, trapped by a demon."

He pulled his pack up straighter, keeping his thumbs behind the straps at his chest. "Well, I see your point. I'm not saying I believe in God, mind you. But you have a point."

I shook my head. "People do change."

"I wish I could figure out whether that's a good thing or a bad thing."

"All depends, my friend." I smiled. "All depends on what you're changing into."

We climbed the mountain pass leading to Ramonth, leaving Jerole and the past behind us.

Thievery's Call

Seth and I crested the top of a mountain pass to discover the path diving into a valley and then winding its way up another mountain.

I sat on an outcropping of rock by the road. "I need a drink and some rest." I pointed to the mountain in the distance. "How many more of these do we need to climb?"

Seth sat next to me. "It's been a while since I've come this way, but I think that may be the last mountain. They shrink to foothills after that one and then we reach the forest and plains."

I drank for a moment and caught my breath. "All right, let's go." I stood up and we headed down the slope. "By the way, I don't know much about you, other than the bits Gabrielle mentioned."

He chuckled. "And likely what she mentioned wasn't good."

I smiled. "Not all of it, but much of that has changed." I glanced at him. "But she does love you very much."

He nodded. "No doubt. Few would stand in the way of a sword. I wouldn't be here without her."

"No, you're right. There's not many who would die for another."

Seth eyed me. "Like you did for me. I'll never forget what you did back in Jerole. That creature would be licking my bones by now if not for you."

"I'm sure you'll get a chance to return the favor."

As we traveled, Seth related stories from his youth. When his father kicked him out of the house, he had almost died the first few nights alone in the forest. Then he stumbled upon a field of crops and took some to feed himself. The farmer never noticed.

When he found other boys in similar situations, they joined him, helping haul crops to their makeshift hideout. Once they had been discovered, they shifted to taking from strangers on the road. To avoid capture, they moved their operations every so often. That's when they found me on the road and tried to take the ring.

I shook my head. "You've lived a hard life. I guess you're glad to be out of that now."

He didn't respond.

"Seth?"

He held his palm toward me and put a finger to his lips. I remained silent, listening intently. Bushes shook and men leaped from them.

"Look out, Sisko!"

A thud echoed on the back of my head, and darkness overtook me.

As awareness returned to me, so did a throbbing pain on the back of my head. Someone had tied my hands behind me. The eastern sky already grew dim as the sunlight fled behind mountain peaks. I sat in a clearing; trees swayed in the gust of wind. A few feet away, men huddled around a fire to fight off the evening chill. Seth sat among them. I listened for a moment, since they didn't realize I'd awoken.

"You mean, you never did get that ring from the fella?"

Seth stared into the fire. "No. It's complicated, but what happened when we reappeared caused me to forget about getting that ring."

The one crossed his arms. "And I thought you were the Dragon Breath."

I swallowed at the mention of Seth's gang name. This was Seth's old gang.

Seth sat up. "I am. And because of it, I can change my mind if I find a reason to do so."

Another of the men stood from the fire and pulled out a knife. "Something about you is different now. I don't see the fire in your eyes."

Seth jumped up. "Try me if you must. Don't forget who it was that gave you a family." Seth pulled a knife from his boot. "I don't want to hurt you, but if you force me..." He waved the knife back and forth.

The man jerked one way and then the other. Seth held his ground, a smile creased his lips. His eyes spoke of calm and patience.

The man lunged toward Seth, his arm swinging from the side. The blade flashed in the firelight. Seth pulled back; the knife crossed in front of his chest. Then he locked his right hand around the man's knife-arm. He swung his left hand around the other side, placing his knife blade against the man's neck, pinning his attacker against his chest.

"Who am I?" Seth growled.

The man mumbled something I couldn't hear.

"Louder!"

"Dragon Breath. You're Dragon Breath!"

Seth shoved him forward, allowing his blade to nick the man's throat, leaving a trickle of blood oozing into his shirt. "And don't you forget it."

The man rubbed his neck and sat beside the fire again. "So, what's to stop us from getting the ring now? We could leave him here for someone to find and be on our way."

Seth wagged a finger. "I've a better idea. Or do you want to end up back at your parents' house like I did?"

A couple shivered. The other two shook their heads.

"As I suspected." Seth rubbed his hands together. "That ring won't come off, and I don't think anyone can get it off. But that doesn't mean we can't use him."

I groaned inside. I tired of people wanting to use me. And now Seth? I couldn't tell if he put on a front to save me or if now that his gang had showed up, he'd forget all that had happened in the last few days.

Seth glanced my way and his eyes froze on me. "Appears he's awake." He rose and approached me, then leaned down to undo the ropes. "Tied you up..." He raised his voice and turned his head back to the men. "...because we didn't want you doing anything nasty to us when you woke up."

Seth leaned closer and whispered. "Follow my lead on this."

I met his eyes and barely nodded. Seth pulled the ropes loose and helped me to my feet. I followed him back to the fire.

Seth pointed at each man in turn. "This is Doodle, short for Doodlebug, because he's the youngest of the group."

The young teen smiled. He couldn't have been any older than me when I entered the steam house. But he stood tall for his age.

"This one here is Elf, because an accident made his ears look elvish."

Elf waved. "My father liked knives, and used them when he chased me from home."

I winced.

Seth motioned to another. "This one's named Troll, for obvious reasons."

The rather large man—appeared to be in his twenties—waved. His large jowls and the small top of his head did give the impression of a troll. I hoped it didn't have anything to do with his personality.

"And finally, we have Arrow." Seth pointed at the man who had attacked him earlier. "He's a bit feisty, as you may have seen, but is as sharp as they come, and *usually* on target."

Arrow rubbed his neck as he stood and bowed.

I nodded. "My name is—"

Seth raised his hand. "Hold it. We all go by ga…I mean, group names here. No real names." Seth tapped his fingers on his chin. "How about Dog?"

I stared at him. "Dog? What's that supposed to mean?"

They broke into laughter as they held their stomachs and slapped their knees. Apparently an inside joke.

Seth drew in a breath. "Just kidding. Now, seriously, what about Whirlwind, because that's what you create wherever you go."

I sat back. "Really? I do that?"

Seth smiled. "Based on my short experience with you, most definitely."

I shrugged. "As good as any, I suppose."

Seth slapped me on the back. "Do I hear a motion from you blokes to induct Whirlwind here into the club?"

Troll raised his hand. "I make that motion."

Doodle stood up. "I'll…I'll…what's it called?"

"A second." Arrow threw up his hands.

"I'll second that."

Seth nodded. "We have a motion and a second. Any discussion?" Seth drew out the last word as if there better not be any. Everyone stared back at him.

"If not, all in favor, raise your hands."

Everyone's hand except for Arrow's went up.

"All opposed, same sign."

Arrow kept his hand down. "I'm abstaining, on grounds I'd rather kill 'im and move on. But I'm not going to say no."

Seth grinned. "Motion passes. Whirlwind, you are now part of our exclusive club, except we've got to decide on an initiation rite."

I sighed. I hated such things, and with a gang of thieves, I feared what they might put me through. I hoped Seth knew what he was doing. Even more, I hoped Seth was still on my side.

Arrow grinned. "I've the perfect thing. While you were gone, Dragon Breath, we came up with a plan to rob a store in Ramonth. If Whirlwind here can do half the things you said, he should be able to help us pull off this pillage."

I swallowed. "I can't guarantee I can do anything. I ask, God does it, if He pleases."

"God?" Arrow leaped to his feet and pulled his knife. "You'll do it or else!"

I glanced at Seth and then back to Arrow. Did he expect me to get up and fight him?

Seth slid his knife out and tossed it to me. "Here you go. You'll need this. A challenge is a challenge."

I stared at Seth's calm face, then at the knife laying on the ground. I knew the second I picked it up, Arrow would attack. I started to reach my hand out for it.

"Of course," Seth interjected, "don't forget what happened to me when I took a knife to the boy. Poof! But I'm sure we'll get along fine without you, Arrow. One less person to share in the bounty."

Arrow gritted his teeth and raised his knife into the air. Then threw it into the dirt by his feet, the handle wobbling as it planted itself into the ground. "All right then. But if we're putting our butts on the line, he'd better come through."

I breathed in fresh air and pulled my hand back.

Seth picked up his knife. "Oh, he'll produce all right. He owes me. Don't ya, Whirlwind."

I opened my mouth to disagree, but his wink caused me to nod instead. "Yes, I believe I do."

"Good. First thing in the morning, we'll be on our way to Ramonth. Let's get some sleep."

I pulled bedding from my pack and rolled it out on the hard ground. My first night sleeping in the open. As everyone stopped talking, the forest noises grew louder. Cricket chirping filled the air, while the wind creaked tree branches with each gust.

I wriggled around, trying to find a comfortable position. But it felt as if the rocks gathered under me like roaches hiding from light. *God, do you really want me out here? Do you really want me to help them rob a store?*

When I sensed a firm *yes* in my heart, I looked at the ring. Was it broken? *Do something if I'm reading you wrong here. Anything. Anytime you wish.*

No reply returned.

Doodlebug stopped with the gates of Ramonth not far into the distance. "We've come all this way without robbing anyone. Maybe we should rest and steal from a few travelers."

Seth shook his head. "No, our job tonight requires surprise. No one knows us here, we don't want to alert anyone that thieves are about until after the job is done."

I plopped onto a rock beside the road. "Though I would vote for a little rest myself." I drained the last of the liquid from my waterskin.

Seth sat. "This is a good time to go over our plan."

The others found seating off the road. Seth examined them each before continuing. "We don't want to attract suspicion, but we all need to be in the city before nightfall. We'll enter by twos, and meet at the *Fisherman's Net*. Once night falls and the city has settled down, Whirlwind will get us into the store. Then we'll move in and take what we need."

I gulped. What did I know about breaking into a locked building? Could I ask God to do that? Would He? I doubted it. Yet, God had told me to go through with this. He must have a plan. I wish He'd fill me in occasionally.

Seth pointed at me and Troll. "You two, you go in first."

I sighed and lifted my pack from the ground. "Away we go."

The city walls grew larger as we approached. I tensed as we passed into the city. One guard glanced at me, but otherwise the pair never paid us any attention. I exhaled once in.

Troll glanced at me. "Didn't think we'd make it?"

I shrugged. "I knew we probably would, but I guess knowing we're coming in for evil purposes makes me uncomfortable. I feel like 'thief' is written on my forehead."

He slapped me on my back; I stumbled forward. "You'll get used to it. I call it redistributing the wealth. Why should the rich get it all? Steal from the rich and give to the poor, which is me."

"I don't think I can get used to that. One shouldn't covet what their neighbor has. Earn what you get. That's the way I was brought up."

We spotted the tavern Seth mentioned. We pushed the door aside and entered a well-lit room. Patrons filled the tables, laughing and chattering. Luckily, Troll and I found a table big enough for the gang, and we staked our claim. A barkeep brought us mugs of ale.

I shifted in my seat and watched Troll. "So tell me, how did you end up in this gang?"

His eyes stared into the distance. "I played in the forest one day when I was fifteen. When I returned home, I saw men leaving my house. They carted away our stuff. When they left, I entered the house to find my parents dead."

He blinked back the hint of tears. "I had no one to take care of me. I tried to craft the swords as my father did, but I never paid close attention when he tried to teach me. My swords broke too easily.

"That's when Seth happened by, with Elf already in tow. He felt pity on me, and I joined them." His eyes focused on mine. "It's the way of the world to take what you need. If you work for it, others will take it. So why work for it?"

I studied his eyes for a moment. While I didn't excuse his thievery, at least I understood its source. And it would probably take an experience of a different kind to convince him otherwise. Words are empty compared to living through such horrors.

I sighed and drank another gulp of ale. "I'm sorry to hear your story. Those in the world can be cruel, but I hope someday you'll discover a reality that exists outside this world."

He shrugged. "You may be right. But I am what I am."

The doors to the tavern opened. Elf and Arrow entered. A few more minutes passed. Then Seth and Doodle arrived and settled around the table. We ate a meal from the gang funds, no doubt taken from others. I didn't like eating the food knowing that. But I didn't have much money to pay for it myself either. What little I possessed I wanted to hold for future needs.

Darkness settled over the town as we chatted away. Elf told a few stories with drama and tension. Seemed he gained the title "elf" for more than the appearance of his ears. Patrons in the tavern left until only a couple in a corner table remained aside from us.

Seth stared out the window. "I think it's time. Are you ready, Whirlwind?"

I sighed. "Sure."

He slapped me on the back. "I like your attitude. Let's do this."

We rose and clomped across the wooden floor and left the building. The moonlight highlighted a man in the distance hauling a bag over his shoulder. He disappeared into a side street.

Seth motioned for us to follow Arrow, who led us down a couple of blocks before stopping next to a building. The sign over the door shimmered in the moonlight the words "Steve's Specialty Shop." Seth led us into an alley next to the store.

He pointed at me. "Your turn, Whirlwind. When you get the door open, signal for us to come. We'll wait here. We don't want a whole group of people attracting attention."

I drew a deep breath and nodded. Troll and Doodle patted me on the back as I left the alley and stepped onto the wooden walkway. As I approached the door, I glanced back to see Seth peering around the corner, smiling.

I stared at the door. A metal handle in the shape of a snake protruded from a shaft. Carved grapevines decorated its border. In the center of the thick-wooded door, a carving of a winged horse glowed in the moonlight.

Not being an expert at picking locks, I wondered how I would open it. Start with the simple solution first, I'd been taught. I grabbed the snake handle and pushed down. It wouldn't budge. Locked, as would be expected.

"Pssst."

I turned my attention back to Seth. He pointed down the street. A man strolled down the walkway a few buildings away. No doubt he'd noticed me. No sense trying to hide. So I strolled to the side and leaned against the wall, whistling.

The man stopped at each building and yanked on the knobs. He approached the store and stared at me as he pushed on the door handle. It didn't budge.

I smiled as he stepped by. He turned and frowned. His badge reflected the moonlight into my eyes. "What are you doing out so late, boy?"

"I'm waiting on someone." I nodded toward the tavern.

He grunted. "Keep your nose clean. I'll see if I can speed them up in there."

I smiled. "Good luck. I think he's a little busy."

The man raised an eyebrow and gave a knowing smile. He returned to his patrol. When he passed the tavern door, he glanced in and then continued checking doors until he rounded a corner.

I breathed deep, thanking God he didn't attempt to verify my story further. Seth's head popped out, and he gave me a thumbs up. But the knot in my gut gave me a thumbs down. I had lied to a city patrolman. Not only did my conscience whip me for it, but if we were caught, I would be in a lot of trouble.

I returned my attention to the door. "Father, I hope you know what you're doing. Each step this direction sends me deeper in." I crossed my arms. "So, what do I do here?"

I thought for a moment, and decided the direct approach might work. I placed my hand on the handle. "Father, open this door for the benefit of the gang." I knew I wouldn't be taking anything. I couldn't go that far.

I wiggled the handle, but it remained locked in place. So God wanted something more than opening the door for them. He wanted to help them in some way. Maybe dealing with their attitude and experience as a gang?

"Pssst."

Not again. I turned toward Seth. He spun his hand in a rolling motion. He wanted me to hurry up. I raised one finger in the air and returned to my thoughts. What would help them?

A thought entered my mind. I wrinkled my nose. Such a non-specific and odd prayer. But my heart said to pray it. "Father, use this building to give them an alternate experience of reality."

I didn't know what God planned, but we'd soon find out. I pushed down on the handle and it gave way; the door cracked open. I pulled the door out and motioned for them to come.

They filed by, slapping me on the back. Seth stood by me as they entered. "I knew you could do it."

I cracked a bare smile before closing the door behind me. The moonlight filtered through the windows to illuminate the room enough to see. Shelves held various items. Pictures and crafts hung from the walls. At the front, behind a glass case, rings embedded with diamonds, rubies, and jade lay on display. A lock kept the case closed.

A scream erupted from a shelf in the back. I followed Seth to find

Doodle sitting on the floor, a sword laying before him. His arms shook as he pointed at the weapon. "It...it...talked to me."

The sword appeared normal enough. Seth knelt beside Doodle. "What did it say?"

Doodle met Seth's eyes. "It said, 'Thank you.'"

"Thank you?" Seth scratched his head. "Why would it say that?"

"I think, because it was taking something from me."

By now, Arrow and Elf had arrived. Arrow shook his head. "Doodlebug, you're losing it." He reached down and picked up the sword. Arrow froze and held it as far away from him as possible. His face grimaced. He grunted and tossed the sword away, and then sank back against a wall, breathing hard.

Seth glanced at the sword and back to Arrow. "What happened?"

He caught his breath as he stared at the sword. "When I grabbed it, a set of eyes and a mouth appeared on it. It said, 'Thank you" and I felt something reaching inside me, taking part of me away. That sword is cursed. Don't touch it."

Seth waved his hand. "We're not here to mess with swords anyway. Let's break into that case and get the expensive stuff."

We followed him to the glass case. Seth pulled out his knife and pushed around in the lock. After a few seconds passed, a click sounded in the quiet shop and the lock popped open. Seth lifted the glass cover, then reached in and picked up a diamond ring.

"Now, this will bring—" His face froze and his smile disappeared into horror. He squeezed his eyes shut and gritted his teeth, but still he held on. He fell to his knees and cried out.

I checked the others. Arrow's mouth fell open, but excitement filled his eyes. Elf backed away. Doodle ducked behind a shelf. Troll covered his ears and mumbled something. I feared that Seth wouldn't let go, maybe couldn't let go.

I grabbed the ring from his out turned palm. The room darkened and the ring lit up. Eyes blinked upon it and a mouth spread across it. Then I felt icy fingers reaching inside me. My legs buckled and coldness shot through my veins as if my blood transformed to ice.

Thank you.

For what? I asked.

For your self-esteem, for your honor, for your soul.

My soul? I pushed back, but the power felt too great. I could feel its fingers greedily grasping what it sought. *Why are you doing this?*

You don't know? When you take what's not yours, you trade something in return. Everything cost something. In this case, your soul.

So that's what God intended. *You don't understand. I'm not stealing you. I'm helping my friend, and you. If you can see into my soul, you should know this.*

The clammy-cold invisible fingers paused in their pulling. A couple seconds ticked by before it spoke. *I'm sorry, I didn't recognize you. Thank you for your help.*

The icy coldness retreated from my body. The eyes and mouth disappeared and the room's moonlight returned to normal. I stood at the case, the ring between my two fingers. Seth, Troll, Arrow, and Doodle stared at me with gaping mouths.

I smiled. "It's really quite friendly once you get to know it." I placed the ring back in the case."

Seth stood up. "How did you do that?"

"Simple. I told it I didn't want to steal it. Then it no longer tried to steal my soul."

Doodle shook his head. "I'm never stealing anything again. Nope, not ever."

I scanned the room. "Where's Elf? He stood here before I took the ring."

Seth searched the area, glancing down isles. Arrow pointed to a corner. "There he is." He dashed to him.

I followed with Seth and Doodle. Elf lay on the floor, a bow and quiver of arrows clutched to his chest. His body jerked and his eyes dilated.

I dropped beside him and pried his fingers off the bow and arrows, then pulled it from his grasp. The room didn't darken, nor did eyes and a mouth appear. I watched Elf shivering on the floor.

I focused on the bow. *Why isn't he getting better?*

I have his soul already.

Give it back.

I can't.

He's learned his lesson. I'm sure of it. Give him another chance.

I can't. It is not possible.

What isn't possible for us, is with God. I placed my hand on Elf's chest. "Father, replace Elf's soul."

The bow quivered and I felt my fingers extend into its fiber, though my hand appeared normal. I felt a glow of energy foreign to the weapon.

Sorry, I'm only returning what was stolen. I yanked, and the soul slid through my fingers, streaming a warmth through my body as it trickled over my neck and across my arm, then into Elf's body. My fingers felt like they shaped the energy as it flowed out my hand, until I could sense his soul had returned.

I breathed deep as I removed my hand from Elf's chest and leaned the bow and arrow against the wall.

Elf stopped jerking; his eyes blinked a few times before he focused on me. Tears formed in his eyes. He pushed himself off the floor and wrapped his arms around me. "Thank you!"

I hugged him back. "Thank God."

Seth chuckled. "I told you guys he's a whirlwind. Stirs up things wherever he goes."

Arrow bumped Seth on the shoulder. "Let's get out of here."

The door-handle clicked and the door swung open. We huddled behind the shelf. I closed my eyes. Getting caught now would ruin everything.

I opened my eyes and could see the doorway from a mirror that leaned against a wall. The patrolman I met earlier waltzed inside, studying the area. I thought about giving myself up in the hopes of protecting the others. God would help me, but these boys would need another chance.

I watched as the patrolman noticed the open case. That would be a dead giveaway. I pushed to stand up, but Seth pulled on my shirt and mouthed, "What do you think you're doing?"

Before I could respond, I watched as the patrolman reached in and grabbed a ring. He jerked back and threw the jewelry back into the case. He held his chest and breathed hard. After scanning the area, he backed out the door and locked it behind him.

I smiled. Another lesson learned. We waited a while before Seth stood up and said, "Let's go."

No one complained, but followed him out the door, locking it behind us. We would have to wait until daylight to leave the city, the gates being closed. So we found an empty alley and settled down for the night.

I smiled as I wrapped my blanket over my shoulders. "Thank you, Father."

The next morning, we left the city and selected the road to Siloest. But a few miles in, we veered onto the road leading to Dark Waters.

Seth walked next to me. "You've done it again."

"Done what?"

"Stirred things up."

"Is that a good thing?"

He smiled. "Mostly. But we don't have the means to feed ourselves. The guys will think twice about stealing anything else."

I met his eyes. "What about you?"

He shrugged. "I'm sort of partial to my soul. I think I'll keep it." He winked.

I allowed one corner of my mouth to turn up. "That's a step in the right direction. But you'll find the way to keep it is to give it away."

He shivered. "I'm not of a mind to have anything grabbing at my soul again."

"There's a big difference between giving and grabbing."

He grunted. "Aren't you full of spiffy sayings today."

"Live and learn, my friend. Live and learn."

Evil's Enchantment

The forest thickened around us as we traveled along the road to Dark Waters. The path grew narrow, and tree branches reached over the road. Sunlight dimmed to dusk under this canopy of leaves, despite being mid-day.

Seth walked beside me, while Troll, Elf, Doodle, and Arrow followed behind in pairs. For most of the trip, they chatted among themselves. Occasionally one of them would relate a tale for the whole group, especially Elf. But as we entered the darkness of the forest, no one said anything.

Sisko, are you there?

I smiled. *Hi Josh. How's my family?*

Doing well. Every once in a while, someone will come by looking for you. They usually go away when they find out you're not here. Josh paused. *So, how are you doing? It's been a while since you've contacted me, and I was starting to worry.*

I frowned. *Sorry. I've been tied up with a gang of late.*

A gang? You can't be serious.

I am, but it's a long story. Remind me to tell you some evening when you have some time.

So, are you trapped or something? I can always try and help you out.

No, no. I'm fine. Besides, your spells are a bit iffy at close range. I'd hate to experience one long distance.

Have it your way. Glad you're fine. I've got work to do. Will catch you later.

Thanks, Josh. Next time.

We approached a break in the forest where light poured through, and the sight lifted my spirits. As we drew near, a large body of black water splashed gently against the shore. The sight drew my curiosity so I stepped to the water's edge. I dipped my fingers in the blackness. When I extracted my hand, a thick, black goo coated them.

Seth peered over my shoulders as the others watched. "What is it?"

I shrugged. "Not sure, but I've heard stories of water like this. It's some type of stuff in the ground that comes up occasionally. Must be one under the lake. It floats on water." I wiped my finger on a patch of grass. "Sticky stuff."

Doodle lifted his right palm toward the lake. "Now we know why they call this place Dark Lake. It really is dark."

We returned to the path and continued our journey. I focused ahead as the road followed the lake's shore. "Have you ever been here before?"

Seth shook his head. "This is way out of my stomping grounds."

"Well, I feel a real evil here, and the closer we get to this Dark Waters, the stronger it feels."

Seth glanced at me. "Yes, it is a dreary place."

I sighed. "No, it's not just the ambience of the forest, I literally feel evil."

He glared at me sideways from one eye. "What do you mean? How can you feel evil?"

I lifted the ring before my face. I realized I'd never told Seth about it. He knew I could do some amazing things, but he didn't know why.

He grunted. "Are you trying to tell me it has something to do with that ring of yours?"

I nodded. "When I was fourteen, I entered the town steam house in Reol. It's called Steamy Realities Steam House, because when you're in there, it reveals your character and either attempts to correct it or enable it. It's a rite of passage for becoming a man in the town."

"So, you were enabled?"

I smiled. "That's the essence of it. When I came out, this ring rested on my finger and wouldn't come off. I was told it married me to God, to be my brother's keeper, and enabled me to perform miracles much as Sampson's hair enabled him to do great things for God.

"It also gives me a greater sensitivity to things spiritual, including the presence of evil. And that's what I'm feeling now."

Seth scratched his head. "Now, that's a story."

"Think back. How do you explain all the things I've done?"

He chuckled. "Whirlwind, there are many wizards in the world, but you are the oddest one I've met."

I raised an eyebrow. I'd never thought of myself as a wizard. Josh,

112

yes, but me? "It's not like I say spells or anything."

"Of course you do. But you call it a prayer."

I rubbed my forehead. "No, you don't understand the difference. I pray to God. He does it. A wizard learns spells in order to control a power in nature God put there. Like learning to whittle so you can make something out of a piece of wood. My best friend back in Reol is a wizard. I know a good bit about it."

"Ah, see. You admit it."

I slapped my head. "No, I don't know any spells, or how to activate them. All I do is when I feel God wants me to do something, I do it and pray for Him to aid me."

"Sure." He patted me on the back. "If that's how you want to frame it."

I sighed. How do I tell someone who doesn't believe in God the difference? I had to admit, from his perspective, it would all look the same.

"That's the truth, at any rate. I'm traveling because God wants me to help people with the ring."

Seth nodded. "Help people? Yeah, I guess you do. By stirring everything up."

I decided to change the subject. "How are we on food? I'm getting a little hungry."

Seth frowned. "I'm afraid we don't have much left. I would stop and hunt, but it would take a decent buck to feed us all. The village isn't far off anyhow."

We followed the road along the lake. Darkness covered the forest to our left, and the feeling of an evil presence continued to haunt my heart. Even the birds in the air flew high over this area as if they knew better than to plunge headlong into some abyss.

We rounded a corner, and a clearing appeared in the forest. In the midst of it, a village rested. Wooden buildings haphazardly lay about, while small paths wound their ways through the town. Like Reol, no wall protected it.

Logs lay piled close to the lake. A group of men carried a tree trunk, freshly cut. Some folks cleaned, others carried items, kids played. On the surface, it appeared as any other small village, but overshadowing the area, malice throbbed like a heartbeat.

As we entered the city, a young teen ran to us and bowed. "Greetings, travelers. Would you by chance be needing room and board for the night?"

113

The child's grin and eyes flashed energy, but his words sounded older. Perhaps the adults taught them what to say.

Seth nodded. "Indeed we do. We don't have much money, but we're willing to work for our stay."

The kid stuck his hand out. "My name's Arnold. I'm sure my father can work out a deal. He enjoys company. Follow me." Arnold turned and headed down the path.

Seth glanced at us and shrugged. "As good as anything, I'd wager."

We trailed after Arnold as he dodged a donkey and the cart it pulled, a couple of workers digging a hole, and kids chasing one another. I shook my head. The outside picture didn't match what I felt inside. I feared some type of deception lay in wait to pounce upon us.

Arnold stopped in front of a larger house. Several windows indicated many rooms. Though not a mansion, it rose above the others in town. Arnold opened the sturdy door, creaking on its hinges. "Father, we have company."

I leaned over to Doodle. "The kid sounds genuinely excited to have us."

He grunted. "I would be too if I were holed up here most of my life. I doubt they get too many visitors."

"I don't know. It's about the only route leading to the seaport from this section of the country. And no one is going to leave the road in that forest."

We entered the house. Pictures hung upon the walls, cushy couches and chairs lined the living room. I felt immediately at home, as if I'd lived here all my life.

A man entered the room, an apron strapped around his waist. His eyes peered from behind wire-framed glasses, while silver-white hair poured from the top of his head into a beard.

The man smiled and bowed slightly. "Welcome."

Arnold bounded up and down. "See, Father, I told you we'd have company today. I felt it in my bones."

His father cracked a smile. "Very well, you were right. Are you going to introduce me to your friends?"

Arnold's eyes widened. "I forgot to ask them, I was so excited."

Seth reached out and the man shook his hand. "My name's Dragon Breath. This is Whirlwind, Troll, Elf, Arrow, and Doodlebug, though we call him Doodle." Seth pointed to each of us in turn.

The man raised an eyebrow. "Interesting names. Mine is Jake."

I grinned. "That's my brother's name too."

He smiled. "Is that so? Well, dinner will be ready soon. Make yourselves at home."

Troll cleared his throat. "Jake, do you have a wife?"

Jake's slight smile faded. "I used to." He closed his eyes for a second, then turned to head back to the kitchen.

Troll grimaced. "Sorry, I didn't mean to—"

"You couldn't know." Jake stopped at the doorway, and without turning to face us said, "It's all right." Then he left.

Troll met Arnold's eyes. "I'm sorry. My parents were murdered when I was about your age."

Arnold waved a hand. "It's a sore spot for him, for sure. But he'll be fine."

Arrow sat on a chair. "What happened to her?"

Arnold shrugged. "One day, she just died. Not much more to it than that."

I shivered. For a second, I felt the evil fill the room, then sucked back out as if someone hid it. The homey feeling swept over me, as if masking a stench. Not all was as it seemed.

Jake ushered us in for a meal. We ate. Jake remained silent while Arnold talked continually, pausing long enough so we could answer his questions. But the flavors of the food delighted my tongue, and I ate way too much as I listened to Arnold's stories.

Arnold showed us to our rooms. He pointed me to a door. "Here's where you can stay." Then he pointed to another door and directed Seth to it.

As he guided the others toward their rooms, I stepped toward Seth and whispered, "Be alert. Something is very off here."

He frowned. "And how am I supposed to be alert when I'm sleeping?"

I frowned. "I mean, be observant. I don't know what, but this place is the focus of the evil I've felt."

He shook his head. "I don't feel that at all. I've never felt so comfortable and at ease. I can hardly wait to sleep upon a soft bed. Do you know how long it's been since I've done that?"

I raised an eyebrow. "Back at your house, I would assume."

He waved a hand at me. "I know, but that's not what I mean. Just that I don't get a soft bed very often."

"Don't go soft on me, is all I'm saying."

"You calling me a coward?" He gritted his teeth.

"No, of course not. I mean, don't trust your feelings. Stay alert."

He opened the door to his room and entered. "There's nothing to worry about. Goodnight." He closed the door.

I watched down the hallway to see the others disappear into their rooms and Arnold strolling back toward me. He smiled as he passed. "Goodnight, Whirlwind. Sweet dreams."

"Same to you." I sighed and entered my room.

A dresser stood in one corner, a couple of soft chairs faced each other in another, and a wood-frame bed resting against a wall welcomed me. A lone window, curtains partially drawn, revealed a deep darkness lurking outside.

I set my pack on the floor and prepared to sleep. A soft bed did sound appealing after the last few nights sleeping on the ground. I bounced onto it, and slid under the covers. Warmth encircled me as if I resided in a womb. I snuggled in and drifted off to sleep.

A forest surrounded me as dreams and reality traded places. Pitch-black darkness oozed from its depths. As I circled around, attempting to discover the growing evil I felt, white eyes blinked at me. They moved forward, and a form emerged into the faint light of the clearing.

"Who are you? What do you want?" I stepped back.

The figure appeared to grow as it moved toward me. "Control."

"Control? Of what?"

The outline of its face sharpened before me. Its white eyes shown from a featureless face, dark robes, and pale, sunken skin.

"Control of you, of course."

I shook my head. "No, you can't have me." A sword appeared in my hand and I raised it.

A black sword materialized in his hands. "You have no choice. You must obey. You are mine."

I jabbed at him. "Not if I can help it."

He dogged and swung his blade my way. Though in life I knew little about fighting with a sword, in this dream-like world I reacted with speed and accuracy. I parried his blow and threw his sword into the air, then drew my edge toward his chest.

But the creature drew back and the blade cut through air. He swung his sword down, and I couldn't get mine back up in time to block. I stood too close to dodge. I thrust my left fist into the air, and the blade crashed into my ring.

The dream world fractured into jagged pieces and fell apart. I jerked up in bed, coughing. Smoke hung heavy in the air. At first, I wondered if the house had caught fire, but I heard a slight whirring noise. I glanced at the ceiling and spotted a vent. Puffs of vapor lazily floated downward.

The hacking cough forced me to pause as I pulled myself from the bed and slid on a pair of pants. I tucked cold feet in my shoes and then cracked the door open, stifling a cough.

The hallway lay quiet. Traces of smoke hung close to the ceiling, but nowhere near as thick as in the room. I slipped out and tip-toed to Seth's room, and pushed the door open.

Clouds fell from his room; the vapor had filled Seth's room as thick as it did mine. But Seth didn't rest in his bed. I checked the next room. Once again, smoke filled it, but Elf lay on the bed. I sucked in some air and scurried to his side. I shook him, but he didn't respond. I fled to the other rooms, and found them the same, all out cold. Except Arrow, who like Seth, no longer resided in his bed.

"Sisko?"

I jerked around; Gabrielle stood in the doorway. "Gabrielle?"

She smiled and hurried toward me. I met her halfway and we hugged in an embrace.

I studied her face. Same yellow hair, same blue eyes. "What are you doing here?"

Her smile faded. "You must come with me. Hurry, before it's too late." She turned and pulled on my hand, but I felt no connection with her soul as before.

"What's wrong?"

"No time to explain. You must hurry."

I let her lead me. "Can't you tell me as we go?"

"It will make sense in a minute. Patience, my love." She focused ahead, guiding me through the hallway, to the front door, and outside.

I held back giving in to joy completely, as I held her hand. I didn't expect to see her so soon, and I couldn't get out of my mind the dream of fighting a demon.

She guided me through the village, and we approached the lake. She stopped at the water's edge and turned toward me. "Do you trust me, Sisko?"

I breathed in. "I trust Gabrielle, if that's who you are. But though everything tells me it is you, inside I'm not so sure."

She sighed. "There is a terrible evil here. To escape it, you must go into the water. If you trust me, trust me now." She stepped backwards and water sloshed about her feet. She held out her hand. "Follow me." Her eyes drooped. "Please?"

I glanced around. I couldn't detect that any evil would soon pounce on me, rather, it permeated the entire area. Yet, she echoed my thoughts. She recognized that there was evil here. I nodded and grasped her hand.

She stepped deeper into the waters, and I followed her as the gentle waves slopped thickly up my calves. A smile graced her face as she focused on me. Her eyes beamed, and I felt myself drawn to her. The murky water rose to my chest.

Sisko, this is Josh. Are you there?

I blinked. *Josh?*

Yes, Sisko, I must talk with you.

I shook my head and released Gabrielle's hand. I rubbed my forehead; she frowned. *Josh?*

Are you with me? Did I wake you up?

Gabrielle's face drew out long, and morphed. I backed away.

Sisko?

Sorry Josh, I'm busy.

Gabrielle's form elongated. Her skin grew scaly, and the head finished its change, revealing a serpent.

It hissed. "I want control!" Its mouth opened and it lurched toward me.

I could hardly move in this thick water, but managed to slide enough to the side that the head missed. I grabbed the neck and locked myself around the beast.

What do you mean you're busy? This is important.

The serpent shot into the air and dove into the water. I filled my lungs with air before we plunged into its depths.

Does fighting a giant sea serpent give you a clue?

That's it. Of course!

I felt branches graze my head. I couldn't open my eyes in this gunk, for fear of losing my sight.

Of course what?

Repeat after me.

I'm under water at the moment.

118

Then think after me! Father. Say it.

Father.

Fill this snake...

Fill this snake...

With light.

With light!

The serpent flew from the waters and into the air. As it did, a glow radiated from it, and I felt the creature's neck shrink. As we reached the apex of the leap and headed down, the serpent diminished until I held the neck of a three-foot snake.

I released it as we plunged into the oily water. I pushed myself back to the surface, sputtering nasty-tasting water as I did.

Sisko, are you all right?

I sucked in a deep breath, then swam for shore. *I wouldn't say all right. But at least I'm not lunch for some devil.*

I dreamed of a devil attacking you. Then I awoke in the middle of the night, and I felt God demanding I contact you and tell you to pray that prayer. But He's always spoken to you directly. Why through me this time?

I stood and trudged out of the water and flopped onto the shore. Oil dripped off me and I felt like I weighed hundreds of pounds.

Something about this place I'm in. An evil presence tried to control me, draw me into the water. I couldn't hear God at that moment, not until your voice broke through the spell.

Did you say water?

Yes. This place is called Dark Waters, and the lake is called Dark Lake.

And you've been in the water?

I watched as the half-moon shimmered against the oily surface of the lake. *Yes, I've got this oily stuff all over me.*

The ring must be protecting you then.

Why?

Milnore has mentioned that place. He says the lake there is evil. It takes living things and changes them into creatures of death.

My eyes widened. *That's why the light changed the serpent into a snake. That's what it was to begin with, before it was controlled by the evil.*

Exactly.

Creatures of death? Oh no. I have friends here who don't have a ring to protect them as I do. I must go find them.

Good luck. I'll say a prayer.

I smiled. *Thank you, Josh. You saved my life.*

As you say, God did, I only followed orders. Take care, and let me know how things come out.

Bye.

I turned toward the village. No telling how many of the villagers were more than they appeared. But Seth and Arrow? Where had they gone? Did the water swallow them already? And who else had disappeared while I fought this evil?

I heard the cracking of twigs. I turned to the sound and saw Arnold leaving the forest and heading back to the house. *What would he be doing out at this time of night?*

Once Arnold entered his house and closed the door behind him, I sloshed over to where the teen had exited the forest. A well used trail wandered into the forest. I stepped carefully, not being able to see well as the dim moonlight barely penetrated the forest canopy. An occasional branch would find its mark upon my head or arms.

After ten minutes of picking my way through the forest, pausing on occasion to ensure I could see the direction the trail led, I entered a clearing. On one end, two trees held the strands of a giant web. From their branches, four web-wrapped bundles dangled.

My stomach knotted. Did Arnold plan on sacrificing us to some giant spider? I approached one web-wrapped bundle, and tore the webbing away until I saw a face. "Doodle!"

His face appeared pale. The pieces fell into place. The smoke in the room poisoned us. I stared at my ring. Somehow God protected me through the ring, though it did mess with my mind a good bit.

I grabbed a sharp rock on the ground and began cutting away the thick webbing. I worked my way up until the body loosened enough to slide it out. I scanned the area. No sign of a spider or Arnold. He must have gone back for the last one.

I placed my hand upon Doodle. "Father, restore Doodle's health." His skin grew pink, and his eyes batted open. I smiled. "Welcome back to the land of the living."

He glanced around. "How did I get out here?"

I lifted him to his feet. "No time for long explanations. We've all been drugged and the plan is to make you a spider's meal."

A younger voice echoed from the forest. "I'd hoped you could have gone out the easy way, the less painful way."

120

I turned and saw Arnold with Elf's body slung over his shoulder. "Arnold, you don't have to be enslaved to the spider any longer. I can help free you."

He laughed. "Free me from the spider? I *am* the spider!" He dropped Elf on the ground, and his body stretched, bulged, and eight legs extended around him, his arms and legs disappearing into the body. He grew rounder, until a ten-foot high spider scampered toward us.

I shoved Doodle to the side and fled the opposite way. The spider followed me. I fled into the forest, away from its nest. Maybe Doodle would have time to free the others. Branches banged into my head and I almost tripped over roots as I pushed through the forest, doing my best to stay on the trail.

The spider sped along behind me, gaining. For a large creature, it could zip among the trees without much effort. It drew close, and I leaped between a couple of trees. The spider whipped around them. I glanced back, and my foot caught a root. I dove into the dirt, rolling up against a tree.

The spider skidded to a halt before me as I lay upon the ground. It prepared to strike. I noticed two trees next to me, growing so close together that they formed a "V" from the ground.

I leaped to my feet and dove between the trees, praying my foot wouldn't get caught. I felt the spider's legs brush against me as I slid between the two trunks, but the spider's head jammed between them and wouldn't come loose.

I fled through the forest once again. Though I gained ground, I could soon hear the sound of several legs approaching. I exited the forest, and sped into the village. The spider rushed up behind me, until it followed about five feet. I raced to the water's edge.

I stopped on the shoreline and turned to face the arachnid. It rushed at me; I dodged and it flew past me. It skidded to a halt, knee-deep in water, but then it moved toward me again.

I pointed my left fist toward the lake. "Father, replace the darkness with light!"

Fire poured from the ring and blasted upon the surface of the lake. Flames leaped into the air, and fingers of bright red raced across the oily film. A glory filled the lake, lighting up the night sky and the small village.

Arnold morphed back into human form and fell limp at the shoreline. I raced to his side, pulled him from the burning water, and knelt beside him.

Tears cascaded down his cheeks. "I'm a horrible monster."

"That can change. You'll see."

He grimaced and squeezed his eyes shut. "I ate her."

"Ate who?"

"My…my…" He broke down in sobs. "My mother."

I closed my eyes and offered a prayer. "You didn't know what you were doing. An evil controlled you. It's over now. It's gone."

"Tell my father I'm sorry. I'm so very sorry." He exhaled and paused. His eyes widened, then he fell limp in my arms.

I slammed my hand onto the ground. "Father, heal Arnold!"

Nothing happened. I checked my heart. I covered my face with my hands. The answer was no. I sat on the shore, my back to a flaming inferno miles long in the lake, but a sickening inferno in my heart.

After a few minutes, I knew I needed to heal the others from the spider's paralysis. I found my way back to the clearing and Doodle sitting beside the bodies. I healed each of them. While I rejoiced that they responded, I felt empty knowing one had died in my hands, and I could do nothing to help him.

I retrieved Arnold's body and we sat in the living room, waiting for Jake to awake. We held a vigil. No one felt like sleeping, nor did we feel like waking Jake. He'd find out soon enough.

In the early morning hours, the sunlight grew into a bright day. Jake shuffled into the room. He saw Arnold lying on the couch. I could see in his eyes that he knew. But he didn't cry. He didn't do much of anything other than release a long breath and say, "It's over."

I nodded. "It's fully over. I've destroyed the evil in the lake. That is, God destroyed the evil." I checked out the window. The fire had dimmed, but it still burned across the body of water.

Jake settled into a seat. "He was the last family I had. I'm all alone now."

Doodle stepped over to Jake and sat beside him, placing an arm around him. "I'll stay with you. I would like a family myself."

Jake closed his eyes and pulled Doodle into a hug. "You would be a blessing to an old man."

Elf and Troll glanced at each other. Troll stood. "I too, would like a family. Can I stay?"

"And me," Elf added.

Arrow's eyes darted around us. "If they're staying, I would like to stay as well. Someone needs to watch out for them."

A tear rose in Jake's eyes. "You're all welcome."

Seth stared at me. "What are you going to do?"

I watched Doodle hugging Jake. "I have a calling to fulfill. There's no family in my immediate future."

Seth slapped me on the back. "I wouldn't go that far. Cause you're practically like family to me, and I'm coming with you."

I smiled. "Thank you."

We helped Jake prepare Arnold's body for burial. Then stayed with him during the service as the priest spoke the prayers, and they lowered the body into the grave. The next morning, I knew I needed to leave.

Doodle, Troll, and Elf all hugged me. I hated leaving them now. I would have enjoyed getting to know them better. But I felt happy knowing they found a real family to be part of that did more than feed their bodies, but feed their souls as well. Much better than living on the road.

Arrow approached me and smiled. "I'm glad I didn't kill you." He haltingly wrapped his arms around me and squeezed. "Keep stirring things up."

I grinned. "Thank you. I will. And keep shooting straight."

They said their goodbyes to Seth. Then Seth and I loaded our packs and followed the trail back out of Dark Waters. I studied the lake as we traveled. The fire still burned here and there, but in many places it had stopped, and a deep, vibrant blue reflected the sun's rays. I couldn't feel the evil any longer.

Seth kicked a rock. "So, where are we going now?"

I shrugged. "Out there, somewhere."

"No plan, Whirlwind?"

"Nope, no plan. And Seth, call me Sisko."

"But I like Whirlwind."

I smiled. "I know, but we're not in a gang anymore. It's me and you. Neither is in charge or over the other. We work together as a team."

He nodded. "I like that, Sisko. But you'll always stir things up."

I grinned. And all this time I had thought it was Josh that kept getting me into trouble.

Faith's Fire

Seth turned his head my direction. "Hey Sisko, where are we going exactly?"

I shrugged my shoulders. "I don't know."

He frowned. "After two years, you think I would know the answer. You're not one for making plans."

"God's making the plans, my friend. I'm just following along." I pointed to the city in the valley as we crested a hill. "But I can say we're going to that city over there. Know its name?"

Seth raised his hand to shield his eyes from the sun and grunted. "Yeah, it's an old backwater town called Dragon's Inn. Used to be a busy town named Crossroads, but fables of a dragon scared everyone away except for a few stalwart villagers. The name gradually changed when the dragon supposedly settled in these hills."

"I take it you don't believe this dragon exists?" I glanced to read his expression.

"Dragons? Really, I thought you wouldn't be taken in by old fables and superstitions." He chuckled.

"I've seen stranger things, like people turning into trees."

"Oh yeah, your steam-house story. Interesting tale, but more superstition if you ask me."

I shook my head and held up the ring on my finger. "Then how do you explain my ring, and the miracles God does through it?"

He stared at it. He couldn't deny the miracles he had watched me do, including those I had done on him and his sister, Gabrielle.

Gabrielle. Thoughts of her flooded my mind. How long before I could see her again? Would God ever finish with me so I could return to her?

Seth stared down the road again. "I guess God can use whatever He wants, but tell me why God would send a dragon to a village?"

I shrugged. "You'd have to ask Him I guess. But God does use many things. You simply have to trust Him."

"Trust Him, huh? I've lived by my wits in the wild far longer than you've been away from mommy and daddy. The only one I've been able to trust is myself."

I chuckled. "All I can say is if you ever visit my village, do not use our steam house. You'll be very sorry."

"Sure, I'll keep that in mind." He pointed to the village gate a half-mile away. "But also keep in mind, this village is very superstitious. I wouldn't talk about your ring openly. Trouble would follow."

We entered the gate to see a few people milling around. They glanced up and scurried away as if not used to strangers. I saw older adults, but no children.

Occasionally, a creaking of rusty hinges would break the silence. Then the villager would jump back inside, slamming the door, knocking pieces of rotting wood onto their porch. Broken shutters swung in the wind and banged upon walls. Not a few houses had leaned slightly to one side. Maintenance hadn't been a high priority, apparently.

"There's the inn. I hope they have a good meal." Seth turned toward it.

I nodded, but the outside didn't seem too promising. The roof waved like a field of wheat in the wind, and holes dotted its surface. The dust swirled around us as we approached the door.

Inside, I squinted to see. At first, I thought the room seemed dark because my eyes needed to adjust. Yet a few seconds passed, and still I could only make out the outline of a counter. Little light penetrated here. A musty smell attacked my nostrils.

We crept to the counter and found a bell to ring. "Anyone here?" I heard something hit the floor, and then a small light flickered on. Soon, a bald-headed man wearing plain, brown clothing exited a room and shuffled to the counter.

"You be travelers, eh?" He squinted an eye at us.

"Yes, Sir," I said. "We're hoping for a place to sleep and..." I scanned the room. "Maybe a meal?"

His mouth opened, and he had to grab the counter to keep from falling down. He bobbed up and down as if laughing, but only a slight wheeze pierced the dank air. After he collected himself, he said, "I have a room you can bed down in, but your meal won't come from here."

Seth frowned at me. "Forget why God sent a dragon here, why did He send us here?"

The old man coughed, and the laughter fizzled to a loud whisper. "Oh, you know about the dragon, do you?" He pointed a long, thin finger at us. "If I were you, I would get right on out of town. The dragon don't take too kindly to strangers."

Seth grunted. "I told you they were superstitious. I would rather sleep outside than in here anyway. Let's go."

He grabbed my hand, but I pulled back. "Sir, when's the last time you saw this dragon?"

"Well…" He scratched his head and stared at the counter. "Been a long time. A very long time. Can't say I recall seeing the dragon. But he's out there. Don't you make no bones about that."

The door to the inn slammed open, flooding the room with light. A young woman stood backlit in the doorway. "Doctor, hurry." She paused as if noticing us for the first time but continued. "It's the baby. She's coughing up blood."

"I'll be right there," the old man said, and he shuffled back to his room.

I blurted out, "You're the doctor too?"

"You betcha, boy. There's not a lot of people here, you know. We do what we're able."

It dawned on me why I had seen no children. Few lived long enough. Sadness filled my heart for these people, trapped in time and superstitions, condemning them to a life of rot and decay. I knew I should go with him.

Seth pulled on me again. "Come on, let's get out of here."

I held up my hand. "Not yet. We need to go see this baby."

The old man had shuffled from behind the counter and headed to the door. "No need, boy. It's the sickness. They all die from it."

"What sickness?" He sounded so ho-hum about it.

He stopped and turned. His eyes blinked as if they had cried for years, and the tear-well had run dry. "Dragon sickness."

"Dragon sickness?" Seth's eyes widened. "I told you they were superstitious."

"We're still coming with you, Sir." I opened the door for him.

"Guess I can't stop you. It's your life you'll be risking. Have it your way." He hobbled out the door.

We arrived at the house and entered. While still darker than I would have liked, at least rays of sunlight shot through the windows and blanketed the floor in patterns. The doctor leaned over the crib and examined the baby.

The woman, red-haired and around thirty years old, stared at the baby, occasionally glancing at the doctor. "Can she survive?"

He shook his head. "Afraid not, Cherie. Too far gone, this one. There's nothing I can do for her." He put a hand on Cherie's shoulder.

She hung her head and closed her eyes. Her shoulders slumped. A vision of Gabrielle crying over our own baby pierced me, and I stopped breathing for a second.

I knew then why God had brought me here: to banish this dreadful disease from these people. And it would start with this baby. "I can help."

Seth grabbed my arm. The others turned their heads, disbelief written in their eyes. Yet, they parted. They had done all they could; why not let the fool have a shot?

I pushed Seth's hand from my arm. "It's all right, I'm meant to do this." I moved to the cradle. The low light revealed a pale figure. Bones thrust themselves against sagging skin, and a trail of dried blood ran from a corner of the girl's mouth. I placed my hand upon the child. "Father, banish the sickness from this baby and town."

For a moment, the baby remained still, and seconds ticked by. Then, a breath sucked in, and a cry rang from the lungs. Color returned to the body, and her eyes opened.

I lifted the infant from the crib and handed her to Cherie. "I believe the child is hungry."

Her eyes beamed as she received the child. She hugged the baby to her chest and cried tears of joy, the first in many years, no doubt. Warmth filled my being at her reaction.

I turned to see the reaction of the other villagers who had watched. An audience had gathered outside the door. They murmured as the news of what had happened spread. But their reaction surprised me.

"Sorcery, that's what this is. Black magic." The doctor pointed his crooked finger at me. "You'll bring down the wrath of the dragon upon us, boy." Fear etched lines upon his sagging face. Those in the room backed away.

"No, God did this, not me." Couldn't they understand? Why would they not trust in what God had done?

"God has refused to answer our prayers for years, boy. Why would your prayer be any different? It's magic, I tell you." He motioned for some men to bind me. "We must sacrifice you before the dragon takes our whole village."

Affirmations arose among the people, and they pressed in to grab me. Seth pressed toward me, shoving people to the ground.

I held up my hand. "No Seth, these people should not be hurt."

He paused for a moment. Doubt filled his eyes. "But—" A pot cracked over his head, and he slumped to the floor. A small swarm of villagers pushed me from the house while others pulled Seth's body into the street.

People jeered and spit upon me. Some hit me, and welts formed on my body. Could I have heard God wrong? Should I have listened to Seth? Questions flowed through my mind as the crowd shoved me to a series of wooden beams sprouting from the ground, topped with crossbeams. The aged rope and weathered wood indicated they hadn't done this in many years.

They placed us under two of the beams and tied our wrists with ropes anchored to the top. They fastened my feet firmly against the beams where they entered the ground.

The crowd moved away and left us there, spread-eagle, awaiting…I didn't know what. They kept crying out "sorcery" and "wizard" in accusation, as if arguing with a judge in their heads about their innocence. Yet they did not attempt to kill us. They waited.

In the midst of the jeering, Seth awoke. "Oh, my head." He pulled on the ropes. "What's going on?"

"I think we're being sacrificed, as best I can tell."

"Sacrificed!" He yanked harder against the ropes; his bulging muscles tightened with the effort. Yet, the cords did not give to his strength. He ended his struggle with a cry of resignation and slumped on the ropes. "I don't want to be a sacrifice!"

"Calm down. I'm sure God has a plan. He got us into this, He'll get us out." I hoped. Somewhere within me, I felt this would not end in death.

128

"What is this plan of His? Why is He doing this?" Seth's voice echoed against the buildings in the street, and the crowd quieted for a moment in response.

I turned my head and locked onto Seth's eyes. Fear born of helplessness raged in them. "I don't know, but He does. However this turns out, His will be done."

He looked at me as if I had lost my mind, but at the same time, I could sense in his soul a desire for such confidence. He stared at me for a long minute until the sound of footsteps interrupted our wordless conversation.

Not human footsteps, but those of a large animal. We both searched in the direction the sound originated, yet nothing could be seen. I heard hard breathing while the ground shook louder and louder with each pounding step as it approached. Still, the beast remained cloaked to my eyes.

In contrast to my talk, the sound and feeling of death approaching tensed my body to flee despite the fact my bonds wouldn't allow it. My legs shook and could barely hold me up.

I felt a caustic breath flowing over me. The creature must be right in front of me, yet it remained invisible. The man told the truth when he said he had never seen it.

The noise of the crowd had disappeared as they waited for the final blow. The creature turned to Seth who cried prayers of mercy. Then the breath returned before me, and the creature materialized before my eyes.

I wished it had remained invisible.

Cries and screams erupted from the crowd, and many ran for safety. My insides turned to water.

A brownish-red head, much like a huge lizard, hung inches from my face. A long neck held up the head. Its flattened body supported wings of skin spanning several feet. It gently flapped them in the wind as if cooling itself. It lifted its head and roared. My body vibrated.

During the roar, I heard shouts of "No!" and "Get away!" from the crowd cowering behind fences and walls. I felt the ropes give way. Seth had already been cut down, and he rushed off toward the crowd. I turned to see Cherie, shaking, holding a sword. She thrust it into my hand. "God be with you." Then she darted away. Genuine love makes heroes from the most unexpected of people.

I turned back as the dragon lowered its head. I had to keep the dragon's attention on me and not on those escaping.

"Sisko, run!" I heard Seth's voice yell from the crowd.

Right. I would be roasted before I could move five steps.

The dragon stared me in the eyes. It lifted its head once again, but this time it inhaled deeply. Everything in me said, "Flee now, this is your only chance." But another calm and sure voice said, "Stay. Your work is not done."

So I stayed. Maybe my death would teach the villagers a lesson. Maybe they would feel sorry and never sacrifice anyone else. The head came down, the mouth opened wide, and I saw the flames forming in its throat and erupting from its open jaws.

I closed my eyes and threw my arm over my head. I heard a loud roar and the sound of crackling wood all around me. Yet I felt no heat, only a cool breeze. Dew formed on my forehead. I put my arm down and opened my eyes. A blanket of flames flowed around me as if it caressed my body and enlivened my soul. After a few seconds, the flames ended.

The dragon reared its head back in confusion. The wooden beams around me crackled with flames. The tip of my sword glowed red from the heat. Yet, my clothing remained untouched, and my hair felt wet as if I had just washed it.

The dragon reared its head back again and blasted another round of fire at me. Again, I felt a cool and dewy breeze while everything else around me burned.

The dragon brought its head back toward me and sniffed. I reached out and caressed its snout. Oddly enough, I heard something akin to a purr. I smiled, and I could have sworn it smiled back.

An impression entered my mind, an impression that I should ride this dragon. I leapt upon its back, and we launched into the air.

Like a soaring bird, we raced into the clouds as the wind whipped though my hair. Perched on the back of such a beast, clinging to its neck, I experienced something few men have: a new perspective on life, both freeing and threatening.

During the ride, the dragon's thoughts and feelings erupted into my mind. I felt its sadness and its rage, but mostly its bewilderment at the villagers. It had been brought to them as a curse, but they had failed to learn from it.

The ride seemed long and yet ended before I wanted it to. The dragon landed back on the village street. I dismounted and petted its back. Then it shot into the sky with a deafening roar. It disappeared over the hills, returning to some forgotten land. It had finished its task.

Seth rushed toward me and nearly knocked me over with his hug. "Sisko, I thought the dragon had fried you for its supper, but like you said, God did have a plan." His eyes blazed from within, as if some spark had ignited a fire.

I had to laugh. "Yes, beyond my wildest thoughts."

I turned to face the crowd as they exited their hiding places. The doctor approached and squinted one eye at me. "Who are you?"

A pointless question. I pointed at the church spiral in the center of the village. "Where's your priest?"

He bowed his head. "He did a miracle, and then the dragon came. We believed he caused it and forced him to leave."

I shook my head. "The dragon said he came because of your reaction to the miracle, and you failed to repent."

Cries erupted from the crowd. "How could we have been so blind?" "We're wrong, we have sinned." "God have mercy on us!"

"You're no different than many whose faith is misplaced." I focused on the doctor. His long face expressed his struggle. "Isn't that right, Doctor?"

He glanced at me, and I saw pride break in his eyes as tears formed. He fell to the ground, joining in the sorrow for past sins.

Yet, it didn't take long for the crowd's sorrow to swell into joyfulness. The crowd clamored to thank me. Next thing I knew, I had been lifted onto their shoulders and carried away.

They celebrated that evening. The Church shone with light, and though no priest officiated, the people rejoiced and worshiped as best they could. Cherie, with her baby, stood at the front, a smile on both their faces. The angels surely rejoiced with us. A smoldering ember had finally ignited into a full fire of life, and a living village emerged from the ruins.

Seth and I hiked up the mountain trail. We breathed hard in the thin air. After reaching the top, we rested on the peak. The valley of Dragon's Inn lay on one side, in a sea of green. On the other, a barren land of rock and shrub spread for many miles. We each took a swig of our water.

"So where are we headed now?" Seth grinned.

I wished I could say back to his house and Gabrielle. I scanned the barren wilderness and swung my finger toward a group of distant hills, barely visible across the plains. "Out there, somewhere."

Seth grinned. I had the distinct feeling he would follow me to the end of the world. And he might very well be required to, but in a way he didn't expect.

"Let's get moving then. We don't want to be up here when nightfall hits." I grabbed my pack and hoisted it on my shoulders.

Where would God take us now? I couldn't wait to find out.

Death's Redemption

The walls of Zureal rose over the horizon. The sight of civilization sent relief over me. Several days over deserted stretches of road, meeting few along the way, had created a hunger for a bed, hot food, and the buzz of people. I had wished we could have taken the direct route from Dragon's Inn to Zureal, but when God says to go one place, I go. The family I helped on a farm did need me, as it turned out.

Seth grinned. "Appears our exile to the wastelands is nearly over."

I nodded. "Not to disdain your cooking, but my mouth waters for a hunk of beef, stewed potatoes, and a mug of ale to wash it down."

Seth walked faster. "Now you've done it. I'm starving!"

I laughed. "It's probably another hour or two before we reach it. Don't die of hunger on me within sight of redemption."

In the days since leaving Dragon's Inn, Seth had remained quiet. The events there had affected me as well. To be enveloped in a dragon's fire and not be burned surprised me as much as anyone. The memory of the dragon ride burned within me. No doubt, in Seth as well.

The hour turned into two before we stepped through the city gates. Zureal sat against a cliff-face. Flat-roofed, stone buildings populated the town. A staircase led up the cliff from the back wall of the city to a set of caves halfway up the mountain. For a city off the beaten path, it boasted a thriving economy and population.

Several eyes stared at us. One man gathered around a group, pointed at us, and talked, causing the others to turn their heads.

"Seth, have you ever stolen anything around here before?"

He shrugged. "I've visited here, but my gang never hung around these parts much. No one here should know who I am."

"These people recognize one of us."

He smiled. "Are you sure it's not the fact that we've not bathed for days?"

I chuckled. "Now that you mention it…"

"Let's get some food in our stomachs."

"I'm for that, but I feel I need to see the priest first."

He raised an eyebrow. "Why?"

"It's that sense I need to help someone, again."

He grinned. "You mean, it's time to stir things up again."

I shook my head. "We'll see."

I followed the streets, leading to the domed building in the center of town. A cross stood atop it, designating it as the local church. The limestone walls stretched high. Windows dotted the upper levels. The door stood open, leading into the narthex.

Upon entering, the smell of incense wafted by my nose. Candles burned in a sandbox. A slight sob could be heard in a distant room.

Seth pointed at the wall. "Who's that?"

I stepped over to him and examined the icon. "It's a martyr."

"You mean he died for his faith?"

"Yes. There have been many such saints."

Seth touched the icon. "Usually dying means you lose. Why would you honor that?"

I smiled. "What would you die for?"

He grunted. "Not much."

"That's the point. These people died for their faith, because they believed it that strongly. Because they believed God conquered death, so physical death held no power over them."

Seth stared as if transfixed. "Most people would say they were deceived, that they were fools."

His use of "most people" didn't escape my attention. "Fools. Yes, such devotion does appear foolish to most."

A voice echoed from one end of the narthex. "Hello. Is there something I can do for you?"

I turned to find a priest approaching. "Yes, Father. My name is Sisko of Reol and this is Seth from Jerole. And for reasons I don't know, God told me to come here."

His eyes widened. "Sisko?"

I glanced at Seth, whose wrinkled brow indicated the same surprise I felt. "Yes, Father. Have you heard of me?"

A smile spread across his face. "Heard of you? Who hasn't? I'm honored to have you here."

I recalled the people who traveled to Reol to have me heal them. Word must have spread that I had taken to the road. "How have you heard of me?"

He laughed. "You don't know? People come through here telling stories of your healings and miracles. Recently, some from Dark Water have related your story in the tavern, and a couple days ago, a man from Dragon's Inn told how you managed the dragon there. I'd imagine these stories are being told in cities all over the land."

Something about that knowledge excited me, but at the same time scared me. I prayed God would receive the credit, but I feared that hero worship would increase for me instead.

A fresh sob echoed through the halls. I turned my head toward the sound. "Who's that? Maybe she's the one I need to help."

The priest sighed. "I'm afraid you're too late for her. She's a widow, and her only son has died, leaving her alone. We're holding the funeral today." He shook his head. "It's a shame. She'll be poor and destitute now. The temptation to prostitution may be too strong for her."

I hung my head. But I checked my heart in case God wanted me to help her in some fashion. I raised my head, not believing what God wanted me to do. "Father, God's telling me she's the one I'm here to help. Maybe there's something I can do for her, even though her son is dead."

He nodded. "Follow me."

He led us through a dimly lit hallway for a few feet before turning into the nave. A large room, lined with a bench and icons along the walls, held a bier upon which a body lay. A woman dressed in black knelt before the bier, as soft sobs escaped her lips.

The son appeared to be no older than fifteen. His pale skin and unmoving chest testified to the fact he no longer lived in this world. My eyes watered, watching the scene.

But what did God want me to do? What did she need? The question stuck in my mind. She needed her son alive. I checked my heart. *Are you serious, God?* I breathed deep. *If you say so.*

I stepped down the center of the nave until I stood behind the widow. I placed my hand on her shoulder. "Don't weep."

She turned her red eyes toward me. Her expression clearly asked, "Who are you and why would you say such a crazy thing?"

Indeed, what God asked sounded crazy. But who was I to argue? I stretched out my hand and placed it on the boy's chest.

"Father, restore life to this child of yours."

At first, nothing noticeable happened, but then color returned to his face, and his chest abruptly rose. He coughed, then his eyes batted open. He sat up as his mother jumped back in shock. He turned to see us.

He sucked in a deep breath. "Wow. That was awesome."

His mother cried tears of joy and leaped onto the bier in her attempt to hug him.

I gazed at the scene. "Yes. 'Wow' is about all I can think of to describe that."

I turned to go back. Seth and the priest sat on benches. Both of their eyes stared at me, their mouths open.

I stopped in front of Seth. "You ready to go?"

He met my eyes and pointed at the boy and his mother hugging. "You resurrected him. How?"

I shook my head. "I didn't do it. I asked. God resurrected him."

He breathed deep. "Who are you?"

I smiled. "I'm Sisko of Reol. Just as human as you."

"But every time I think I'm beginning to figure you out, you do something like this, though I'll admit this tops anything to date."

I patted him on the back. "You're making this too complicated. There's nothing to figure out about me. You're trying to figure God out. That, my friend, takes eternity to do."

He nodded. "I'm starting to get that idea."

The priest slipped next to Seth. "Do you have a place to stay? I'd be honored if I could provide your needs while you're here."

I grinned. "I'd be honored as well, Father."

He bowed. "My name is Father Anthony. If you'll follow me."

I felt a tug on my sleeve. I turned to see the mother and her boy beside me. He smiled but stared at the floor. "Sir, I want to thank you so much for—"

I wrapped my arms around him and squeezed. His mother enveloped us in a hug as well. I pulled back. "Thank God. He's the one that did it."

The boy nodded. "I wanted to ask you something."

"Sure."

"I want to know...can I be your disciple?"

I stopped breathing. Disciple? To me? I sat on the bench. "God sent me to be my brother's keeper, not to start a school or movement. I help who I can with the ability He's given me. That is all."

He pointed to Seth. "But he's following you."

Seth nodded. "I have learned a lot."

I sighed. "He's a friend. He's not a disciple or anything." A thought broke into my consciousness. "Besides, part of the reason God has brought you back is to take care of your mother. You can't leave her now."

His shoulders sank and he nodded. "Yes, you are right. I can't leave her."

I patted him on the back. "Remember, no matter who your teacher is, you're first and foremost a disciple of God. I'm sure Father Anthony here will do a good job guiding you."

He smiled. "Thank you for everything."

We followed Father Anthony back down the hallway, into the narthex and out the door. I jumped back when I exited the building. A crowd waited for me around the steps of the church. When they saw me, they pulled in tighter and called out to me.

I glanced at Father Anthony. He smiled. "I'll keep dinner hot for you."

I felt God wanted me to help these people, and I couldn't turn away from them. I sat on the steps. "One at a time, please. No need to push in."

For four hours I healed diseases, broken bones, blind eyes, and problems I hadn't known existed. As darkness settled over the city, and the last few left whole, I pulled myself up and slogged to the house I'd seen Father Anthony and Seth enter.

I entered as the door opened. A brown-haired woman of medium build and a kindly smile ushered me to a seat at the kitchen table. Father Anthony and Seth sat chatting over cups of tea.

Father Anthony rose. "I see you're finished. This is my wife, Rhoda."

I bowed. "It's so nice to meet you. Thanks for giving us a place to stay tonight."

She blushed. "We're glad to have the company. Sit and I'll get you some stew."

I pulled out a chair. "So, do you have any kids?"

Rhoda paused, and Father Anthony bowed his head. I gulped, knowing I must have hit a sore spot.

Father Anthony sighed. "We do, but I'm afraid our son is being held captive."

"Captive? How?"

He swallowed a gulp of tea. "There's a group of men, raiders, who are no friends of the Church. They took our son as a slave, to bring him up in their ways. Said they were saving a soul from death."

Seth shook his head. "How backwards is that?"

I glanced at Seth. "You think so?"

Father Anthony nodded toward Seth. "He was telling me about his time as a gang leader, and what you had done. Wouldn't you think he would know more than either of us about that life?"

I smiled. "I suppose so." But that Seth said it surprised me more.

Seth sat up. "What is your son's name?"

"Quin. He's about five years old now."

A sob escaped Rhoda's lips before she pulled it back in.

"When did they take him?"

Father Anthony fingered his cup. "About a year ago."

Seth shook his head. "Any idea where they are? Have you tried looking for them?"

"They said if we followed, or they so much as saw us coming, they would kill him. We've tried to get news from traders and other travelers, and paid money for someone to find him and bring him back. But no one's been able to."

Seth met my eyes as I spooned stew into my mouth. "Can't we go find him? This is something God could have us do? Right?"

I felt the expectations of Father Anthony and Rhoda waiting for my answer. And yes, I felt God wanted it too. "Yes, I believe so."

Rhoda turned toward me. "Thank you so much. May God grant you abundant blessings."

Father Anthony and Rhoda fed us breakfast, filled our packs with food and supplies, and prayed prayers over us. Seth and I stepped onto the street. Carts pulled by horses and donkeys entered and exited the gates while people scurried about their business.

Seth shook his head. "So how do we pick up year-old tracks? I wouldn't know where to begin."

"God knows." I closed my eyes and searched into my heart for direction. A minute passed before I opened my eyes again. "This way."

I started to step forward, but stopped when I saw a contingent of young men standing in front of me. The young boy God had brought back to life yesterday stood in the center of them.

I nodded to them. "Good morning. Is there anything I can do for you? Someone need more healing?"

They all shook their heads. The boy spoke up. "Sir, we want to follow you wherever you go."

I breathed in and slowly let it out. "Don't you need to stay with your mother?"

He smiled. "She said the harvest wasn't for a couple months yet. Why not follow you for a while and see where God leads me?"

I scratched my head. I didn't know what danger we'd find ourselves in if we found these raiders. The last thing I needed was a group of boys who could potentially be used as bargaining chips, or worse, be killed.

Seth raised a hand. "I don't think we have enough food to feed you all."

One of the boys frowned. "If he can raise the dead, certainly multiplying some food wouldn't be an impossible task."

I figured honesty might be the best policy with them. "It's not that God couldn't do that, I simply can't guarantee that He will. It's also a sin to presume on God. The fact is, we're likely going into danger. We're attempting to rescue a boy from some raiders. If you're all right with dying, you're welcome to come."

Several of the boys glanced at each other. One of them waved his hand. "I'm going to get in trouble if I don't do my chores. I think I'll pass on this adventure." He turned and scurried away.

Another shrugged. "You know, I remember I said I'd meet the butcher and help him clean his shop this afternoon. I'd hate to disappoint him." He left.

One by one, they gave their excuses, and departed. Except for the boy who had been dead, but was now alive. He frowned. "They don't know what I know. I'm following you. Death doesn't scare me."

I sighed. "I don't suppose it would. What's your name?"

"Everyone calls me Shad. So, can I come?"

I shrugged. "This isn't easy. And I'm no teacher. Just a follower of God."

He smiled and nodded.

I glanced at Seth, who grinned at me.

"What?"

"You aren't going to win."

I stared into the sky for a moment before focusing on the gate and moving forward. "Come on, then. But don't expect any sermons."

The two followed me out the gate. I paused a few feet out, then turned and headed to the north-west.

"Where are you going? There's no road that way," Seth said behind me.

"I know that, but this is the way God says to go."

We followed the city walls until they merged with the cliff-face. A few feet from the wall, a small rabbit trail cut among the bush and cactus and followed the mountain chain.

I stepped onto the trail and followed it. It grew to a small path, then widened enough for two or three to ride abreast.

Seth stepped up beside me. "This road isn't on any of the maps. How did you know it was here?"

Shad laughed. "He's Sisko. That's how."

I spun around, and Shad stepped back, the merriment falling off his face. "I said no sermons, but I will offer this teaching. I don't do these things. God does. I only ask." I raised my left hand before his face; the ring shown against the sunlight. "I went into a steam house and came out with this ring. The priest said it married me to God, to do His will, and enabled me to do miracles. But it isn't me that does them. Do you understand that? All I do is ask."

His blank stare pierced me. He barely nodded his head.

I sighed. That had sounded harsher than I intended. But he should have stayed with his mother. "Are you sure…" I hung my head. Was I sure? I had never checked my heart. I squeezed my eyes shut and rubbed my forehead. After mentally kicking myself for forgetting, I asked God what He wanted me to do.

I opened my eyes. "I'm sorry. I reacted too strongly. But everyone treats me like a god or something. I'm human, just like you. Why God chose me, I don't know. But it could have been you as easily as me."

He relaxed. "I didn't mean to imply anything bad."

I placed a hand on his shoulder. "You'll be glad to know that God does want you to come with me. But we'll treat each other as equals."

A smile broke out on his face, and his eyes sparkled. "Thank y—"

I thrust a finger to the sky.

"I…yeah, I mean, thank God."

I grinned and patted him on the back. "Let's get going."

I straightened my pack and headed down the road.

Seth whispered behind me, "He gave me the same speech."

The path wound its way among the foothills of the mountains to our right. A few clouds raced through the air, giving us momentary relief from the sun. Birds squawked overhead, and an occasional animal would dart away through the brush.

The day slipped by before I realized it. Seth told an occasional story now that he had a new listener. I kept a close check on my heart, in case I sensed a new direction or to stop. But the direction God led continued along the path. A forest thickened into the foothills as we traveled. The shadow of the mountains fell over the hills and the western sky dimmed to starlight.

We stopped to set up camp. After a fire blazed and Seth brewed tea, we dived into the supplies Rhoda had provided: dried beef and cheese. At first, no one talked, but as bellies filled, the chewing slowed and gave way to conversation.

"Sisko?" Shad fixed his eyes on me.

"Yes?"

"How does a steam house give you a ring?"

I smiled. "Can't describe how. It's a mystical steam house. Whoever goes in, it reveals their character, tries to correct the bad traits through repentance, or enhance the good ones. I've seen a person turning into a tree in there."

His eyes blinked. "A tree?"

I nodded. "I know, hard to believe. But it's true. Like I said, I can't explain how. But if you ever visit Reol, don't go in expecting to get something like my ring. Too many people think they have great character, only to find out it reveals something they've hidden from themselves and others."

He set his chin in his hand, his elbow propped on his knee. "You should hear the stories being told about you. There's the one how you took over a circus and healed everyone in the area, and turned the circus owner into an elephant."

I jerked back. "I did no such thing!"

"And there's the story of your big fight with the creature in Jerole. Wrestled with him for five days and nights before slaying the beast. After they threw you in, they've never heard from that creature since."

Seth laughed. "Sisko? Wrestling with a creature for five days and nights? I could knock him out with one punch."

I grinned. "You probably could. I didn't wrestle with the creature at all. Just cast the demon out controlling him."

Seth shook his head. "How does such a story arise? No one was down there but you, me, and the creature."

I shrugged. "Who knows what the man I healed told people after we left?"

Shad pointed at me. "And the one about turning Dark Waters into Clear Waters, and the giant fireballs you threw to defeat the evil creatures terrorizing the village."

I groaned. "That's not how it happened."

"So when you showed up on the heels of hearing how you'd slain the dragon at Dragon's Inn—"

"I did not slay the dragon!"

"—and then you arrive and raise me from the dead, it's easy to see why people are treating you as they do."

Seth nodded. "I don't know why they make up that stuff, because the truth is amazing enough from what I've experienced."

I pointed at Seth. "As long as that truth includes that I'm doing what I'm told, and that's it."

Seth grinned. "And from my experience, I'd say your obedience is pretty amazing."

I shook my head. "If I can't trust God, then I can't trust anything."

"Even in the face of death." Shad stared at us.

I patted him on the back. "Yes, even in death."

I awoke to someone jerking my hands behind my back. My legs wouldn't move; they'd been tied. I craned my neck to get a better view. I could see at least eight men dressed in green tunics and brown trousers either standing or sitting on logs around the camp.

The one tying my hands jerked me to my feet. "That's the last one."

Once turned around, I saw Seth and Shad bound and being held by two of the men. Were these the rangers we wanted to find? "What do you want?"

"That will be revealed in good time," a child's voice spoke to my left.

I turned to see a five-year-old child. "Is your name Quin?"

He cocked his head to one side. "Strange, I don't know you, but you appear to know me. Did my father send you?"

I glanced at the other men. None of them acted at all concerned that we conversed. "Yes. He's worried about you. You were taken from him by these men, were you not?"

Quin smiled. "Yes, and it's a good thing they did. They saved me." He strolled around Seth for moment before moving his attention to Shad. He stared Shad in the eyes. "This one is promising."

Shad clenched his teeth together. "Promising for what? I don't need 'saving.'"

Quin nodded. "That's what I thought initially. You'll see the light soon enough."

I worried what he meant by that. But then Quin turned his attention to me. He wrinkled his forehead. "There's something odd about you. I can't place it." He frowned. "No matter. The test will reveal the truth, and you'll either accept it, or be judged by it."

Quin marched into the forest. "Bring them along, men."

One flung me over his shoulders. I bounced along as they trotted through the forest. I couldn't make out any markers to keep track of their turns and twists. Before long, I couldn't tell among all the trees which direction we headed other than in general based on where the sun shown through the canopy of leaves.

After a couple of hours, we entered a clearing. A group of tents sat around a fire pit. Against a rise in the hill, a cave opening loomed over the area. I felt an evil from it. I groaned inwardly. I ran into these evil places way too often. Came with the territory, I supposed.

They laid us side by side against a log. Quin stood before us. He pointed at Shad. "Let's do him first."

One of the rangers flipped out a knife and stepped toward Shad. He closed his eyes and turned his head, but the man cut the cords around Shad's feet and hands.

Quin grabbed Shad's hand and pulled him up. "How old are you?"

Shad stared at him for a second before answering. "Fifteen."

Quin nodded. "About right."

"Right for what?"

Quin grabbed Shad's wrist. "Come with me and you'll see."

Shad pulled away. "No, I don't want to!"

Two of the rangers pulled knives and approached Shad. Shad swallowed and stopped struggling.

Quin held a cup. "Take this and drink it."

Shad glanced at the drawn knives waiting for his protest. He frowned, grabbed the cup, and drank. He grimaced and wiped his mouth.

"That's enough." Quin took the cup from him and pulled on his hand.

I jerked on my ropes as did Seth, but we watched helplessly as they entered the cave.

Seconds turned to minutes as we waited. None of the men around us talked. Birds, the scurrying of animals along the ground, the buzz of flies filled their silence. Musty dampness crept around us.

What mystified me most was Quin. He acted as the leader of the group. But that didn't make any sense. Why would a captive, and a small child at that, end up being their leader? And why did these men act so half-dead?

After about half an hour, Quin and Shad returned. Shad glowed with a smile. Quin placed a hand on Shad's shoulder. "I'm happy to report that Shad has seen the light. He will be my assistant, since he is younger than you all, and older than me."

Shad nodded. "He speaks the truth." Shad stared at Seth and I. "You would be wise to humble yourself and see the truth."

I sighed. This appeared more like a cult than a gang. I expected at any moment they'd say the name of their group was "And a child shall lead them."

Quin pointed at me. "He's next."

I didn't bother resisting. He gave me the cup, and I barely sipped it.

"More, I don't see your throat moving."

I swallowed a gulp. A bitter taste slid down my tongue. I grimaced.

"One more time."

I swallowed again and gagged, but managed to choke down the liquid.

Quin yanked the cup from my hand. "Follow me."

The entrance led into a tunnel. Torch flames flickered off the variegated cave walls. As we walked, the torches grew farther and farther apart, until we passed through pockets of dusky darkness. I felt the sense of evil grow stronger the further we sank into the mountain.

We approached a doorway on the edge of the last torch's light. As I stared at it, I realized the door appeared to waver with the firelight, causing me to steady myself against the cave wall.

Quin turned to me. "You are about to see the truth of the universe. I do hope you can handle it." He opened the door and we entered.

We stepped into a vast room, though I couldn't tell how big as darkness shrouded everything. But countless points of light and small balls colored green, brown, blue, orange, gray, and many other variations, floated in the midst of the void so that I stood as a giant in the middle of a galaxy. But a throbbing light, multiple times bigger than any of the "planets," hovered in the center of the room.

"Who stands before me?" a deep, bass voice reverberated through the room. With each word, the light in the center grew and fell with the syllables.

"I am Sisko." The planets and stars spun around, then stopped. "And who are you?"

"I am the master of the universe, orderer of creation, fulfiller of reality, and worthy of your worship."

I shook my head, trying to clear it. "You mean, God?"

"If you wish to call me that, I will not object."

The planet and stars spun around again, then froze. My mind spun around too, yet through the fog I knew this couldn't be God. Aside from the sense of evil the ring provided, God wouldn't have to ask me my name.

I breathed deep. "I don't believe you."

"Don't be hasty. Believe in me, and you will become the ruler of a world." One of the balls grew until it filled the room. Misty blue clouds, striped with orange bands, rotated before me as if on display. "This world, for instance, filled with a primitive race, would be perfect for you. I can sense you have power."

The ball of blue and orange wavered, and I rubbed my forehead. "I don't have to think about it. I know you are not God or a god. A demon, perhaps." At least, I thought that might be the case. And I felt as if I should be doing something or saying something, but I couldn't think.

The planet shrunk back to a small ball in the room, but the throbbing light in the center doubled in size, and the light blasted forth so that it felt like being too close to a big fire.

"You have chosen the wrong path. You are an unbeliever and are found wanting!"

The light died back to the ebbing glow as when first I had entered. Light appeared at one end of the room as if someone had opened a door.

Quin pointed toward the light. "You can leave now."

I guessed a punishment awaited me once outside. I stepped toward the light, but stopped when I didn't hear him following. "Are you coming?"

"I'll be out in a minute. I must converse with god to determine your fate."

A fleeting thought forced its way into my mind. "Why doesn't 'god' do it himself?"

Quin scowled and pointed to the light. "Leave, unbeliever."

I wavered for a moment, feeling like words lay on the edge of awareness, that needed to be said, but I couldn't force them to the surface. I sighed and turned toward the light.

Noise echoed and a door banged open behind me. I heard voices echoing down a tunnel, saying, "Stop! You're not prepared! You cannot go in there."

I turned to see Seth barging into the room. Two men fell upon him, but Seth elbowed one in the gut and flipped the other over his shoulder, landing him on his back.

Quin yelled, "You must leave! Both of you."

I waved to Seth. "This way, the door is over here."

Seth sped toward me. "No, Sisko! Don't move."

I nodded. He followed me, so I continued on.

"Sisko, stop! Now!"

"This way, Seth." I put my foot out, but the floor disappeared on me. I felt the edge of the floor with my other foot, but it scraped off as my weight fell downward. The stars and the planets spun again, but for a different reason.

My fall halted as someone grabbed my arm. I glanced up to see Seth's hand wrapped around my wrist, and his other clinging to the edge of an invisible ledge.

"What's happening?" I called up to him.

Seth grimaced. "You've been drugged. Ask God to clear your mind."

"My mind feels clear enough...I think."

146

Quin's head appeared into view, as if someone had lowered a wall. "It appears you have both been judged and found wanting." He slammed his foot onto Seth's fingers.

Seth winced and groaned. "Father, clear Sisko's mind."

The stars and planets vanished. The ebbing light in the center of the room shrank to a bare glow. But below me, a river of lava bubbled. Seth's hand grasped the edge of a cliff jutting out.

I closed my eyes to search what I should do. "Let go of my hand and save yourself."

He swung me back and forth as Quin continued to stomp on his fingers. "I'm not afraid…" Seth grunted and jerked me upwards. His muscles bulged and he cried out as if the effort hurt every part of his body. "…of death, any more!"

I grabbed the edge of the cliff and pulled myself back onto the cave floor. Quin slammed his foot onto Seth's hand, and his fingers slipped.

"Seth!" I crawled to the edge to watch Seth fall, and then plunge into the river of lava. I felt helpless. All I could do is pray. "Father, save him."

Quin stood over me. "No one can save him now."

Seth had prayed for me, and God granted his request. "There is someone who can. Let me introduce you to Him."

More of the Rangers swarmed into the room. Quin pointed at me. "Kill this one." They drew their swords and raced toward me.

I breathed in deep. "Father, fill this room with Your light!"

I flipped over on my stomach and covered my head. A warmth filled the room, and cries soared to the ceilings of the cave, echoing back and forth as the men screamed and cried for the fire to stop. But one bass voice boomed within the room. It careened to an agonizing scream, hurting my ears. Then it died off, leaving the pleadings and tears of the people echoing in the cave.

I felt the warmth leave and peered out to see a deep darkness accented by a reddish glow faintly outlining the ledge and the ceiling. A faint light from a torch flickered from the doorway that Seth had entered.

A child cried beside me. I sat up. Quin huddled on the floor in a ball, whimpering. "I want my father. I want my mother. Where are they?"

I sat beside him and held him in my arms. "I'll make sure you get to them. Everything's going to be fine." My heart sank. Not everything. Seth wasn't fine.

I heard falling rocks. I glanced over to the ledge. A hand grasped its edge, and pulled up. Seth's head popped up.

I jumped into the air and raced toward him. "Seth! What happened? I saw you fall into the lava."

He laughed as he pulled himself onto floor. Globs of glowing red lava dripped from his skin. "You of all people shouldn't be surprised."

I touched him, and it burned my fingers. I shook my head. "But you don't have a ring like mine."

He focused on my eyes. "I asked, He did it. I believe."

I smiled. "You believe?"

"You said He did it. So I figured He'd either save me or not. But you have a mission to fulfill. That was worth dying for." Seth scanned the area. "Besides, I knew you'd stir things up once your mind was clear. And I can see I wasn't wrong."

"Comes with the territory, I guess." I helped Quin to his feet. "Come on. Let's get you to your parents."

We helped the other men out of the cave. They were as disoriented as Quin. Each of them had come in as a child, and the demonic influence convinced them that it was God. Preying on little ones who have great faith, but little discernment, the demonic being had created its own cult following in the mountains.

So Seth and I gave them instructions on how to reach their home, once they remembered the name of their town. Eventually they parted ways, and the camp grew empty, leaving me, Seth, Shad, and Quin. We worked our way back to the road.

I turned to Shad. "Well, how do you feel about this traveling around with me now?"

He stared at the sky. "Well, it was certainly…different than my normal chores."

Seth laughed. "Now that's an understatement."

Shad glanced at Seth and smiled. "I think I need to stay with my mother, at least for now. But I thank you for letting me come along. I learned a valuable lesson."

I raised an eyebrow. "Oh? What's that?"

"Don't drink something that will mess with your mind. It will deceive you."

I smiled. "Not a bad lesson. So, can you take Quin back to his parents?"

Shad grinned. "I'd love to. Father Anthony will be so happy."

I laughed. "I would like to see that, but I'm afraid God has us going the opposite direction. So I'll leave him in your care."

Shad nodded, then hugged both me and Seth.

I squeezed Quin. "Tell your father we'll look him up next time we're around."

He hugged my neck. "Thank you." A grin spread across his mouth.

Then Shad and Quin turned and headed down the road.

After a final wave goodbye, Seth and I stepped toward the opposite horizon, keeping the mountains to our right. We traveled in silence for a few minutes.

Seth sucked in a breath. "You were right."

I glanced at him. "About what?"

"Back after we left Jerole. You said people change."

"So, do you like what you're changing into?"

He smiled. "Yes, I believe I do. I believe, so I do."

I slapped him on the back. "You might make it after all, my friend."

Ego's Conflict

"Where are we?" Seth stood on the ledge of a mountain, gazing at the neverending rows of peaks rising into the distance.

I chuckled. "If you don't know, I sure don't."

Seth grabbed his water-skin. "Not that I don't trust your sense of direction, but when you said we should head into the mountains with no road or path to follow, I questioned your sanity."

I shrugged. "I still feel this is the direction God wants us to go."

"But why? I thought He wanted you to help people. We're miles from anyone out here."

"I'm as much in the dark as you are. But all we can do is follow. Leave the rest up to Him."

Seth nodded toward the sinking sun. "We'd better find some shelter. It's cold enough up here while the sun's out. No telling how bad it will get at night, and we don't have time to reach a valley."

I pointed several yards to our right. "How about that cave?"

Seth nodded. "It'll do. Why don't you set things up? I'll see if I can hunt some game before it gets dark."

He placed his pack in my hands and pulled his bow and arrow from it. Then he strolled toward a group of trees down the trail.

I reached the cave and dumped our things against the wall, then searched until I found dry wood lying about and coaxed a fire into existence close to the cave's entrance.

Once satisfied with my work, I sat against the rock and waited for Seth to return. I stared at the cave walls, and my eyes searched for anything interesting. I sighed and squirmed into a more comfortable position.

A glint of reflected firelight caught my eye further into the cave. I froze, afraid it might be an animal, but nothing moved. Then it flickered at me again. I stood and approached it. As I drew near, a faint outline revealed itself on top of a rock.

I reached out and felt a handle. I pulled it into the firelight and smiled. "It's a bell!" My voice echoed in the empty cave. What would a bell be doing in a cave miles from anywhere?

I turned it around. Two inches in diameter, wavy lines graced the bottom and top of the bell, and four symbols decorated the golden metal between them. One appeared to be a leaf of some type. Another a grapevine, the third a wing, and the last a flaming sword. Yet, dirt clung to it, obscuring the brilliance breaking through at various spots. I pulled it to my shirt to clean it, and the clapper banged against the bell, releasing a pure resonance echoing through the cave.

A light burst from nowhere before me. I jumped and fled to the cave opening, skidded to a halt, and peered back in. The light died and a well-built man stood in the cave, stooped over, a paint brush in his hand.

He pushed the brush down, then froze. He straighten up and scanned the area. "Ahhhh! Now? After all this time!" He threw the brush down. "A few more stokes and I would have finished."

He stared at the fire. "All right, who rang my bell?"

"I did." I entered the cave again, but remained close to the entrance.

He shook his head. "Over one hundred years that bell has sat in this cave undisturbed, until you found it and rang it."

"I'm sorry, sir. I didn't know it would do anything."

He laughed. "Right. You search high and low for my bell, then finally find it and act all innocent?"

I rubbed my chin. "Are you saying this is a sought-after bell?"

"The Bell of Dreams? You've not heard of it? Surely you jest."

"I believe maybe I've heard of such a thing in old fables my mother told me as a child. But you did say it had been one hundred years. Why would I search for an old fable, or know to look out here?"

"Well, fess up. How did you find it?"

"God led me to it."

The strange man stared at the ceiling. "I'd believe that. Just like Him to do something along those lines." He sighed. "I guess it was bound to happen eventually, and eventually has arrived." The man sat beside the fire.

I sat across from him. "My name is Sisko."

"You can call me Joel. Everyone else does."

I wrinkled my brow. "Is that your name?"

"Yes, now that you mention it, it is."

"Then it would make sense that everyone calls you that."

He pointed at me. "I see I have a live one, I do. Go ahead, ask the question."

"You mean, about this bell?" I lifted it in the air, and as I did, it rang out again. A light enveloped Joel, causing me to shield my eyes. When it dimmed, Joel no longer remained.

I waited for a moment, but he didn't return. I rang the bell again. The blinding light flashed across the fire and left Joel sitting, his chin in his hand and his elbow propped against a knee.

Joel frowned. "Are we going to act like children? One kid must have called me and sent me back a hundred times before he tired of the game."

I smiled halfheartedly. "Sorry. I'm not familiar with how this works." I grabbed the clapper and unhooked it from the bell. "There, no more accidents."

"Thank you." He sniffed. "You want some tea?"

I turned to my pack. "I believe I have some tea here, though we'll need to go find a stream to get more water." I turned back with my tea leaves to find two cups of hot water sitting on a rock by the fire.

Joel dropped leaves into the steaming liquid. "Never leave home without my tea."

I pointed at the cups. "Where did those come from?"

He threw his hands up. "What did I say? Never leave home without them, and that includes the water and cups."

I stared at him. "Who are you? I mean, why does the bell control your appearance?"

His mouth curved into a wave. "That's not the first question I thought you'd ask."

"Should I have asked a different one?"

His voice rose to a high pitch. "Oh, Mr. Joel, whatever did you mean by Bell of Dreams? Are you like a genie and I get three wishes?" He grunted. "That question."

I scratched my head. "Well, now that you've asked it for me, what about it?"

He removed the tea leaves and handed me a cup. "No, of course not. What a silly question!"

I started to point out that I hadn't asked that question, but he didn't pause.

"The reality of it is I was a bad boy, so God gave me this penance. Whenever someone rings the bell, I have to do something for them, though that is of my choosing."

"But I have some input, I presume?"

"Not strictly speaking, but in practice, yes. Some have rung for me over and over until I gave them what they wanted." He circled a finger around his ear. "And some of them realized too late it would make them crazy. But do they listen to me? No."

I sipped some of his tea. I straightened my back. "Wow. This is great tea!" I sipped some more. "The best I've ever drunk."

He flung his fingers out as if brushing dust off a shelf. "My own creation. The, uh, environment gives it a unique flavor."

I sipped some more. "This is absolutely heavenly." I set the cup down. "So, do you have a clue what you're supposed to do for me?"

"I'll have to check." He shook his head. "Usually the Big Guy upstairs gives me a heads up." He stared at the ceiling again. "So I'm not in the middle of something when I get yanked away." He focused on me. "Hold on a second."

Joel closed his eyes and stayed motionless for a few seconds. Then his eyes flashed open. "I'm supposed to take you to Belenor. Apparently you're needed there."

"Really? You can do that?"

Joel snapped his fingers. A blinding white light enveloped us, and when it died, we sat in the middle of a street. People scurried by, but one child's eyes widened and he yanked on his mother's dress, pointing at us.

A team of mules pulled to a halt and a man peered over them from a wagon. "Hey, the middle of the street is no place for grown men to play. Get out of the way, you fools!"

I scurried to my feet, Joel following suit. "I'm sorry, sir."

He grunted and nudged his mules onward.

Joel dusted himself off. "So, do you know why God wants you here?"

"Not a clue."

Joel frowned and sighed. "He's like that. Likes to keep you in the dark, and then at the last second, BLAM."

I nodded. "I've grown used to it. I don't worry about seeking out who I'm to help anymore. God always sends them across my path." I

153

gestured toward the tavern. "Want a drink?"

Joel stepped toward the *Leafy Brew Tavern*. "So, how is it you help people?"

"God's given me the ability to do miracles. Mostly healings, but sometimes other things. Whatever people need to set things right." I pushed my way into the tavern. We obtained our drinks and sat at a table.

"Ah, miracles. So I suppose you're pretty good doing those?"

I shrugged. "It's not like I practice. I ask and God does it."

Joel laughed. "You make God sound like some kind of barkeep. 'Another ale, God! Get a move on, I don't have all day.'"

This man viewed ideas from a different perspective. "Not like that at all. He usually—"

A whimper wafted past my ears. "...tells me." I turned toward the sound. Behind me a man leaned over a table. A bottle of whiskey sat beside him, half drained.

I scooted beside him. "Sir, what's wrong?"

He lifted his eyes from under his folded arms. They stared at me, bloodshot and wet. "My...my daughter."

I glanced at Joel, who stared blankly back at me. "What's the matter with her?"

"I...I..." He broke into fresh sobs for a few seconds before regaining his composure. "I nearly killed her. I didn't see her. Turned my head for a second. Just one damn second!" He sank his head back into his arms.

I patted him on the back. "Why don't you take me to her. I can probably help." Maybe God brought me here for this child.

His voice sounded muffled under his arms. "Who are you?"

"Sisko."

He jerked his head up and peered into my eyes. "Sisko of Reol?" I could see hope welling up in him.

"Yes."

He reached over and wrapped his arms around me, burying his head in my chest. "Oh! Thank the Lord you are here!"

Joel's eyes widened, but he continued watching.

I stood up, prying his arms from me. "Now, now. Take me to her."

He nodded vigorously, then rose from the chair and led us out the door. Joel and I followed him across the street, down a couple of blocks, then veered into a side-street.

Joel whispered to me, "Does everyone treat you like that?"

I nodded. "Most."

His mouth twitched. "Hum. Interesting. I don't think I've ever received that kind of praise."

I glanced at him. "Haven't you been painting the last hundred years?"

"Not painting. Done a lot of other things, like watch the moons of Jupiter dance."

I raised my eyebrow. "Jupiter? What's that?"

"Forget it. Point is, I've been busy."

"But you've not helped anyone in the last hundred years?"

He put a finger to his lips. "Well, there was that one time…no, come to think of it, I didn't do that one." He raised his finger. "Ah. I helped an old beggar once."

"You gave him some money?"

Joel waved a hand at me. "Heavens no. I took his bottle from him. Probably prevented alcohol poisoning."

"And what did you do with the alcohol?"

He smiled. "It went perfectly with my roasted lamb that evening."

I shook my head. I couldn't believe this man. "And the last few times someone rang your bell, I bet you only did one thing for them."

"Well…" He leaned his head to the side. "Yeah."

"It's no wonder you're not as popular as I am." I chuckled under my breath.

The man directed us into his two-room house, and led us to a bed. A blonde-haired girl lay upon it, barely breathing. Bandages had been wrapped around her chest and arms; splotches of red blood stained their surface.

I lifted my hand to place it on her head.

Joel waved his arms. Her eyes popped open, the scars on her face healed, the pale color of her cheeks turned to ruby-red. She sat up.

The man leaped toward his daughter and hugged her. I stared at Joel. He grinned from ear to ear, and stuffed his hands in his pockets.

The father turned to Joel. "I don't know who you are, but thank you so much! I can't begin to express my gratitude!" He grabbed Joel and hugged him. Joel soaked it all in.

After turning down his attempts to pay us, we left his house. Joel pointed at me. "Why did you not accept his gift? Don't you realize how rich you could be?"

I stopped and spun toward him. "Is that what you're doing? Trying to

155

get rich? If so, I'll ring your little bell and send you back."

He waved his hand. "No, no. I don't need money. But I thought you would."

"What was with the jumping in and healing that girl, then? Why did you preempt me?" I stared at his eyes.

"I wanted to experience being the hero for once. And I have to say, it was pretty nice. I can see why you do this."

I threw my hands into the air. "I don't do this for that reason! I do it because God gave me a ring. He literally conscripted me into this job!" I thrust my left ring-finger in front of Joel's eyes.

Joel smiled. "Oooo, pretty." He snapped his left hand and a similarly styled golden ring appeared on his left ring-finger. He grinned.

I threw up my hands. "You're hopeless." I started walking down the street.

He stepped up beside me. "What's the matter? Don't like some newbie with more power muscling in on your territory?"

I stopped, jammed my hands into my pocket, and pulled out the bell in my right hand and the clapper in my left. "Does this look like I should be worried? One ring and you're gone until I'm ready for you to come back." I moved my hands together.

He shot his palms toward me. "All right, already! I can see you're not up to any friendly competition. A scaredy-cat is what you are."

"I'm not scared of anything."

"Great! Then we'll race. Let's see who can heal the most people before sundown." He dashed toward a group of people.

"Joel, that's crazy." I watched as he stopped and chatted. A man holding a crutch pointed at his bandaged leg. Joel snapped and the leg straightened. The man put weight on his leg, then jumped up and down, his face full of joy.

Joel winked at me and put one finger up. Then he headed down the sidewalk to find more.

I shrugged. Maybe God sent us both here to heal everyone in town, within a day. I couldn't let this crazed miracle worker beat me. We hadn't found all the problems in the tavern, no doubt. I jogged toward its doors.

156

After searching the city, and healing thirty-five different ailments, I returned to the *Leafy Brew Tavern*. Joel leaned against a pole, waiting for me. The sun touched the horizon like a giant ball balancing upon the edge of a distant mountain.

Joel chewed on a blade of grass. "I did thirty-six. How did you fare?"

I glanced around and saw a wilting flower. I laid my hand on it, and prayed for its reviving. It brightened, straightened, and a fresh scent of sweet nectar floated from it. "Thirty-six myself."

Joel frowned. "You can't count that."

"Why not?"

Joel lifted his finger to say something, then pointed at the sun. "It's too late. The sun is setting."

I held up a finger. "Ah, but you didn't say whether the sun had to be totally gone or start to be gone. I don't consider it sundown until the sun has gone all the way down."

He chuckled. "I left that ambiguous so I could twist it to my advantage if need be. And I need to, so there."

I patted him on the back. "Joel, I don't know about you. But we did make a lot of people happy today. That's got to count for something." I stared at the flower. "But that's really getting too close to cursing myself. I shouldn't have done that."

Joel rubbed his chin. "I don't know. Plants have feelings too. I'm sure it's happy to be vibrant and alive again, even if it will only be for another day."

"I know, but it's more why I did it than anything. Using my gift isn't a game."

He grinned sheepishly. "Now you know why I ended up with that penance."

A male voice broke into our conversation. "Did either of you see a man run by here the last few minutes?"

I turned and shook my head. "No, sir. I arrived moments ago."

Joel waved his hand. "I didn't notice anyone."

The man growled. "The scoundrel stole our valuables, and nearly killed my wife. Luckily his knife missed her heart and landed on her shoulder."

"Oh dear." I gasped. "That's horrible."

"But what gets me is the authorities broke his leg because of his crimes. How he was healed I don't know, but if I find out who did it, I'll wring his neck." He appeared big enough to do so.

I frowned at Joel, who gritted his teeth together and stared at a distant building. I placed my hand on the man's shoulder. "I'll keep an eye out for both of them. If I see anyone healing anybody, I'll let you know."

He nodded. "Thank you." He spotted a group of men and headed toward them.

I nudged Joel. "Don't you think you'd better go heal his wife, being you healed her attacker?"

He muttered something I couldn't hear. "I suppose so." He vanished.

I sat on the wooden sidewalk and watched the people strolling by, and the carts carrying people and supplies about town. On one street a ways off, amidst wood-frame buildings with steep roofs, vendors packed up the market.

Joel materialized before me. "Happy?"

"Sure, but you don't seem to be."

He sat beside me. "I've not been myself. I guess after one hundred years, I'd pretty much forgotten about that bell. To have it ring again and yank me away, demanding that I do something for someone, it's like being thrown back into prison."

"Prison? That's not how I think of this. It's a ministry."

"Really? What did you mean about being 'conscripted' into this 'ministry' earlier today?" His eyes bore into mine.

I scratched my head. I did say that. What did I mean? I frowned. I couldn't put a positive spin on that one. "Maybe I do feel trapped to some degree. I didn't ask for this ministry. Yet I feel honored that God gave it to me, and I do enjoy helping people. I think that's why the steam house gave it to me."

His eyes widened. "The steam house?"

"Yes, a steam house in the town of Reol that—"

"Yes, yes, I know all about the steam house. I…" He stared at the sky for a moment. "…had a hand in what it became."

I laughed. "You did not. What a crazy claim. I've never met someone as full of hot air as you."

He chuckled. "Yeah, you've got me pegged." He stared at the ring on my finger. "But that explains a lot. That's the ring…" He shut his mouth.

"What? Do you know something about this ring?"

He sighed. "Yes, but I can't say. I work under restrictions, believe it or not."

I studied my ring, wondering if what I wore possessed abilities beyond simply producing miracles. "So, can you see the future?"

"Only what God allows me to see."

I thought for a moment. "Will I have children someday?"

Joel smiled. "You want to know?"

"Would I have asked if I didn't?"

"I think I can tell you that." He held up two fingers. "That many. A girl and a boy."

My mind drifted back to Gabrielle. Would she be the mother? Did I dare ask? No, I shouldn't ask that. Let things happen as they may. I can't easily control what children are born, but who I marry could easily be influenced by such knowledge.

I patted Joel on the back. "You ready to return to the cave? Seth must be worried sick about me."

He gazed into the clouds. The sun hiding behind the mountains etched the blobs of vapor with red paint. "I don't think you're done here yet."

I jerked my head toward him. "What? We just healed everyone in town we could find. Who else is there?"

He focused on me. "There's you and me."

"What do you mean?"

"You need to learn humility."

I jumped up. "You of all people say I need to learn humility? How dare you, you hypocrite!"

"Answer me one question, then I'll say no more."

I waited, attempting to unclench my jaw.

"Of the people you healed today, how many of them did you check with God if it was all right to heal them?"

A sick knot wrapped itself around my stomach. I plopped down onto the sidewalk and wrapped my arm around a pole for support. "None. Not one single person." I closed my eyes. "I was too wrapped up in trying to beat you."

Joel nodded. "You have no clue if any of those people will be spiritually worse off or not because they were healed."

I frowned. "You egged me on."

"You had the bell."

I growled. "Why do you keep one-upping me?"

159

"Now, now. Watch that humility level there."

I ground my teeth together before relaxing. "So, what is it you need?"

He pointed to my pockets. "To be free from the bell. I was told when a man obtained my bell, wearing a miracle-producing ring from the steam house, he would be able to relieve me of its call."

"So you're saying God wanted you to send me here, so I could learn a lesson and you could be freed of the bell?"

He nodded. "That's pretty much it, in a nutshell."

"So, you need me?"

Joel rested his chin in the palm of his hand. "Yes. We need each other. That's the nature of things. We're all obedient to someone, accountable to another, to meet their needs before our own. Humility."

I stared at the few people still on the streets scurrying to and fro, as darkness deepened over the city. "I'll do it upon one condition."

Joel raised an eyebrow. "A condition?"

"I'll keep the clapper with me as a reminder. When I have kids, you'll watch over them." I lifted my left ring-finger up. "Especially whichever one might end up with the ring."

"You think another will eventually wear it?"

I shrugged. "I have a strong sense that the ring's journey will not end with me. Who will wear it and when, I don't know. If one of my children ends up with it, it will be a heavy burden, a grave responsibility. They'll need all the help they can get."

He laughed. "And after all this, you think I'm the one who can help them?"

I met his eyes. "You've helped me. I've become complacent. People praising me everywhere I go, it becomes harder and harder to divide the ministry from me. Maybe you can get through to whatever issues my children might face with the ring."

Joel grinned. "I'll do it, until the ring has finished its journey. But I do it out of love, not due to demand."

I stood. "Well, then. I say let's get back. Then I'll take care of your bell."

He slapped me on the back and a white light filled my vision. "So it is done." The light died off, and I saw the cave walls reflecting firelight, and Seth staring at us with his teeth sunk into a meat-covered bone.

Seth extracted his teeth from the juicy meal. "Uh, where did you go? And who is this?"

I smiled. "Belenor, and this is Joel."

"Belenor? Do you know how far away that is?"

I pointed to Joel. "This man can do miracles."

Joel bowed. "Runs in the family." He pointed at my pockets. "The bell?"

I dug it out and held it up with my right hand. I placed my left hand on Joel's head. "Father, release Joel from the demands of the bell, but not from the demands of your justice or mercy."

The bell twirled and I let it go. It hovered in the air, spinning faster and faster, until in seconds it blurred and then disappeared into nothingness.

Joel smiled and hugged me. "Thank you so much. You don't know what this means to me."

I shoved his arms off. "Now you're doing it!"

He laughed. "So I am. But I do thank you." He shimmered and then faded away.

Seth handed me a piece of meat. "What was that all about?"

I accepted his offer. "A reminder to stay submitted."

He chuckled. "You don't need a reminder of that. You do whatever God tells you, all the time, no matter the apparent consequences. I've never seen a faith like yours."

"And that's exactly why I needed the reminder." I sank my teeth into the juicy meat. *Thank you, Joel, wherever you are. Thank you.*

Fear's Blinders

After ten years of healing sicknesses and pointing to God, the only person anyone pointed to was me. They sought after the power I possessed, that I might heal them. A heavy weight for a twenty-four year old.

"Please," one woman cried out, "my husband is near death. Please heal him!" Her pleading eyes dripped tears across her cheeks.

I nodded. "Lead the way."

Seth spotted me and the crowd moving as he browsed through Holoroth's market. He jumped to follow us.

The woman, covered in a black shawl over a brown dress, led us across Holoroth's main street and down a side street. The crowd followed behind me. Some needed a miracle themselves, but many also came to watch me do miracles. More for entertainment than anything. Some of these people probably remembered me from several years ago when the circus had kidnapped me and I reattached Josh's arm under the big tent.

The woman turned and led me to the front door of a house. I halted and raised a hand to the followers. "Wait out here. We can't have a crowd in this woman's house."

Several nodded. I entered the house with the woman. A pot over a fire under the mantel, a table with five chairs around it, some cupboards, and a bed against a wall constituted the sum of the room's decor.

Upon the bed lay a man. I stared at him. His eyes, barely opened, sunk into sockets surrounded with pale skin. His hand that previously must have been strong, grasped my fingers feebly. He stared at me a moment, then a smile spread across his lips.

I placed my right hand over his forehead. The ring that started this journey glistened in the shards of sunlight filtering through the shadows. How many times had I done this? I had never kept a count, but this was my ministry. If I didn't do it, who would?

"Father, heal this man of his sickness."

His pale skin smoothed out and flushed with a reddish tone. His grip grew firm on my fingers, and his muscles bulged.

I pulled him upright. "Give him some water and food. The poor man must be starving."

The woman threw her arms around me and wept on my shoulders. I patted her head. "It's all right. You'll be fine."

"How can I ever repay you?"

I smiled. "You can't. Minister to others, and that will be payment enough."

The man joined his wife in the hugging celebration. He opened his mouth to speak, but before words could form on his lips, the room darkened into blackness. I tried to move, but could find no reference to tell that I had.

Sisko?

Josh, are you doing this?

The darkness burst forth with a white light, then dimmed to reveal the form of Josh standing before me.

I stared at him. "How did you do this? I thought all we could do was communicate."

He smiled for a moment. "I've gotten better."

I sighed. "This wasn't the best time. I was in the middle of a conversation."

He breathed in deep. "This is important. It's about your mother."

My gut sank. "What about her?"

"A rogue wizard came looking for you. When he didn't find you, he attacked your family, hoping you would arrive to save them. I discovered the attack and fought him in battle, and defeated him."

"And my mother?"

His head sank. "Before I could reach them, the wizard had cast an evil spell, which we call *Utter Darkness*. It sends a person's soul into utter darkness until it can be released."

I gritted my teeth. "Can you do anything?"

"I can't."

"What about Milnore?"

Josh closed his eyes and paused for a second. "Milnore has passed away."

I gasped. "Passed away?" I couldn't believe this. "I'm about four days away, three and a half if I hurry. I can—"

Josh held up a hand. "No!"

"But I can heal her. I know I can!"

Josh shook his head. "No, you cannot."

I stomped my foot. "You know what I can do. I'm coming."

"Did you check with God?"

I opened my mouth but didn't say anything for a moment. Then I pointed a finger at Josh. "No, but she's my mother. I have to come and help."

"You can help, but not by coming here. For one, I can't guarantee that the wizard is gone. He may be waiting to see if you return, and if you do, word will get around that you have a means to be summoned, and you'll put your family at greater risk. Do you want that?"

I rubbed my forehead. "No, of course not."

Josh paced. "What you can do is go find a hermit by the name of Fensoow, and retrieve from him the antidote. He is the only one who can give it."

I studied Josh's face. "If I can't come to Reol, how am I supposed to bring an antidote to you?"

Josh shook his head. "It's not a substance. It's an energy of the soul. He will pass it to you, and then you can pass it to me by meeting me again like this."

I breathed deep. "All right. So where do I find Fensoow?"

"In the Forever Forest."

I blinked. "Do you know how big that forest is? I could spend years searching for him in there. Can't you narrow it down?"

He shook his head. "Sorry. That's all anyone knows, is that he resides in the Forever Forest. He moves around." Josh paused. "But if anyone can find him, you can."

Josh breathed deep. "One other thing. If she stays in this state for three days, she'll die and be lost in the darkness."

"Three days!" I doubled over, holding my stomach. "Josh, you were supposed to protect them. What happened?"

"I...I...did my best. I can't keep an eye on them every second." He squeezed his eyes shut and a tear rolled across his cheek.

I slammed my fists onto the bland, white floor. "What's done is done. I'll find this hermit. God has to help me. He has to."

Josh nodded and sniffled, rubbing his nose. "Contact me when you have it. And may God be with you."

"I will. Be by her side, waiting for me."

"I've not left your house since it happened, and I promise you I won't until she's whole."

The white room filled with light, blocking out Josh's form. Darkness swooped in, then beams of natural sunlight pierced the void, tearing it open, dissolving it into nothing.

Seth stood before me, his hands holding my shoulders. "Sisko, are you all right?"

I blinked and focused on him. The crowd peered in windows while the man I healed moments ago sat on the bed. I focused on Seth. "We have to leave. Now."

Seth's brow wrinkled. "Why? You're not done here."

I stood, and steadied myself as my balance returned. "I'll explain on the way. This is urgent." I lurched toward the door.

Seth steadied me. "I can see you're about to create another whirlwind."

I left the house, and the crowd cheered. I turned to see the man I'd healed standing on the porch, waving at everyone. I motioned for Seth to follow and proceeded to push my way through the throng.

One young child held up her doll. One arm had fallen off. "Can you heal Amanda?"

I glanced at her. "I'm afraid not, dear. I'm sure your mother can help you." I led Seth down main street and through the gate heading south. Around twenty people followed behind me.

Seth spoke softly. "Why didn't you help that girl out."

"It's just a doll."

"But it's not like you to—"

I stopped and spun around. "My mother is dying! I have three days to get what she needs to be healed."

Seth's shoulders slumped. "I'm sorry."

"Apology accepted." I turned to face the crowd. "I'm heading into the forest. It won't be easy, and some of you may well die if you follow. Please, return to your homes."

They all glanced at each other as if not sure what to make of my words.

I waved a hand. "Bye." Then I turned and plunged into the

underbrush. Seth followed, but the rest watched as we disappeared from view.

Our steps crunched upon the dead leaves lining the forest floor. We circled bushes and thorns as the rays of sunlight filtered through the canopy and drew fractured patterns upon the ground. Wind gusted through their branches, while birds and animals scurried about the leaves.

After a few minutes, Seth said, "Where are we going?"

I stopped and scanned the area. "I haven't a clue. Guess I'd better check." I closed my eyes and listened. Nothing. I searched my heart. I could feel no sense of leading.

I stomped my foot on the ground. "Don't desert me now, God!"

Seth leaned against a tree. "Maybe the pressure of your mother's life hanging in the balance is distracting you?"

I sat on the grass. "Maybe." I stared at the forest. Miles of trees lay before me in all directions. The hermit could be anywhere. Unless God directed me, I had no hope of finding him, assuming he camped within a two-day traveling distance from us. Three if he willingly helped us once we found him.

Josh, why did you let this happen? I sank my face into my hands as I tried to keep back the tears.

I really am sorry, Josh's voice rang back.

I gritted my teeth. I hadn't meant to call him. Not now. My thought echoed back to me. Not now? Did Josh hear that? I knew the thought sounded raw and harsh, but part of me didn't care. Another part did, said I was better than that. But the whole point of me leaving was to protect them. And now it appeared I would have been better off staying there. Maybe I could have prevented it.

I sucked in air and released it slowly. *It's just as much my fault as yours, Josh. I left Reol, hoping to save them. It was unfair of me to put the whole burden upon you.*

I do feel extremely guilty if that helps.

As if my brain came to life, I saw my problem. *Josh, I forgive you.*

He said nothing for five seconds. *Thank you. That means a lot.*

My heart leaped within me. I stood and pointed. "We're going that way." *Thank you, God, and thank you, Josh.*

You're welcome. Now find that hermit and the antidote. Contact me when you have it.

Will do. Later.

Seth marched ahead of me. "What changed?"

I followed. "Me. I had a forgiveness blockage. Makes it hard to hear God when that happens."

Seth nodded. "I'll keep that in mind."

We traversed streams and hills until the sun hid from the moon. After a meager meal, we bedded down for the night. But sleep escaped me. I lay staring at the stars gliding through the sky, partially obscured by leaves. By the time the sun chased away the points of light, Seth rose and packed. I yawned and rubbed my eyes, then helped him. We continued our journey through the Forever Forest, hoping it wouldn't take us forever to find the hermit.

The sun climbed high in the sky. The canopy prevented its heat from burning us, but the forest air hung heavy with moisture, forcing me to pant as we pushed through the underbrush.

A meadow about ten feet wide broke into view. We stopped on the edge of it. I slid my pack off and dug out some dried beef and cheese. "Lunch time."

Seth nodded and followed suit. "Have any idea how much further it will be?"

"Not a clue." I glanced around. "But if we can't find him by tomorrow, we might as well give up."

Seth shook a piece of cheese at me. "One thing I've learned from you so far, is that God doesn't lead you where you don't need to be."

I smiled. "Why Seth, your faith is developing quite nicely."

He shrugged. "You're rubbing off on me, I guess."

A low hum tickled my ears. I jerked my head toward the clearing, but the grassy meadow stood empty as wisps of wind swirled the grass.

Seth followed my gaze. "What?"

"Do you hear that hum?"

He focused for a few seconds. "No. Don't see anything either."

I kept my eyes fixed on the meadow and slid another chunk of cheese into my mouth. As I chewed, something moved among the grass, as if a patch of it shifted enough to form an outline. I swallowed. The outline of a man standing in the grass. But no sooner had it happened, than it blended back into the meadow.

"Someone's out there."

Seth stared at me. "I don't see or hear anything."

"Someone's there. I'm sure of it."

"But how can—"

A form materialized in the middle of the field. A white-bearded man, with white hair flowing over his shoulders, frowned at me. "I nearly had it. How did you see through my bending disguise?"

I smiled at the sight of him. "Would you happen to be Fensoow?"

He stroked his beard. "Why, yes. I believe I am."

"Believe? Don't you know?"

He cast a finger into the air. "Ah, now there's the question, isn't it? Do we know because we believe, or believe because we know? And if I believe I am this Fensoow, then naturally I know, for then, why would I believe?"

I stared at him. "What?"

Seth no longer chewed, but his eyes remained fixed on Fensoow. "Why couldn't I see you?"

"Oh yes, the mysteries of the universe are wrapped up in such questions. Why can we see anything, or why do we not see what we should? I bent the light to cover me up." He snapped his fingers. "I recall a story that you might find enlightening. When I was younger—"

"Sir?" I broke in.

He closed his mouth and stared at me. "Are you not ready to be enlightened, my child?"

I sighed. "Pardon me if I seem rude, sir, but my mother will die tomorrow, and I've been told that you have the only antidote."

He frowned. "My, my. And where is your mother?"

"In Reol."

He shook his head. "Too late for her, then, being we're several days from there. Such a pity." He straighten his back. "Now back to my story. I was—"

"Sir?"

He rocked his head from side to side. "Who's in trouble this time?"

"It's still my mother. You see, I need to get it from you, so I can pass it to Josh, so he can pass it to her."

"I don't see how that will help matters."

"Josh and I are linked, we can meet each other mentally."

He chuckled. "Ah, the old mind linking spell. Never used it myself. Never found anyone I wanted to share a mind with."

"Please, sir." I drew in a deep breath. "Can you please give me the energy to heal the *Utter Darkness?*"

"Can I?" Fensoow nodded his head. "Now there's a question worth asking. For if I can, it would resolve your concern. But your concern may mean I can't."

I huffed. "Either you can or you can't. Now can you give it to me or not?"

He scratched his beard. "No."

I sank my head into my hands and squeezed back a flood that wanted to escape. "Then my mother will die."

"She doesn't have to."

I jerked up. "But you said—"

"That I can't. Doesn't mean I won't." He pointed at me. "Got you that time. I interrupted you!"

"But you're talking in riddles! Can't you say what you mean?"

"Then how would you learn?" Fensoow cocked his head to his right.

"I'm not interested in learning right now, I just want to save my mother. Please!"

He nodded. "I will do my best." Fensoow pointed at one edge of the clearing. "If you cut the grass in a ten-foot wide area and build a hut, I may be able to give it to you."

I threw up my hands. Fine, so he wanted payment for his gift. I never sold my gift. Memories of the circus returned to me, but I shoved them away. I didn't keep that money, so it didn't count. But if I worked hard, and Seth helped me, we could probably finish his hut before the sun sank.

I rose to my feet. "Come on, Seth. Let's build this hermit a hut."

A grin spread across Fensoow's face. "Excellent. Work is good for the soul." His mouth twitched. "Then again, without a soul, work would be worthless. But since I have some here, it should be beneficial." The strange hermit recounted tales of spiritual battles, often stopping to fill us in on the eternal value and thoughts of the stories as if Seth and I were his disciples.

As Fensoow rambled on and on, Seth and I worked to clear an area. I gathered the grass in my arms, and Seth chopped it down with his sword. After an hour, we finished preparing the spot. Seth helped me construct a decent hut for the hermit. Hours passed before we threaded the last few pieces of wood into place.

Seth stood back and admired his work. "Should keep the rain off of him, though I wouldn't guarantee it in a strong gale."

Fensoow nodded. "Very nicely done. A hut shouldn't be permanent, my friend. It will provide shade while I mediate."

I studied the old man's face. "Now that we've built what you asked, can you give me what my mother needs to be healed?"

His eyes darted across me, as if sizing me up for a sale. He wiggled his finger to draw near. When I stepped forward, he placed his palm against my forehead. Fensoow closed his eyes for a moment. I couldn't feel anything different, but waited patiently.

Fensoow's eyes opened slowly. "I can't give it. You're still not ready."

I raised an eyebrow. "I'm not ready? What does that mean?"

He raised his index finger. "Ah, another outstanding question. For if one is said to be not ready, there are many reasons for such a state of existence, and may not apply to another at all. But to be ready? How to know?"

I plopped onto the ground beside the hut. "Indeed! How would I know why I'm not ready. You'll give me no answer I can understand."

Fensoow shook his head. "So you have learned little building the hut?"

I threw my hand into the air. "I learned how to build a hut, yes. Thanks to Seth."

Fensoow tightened his lips and stroked his beard. "That's a shame. Did you think I asked for this in exchange for the antidote?"

"You're not going to back out, are you? A promise is a promise."

"The question of the universe. What is, is. What isn't, isn't. But to know the difference, is the choice of belief. Do you believe I needed you to build that hut?"

I rubbed my forehead. "So, you're saying I was supposed to learn something in building that?" My mind thought back, trying to discern what I should be learning, but nothing obvious came to my mind. I sweated over it for another minute, but in the end I slumped over. "I'm tired of playing these games. My mother's life is on the line! Please give it to me."

"That's why I can't."

"What? Because my mother's life is on the line?"

Fensoow sighed. "Beyond that."

"What!"

"I can't tell you, or the door will shut."

I glanced at Seth, who appeared just as in the dark as I was. "I don't know."

Fensoow nodded. "That's the first sensible thing you've said all day."

I sank my head into my palms. Why couldn't he give it to me?

Everything would be solved. Seth patted me on the back.

Fensoow gazed at star-spotted ink darkening over the evening sky. "We should eat and sleep. The morning may reveal truths hidden in darkness."

Seth rose to prepare a fire.

Fensoow smiled. "I recall when as a young novice, I strolled…"

I rose the next morning, with no better answer than I had going to bed. The hermit lay in his new hut, sleeping or meditating. Probably hard to tell the difference. But today, at some point, my mother would be forever trapped in the *Utter Darkness*. With each second, I feared hearing the news from Josh that she had passed away.

I couldn't stand the thought of losing her like this. My mind froze in its thoughts, and focused on one specific reality: I couldn't stand it. Could that be blocking it? I always trusted God for everything else, why did I have a hard time when it came to my family?

The reality hit me like a giant's fist. I stood and paced the ground. "I can't stand the thought. Does that mean if God lets her die, that I couldn't stand Him? What would I do?"

I had placed my family in God's hands, only to yank them back out again. I would judge God, if He failed to keep her alive. The ludicrous idea grew fully formed. Me judging God?

I rubbed my forehead. "Of course, I'm not content."

"Brilliant!"

I spun around to see Fensoow standing behind me. "You surely know how to sneak up on someone." I stared at the ground. "So, am I ready yet?"

"And if I say I'll give it to you tonight?"

A tear forced its way onto my cheek. "Then I guess it would be God's will that she die tonight."

He placed his palm on my forehead and closed his eyes. A moment passed. "You are ready enough. But be forewarned, your weakness is that the love for those close to you can grow stronger than your love for God. Evil can use that."

I nodded. "I understand." Though I didn't fully grasp the totality of what he meant.

Fensoow's eyes locked onto mine. "Father, pass your energy onto this one."

Searing fire filled my mind and body. I cried out, writhing in invisible flames. The agony lasted for a long minute, then it mellowed out into a deep flow of sparkling glory, as if swimming in a sea of light.

Fensoow smiled. "Make sure this Josh you give it to can handle it. If he dies, both he and your mother will listen to stories like mine for eternity."

The energy within filled me with joy, peace, and love. "Of course. And thank you."

He bowed. "Thanks offered to creation reflects upon the Creator. He appreciates your service."

I sat against a tree. *Josh, are you there?*

A few seconds passed. *Yes, I'm here. Do you have it?*

Yes, I do.

Darkness swooped in upon me, followed by the bright light, which dimmed to a featureless white void.

Josh tapped me on the shoulder. I swung around. "There you are."

He nodded. "I'm ready. Give it to me."

I placed my hand upon his head. "First, I have to make sure you're ready."

I closed my eyes and sank into his mind. I flung my eyes back open. "Josh, you're not only ready for this, but should be teaching me. How did you get like this?"

He waved a hand. "I'll tell you the story sometime. But first things first."

I nodded. "Father, give Your energy to Josh."

The burning warmth streamed through my arm and into Josh's head. Josh's eyes widened, but otherwise I couldn't tell if he had it or not.

When the last of the energy flowed out, I lowered my hand. "Did you get it?"

He patted his head. "Yes. All up here."

"But you didn't hardly react. I felt like a burning fire had enveloped me for a long minute when I first received it."

"Spiritual development. I'm used to that fire now." He stepped back. "But first things first. I'll let you know how it goes."

The room flashed into a blaze of glory, darkened to black, and then the forest returned to my visions, with Seth standing over me.

Seth lifted me to my feet. "Well?"

"Josh should tell me something. Soon I hope." I met Seth's eyes. "One other thing."

"Yes?"

"Don't ever tell anyone that Josh and I can communicate. Especially Gabrielle. If anyone thinks I know what's going on in Reol, they'll use my family as bait."

He held up a hand. "I'll never say a word."

I patted him on the back. "I know you won't. I trust you."

He smiled. "Thanks."

I pointed toward the road, a couple days' journey back. "Might as well return the way we came." We pushed our way into the underbrush and trees.

In fifteen minutes, Josh called. *Sisko?*

Yes, Josh.

It worked! She's up and eating. She's going to be fine.

I sighed. *Thank you Josh. I owe you a giant hug someday, if we should ever see each other again.*

That would be good. Talk with you later. Bye.

Goodbye, friend.

I turned to Seth. "Josh says she's fine."

Seth smiled. "Good. So, where to now? Any idea?"

I grinned. "I think there's a little girl in Holoroth with a doll that needs healing."

Seth patted me on the shoulder. "Good to have you back, my friend. Good to have you back."

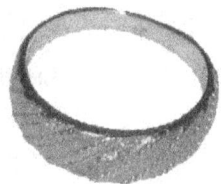

Love's Sacrifice

Seth's face glowed in the light from the campfire as he played with his flatbread. He glanced at me and back to the fire. Crickets chatted away in the background, but Seth remained silent.

"Something bugging you?" I dipped a piece of the flatbread into the stew and stuffed it into my mouth. A rare treat for us on the road, so it seemed strange Seth didn't eat.

He glanced at me. "Sisko…" He paused as if collecting his thoughts. "We've been on the road together for almost five years now. We've been through a lot. You've taught me many things about life, and I've seen you do some amazing miracles with your ring."

Light danced on the ring's golden surface, highlighting the inscription in Hebrew, "It is better to give than to receive." The words of the priest seemed a distant memory now. If I used the ring for others' benefit, I would be blessed. If for myself, I would be cursed.

Yet, in a way, I did feel cursed. Seth reminded me of his sister, Gabrielle, whom I hoped one day to marry. But five years is a long time. Would she still be waiting for me? The memory taunted me. A curse I would bear until God released me from my task of seeking out people to help.

Not that I needed to find them any more. Word had spread during the last few years, and people would seek me to ask for, even demand, a miracle.

Seth continued ripping his flatbread into tiny pieces as he talked. "But it has been a long time since I've seen Gabrielle and my father. I need to return, at least to visit."

How I would have loved to join him. I stared into the moonlit night.

A vast and empty desert stretched into the horizon, rimmed by soft light. "But my path takes me across the desert, not back to your house."

"I had a feeling you would say that." He focused on my eyes. "But, as much as I hate leaving you, I feel I have to. I'm sure of it."

He would leave. I could see it in his eyes. It would be lonely without him. "You've got to do what you've got to do. Just one thing."

"Name it."

"Tell…" It seemed hard to tell something this personal to her brother. "Tell Gabrielle, if she is still waiting for me, I will come back."

A grin spread across his face. "Consider it done." He finally dipped a sizeable piece of flatbread into the stew and ate.

The next morning, we packed, we hugged, we turned, and traveled our separate paths. I wished I could go back with him, but my heart pointed me across the desert. I knew from experience to follow, but who out there needed my help?

So I walked. And walked, and walked, and walked. Hours grew into days, and days blended into a never-ending succession of cold nights interrupted by a burning sun.

After several days, my food supplies dwindled to nothing, and hunger gripped my stomach like a vise. I had depended on Seth's hunting skills for my food. I attempted to catch what small animals I could, but frequently missed.

Though I still had water left, I could only now see the outline of distant mountains indicating the end of the desert. It would still be many days till I reached them. Unless I found more water, I would be dead long before then.

The hunger lessened, but I felt weak. I rationed my water and found what edible vegetation I could. As each day wore on, I knew I would not last. I would not make it.

One day, the last drop of water dripped onto my parched tongue, seeming to vaporize on contact. Death would soon come. But I kept moving in the slim hope I would find water.

The next day, the hunger returned. My body felt like freshly cooked noodles as I baked under the relentless sun. Each step sent aches through my limbs; my feet dragged like heavy weights.

I stopped to rest more frequently. Each time, I struggled to rise and continue. But hope and faith that God wouldn't end my ministry in this desert pushed me on.

However, the time came when I could barely hold myself up. I sat down on a rock. My body demanded I lie down and die. I wavered in the wind as did my beard and hair.

"Father, I've done so much for others. Am I to die now? Why did you send me out here? To become food for the vultures circling over me?"

The ground swam. I shook my head. I had to do something, or I wouldn't last much longer. How many people wouldn't receive a blessing if I didn't survive? Certainly I helped others by ensuring I lived on. It couldn't end this way.

"Father, provide me with food and drink."

A loud crack tossed my limp body off the rock and onto the ground. Water flowed from a crevice in the rock. A primal craving took over. I crawled to the water, placed my parched mouth into the stream, and gulped, wetting my mouth and cooling my throat. Strength flowed into wasted muscles. After several minutes, I laid back against the rock, sated.

Well, Father, that's half the request.

With water no longer a problem, hunger took center stage. Then I saw them, two chicken-sized birds, pecking at the ground by my feet. They ignored me as I drew my sword and brought it down on their heads.

I built a small fire from the scarce, dried brush and feasted on wild bird. From the first bite, the succulent meat danced on my tongue. Before I came to my senses, I had stuffed myself.

Now I needed rest. I saw a clump of trees not too far away. They would make good shade to take a nap. After filling my flask with water, I struggled to reach them.

I had not gone far when I heard voices. The closer I came, the more it dawned on me what I had done.

I climbed the small sand dune bordering the trees. Peeking over the top, I saw a caravan. A small group of people worked on various chores. In the midst of the trees, a small spring-fed pond lay placid in the center. Fires cooked food, wafting sweet smells upon the air I breathed.

My stomach wrenched. It turned, and a pain like none I had felt before wrapped itself around my abdomen and squeezed me hard. I vomited out the food I had eaten.

After the wrenching subsided, I watched the people again. God had already provided; I had broken the vow for nothing. I slammed my fist into the sand and laid my head upon the ground. I had failed to trust and sealed my own fate in the process. I now stood a cursed man.

But the food and sound of people drew me into the camp. I scrambled over the top of the dune, and the people soon jumped from their activities to help a sick and lost young man.

Helen wiped a damp cloth over my forehead. "I can't believe you crossed the desert. You picked one of the worst routes to do so."

"I didn't pick it. Must have been the only way to reach you."

She wrinkled her brow. "Me?"

"I mean everyone here. My name is Sisko."

She stared into the distance, and then her eyes widened. "You don't mean the young man who does miracles?"

"Ah, I see you've heard of me." It had become commonplace now; it no longer surprised me.

She dipped the towel into the pond and squeezed out the water. "Well, maybe you have been sent then. We do have sick here." Her brown eyes flashed with hope.

A husky man approached the pond's edge. His face carried dirt and scars, yet he bore the eyes of a young man. "So, it is true what people are saying. You are here."

I stared at the man. "Have we met before?"

"Yes, back at Dragon's Inn. The miracles you did there totally changed the village for the better." He cracked a slight smile, but worry shone from his eyes. "My name's Jack."

"Oh yes, I remember now." That had been three years ago.

"Look, my wife is desperately ill. Can't you come and heal her?" His gaze fixed on me, as if he feared I would say no.

"Of course. I'm not feeling too good myself right now, but I can come."

I struggled to my feet with Helen's help. The potato soup they'd given me had stayed down, and I felt better. Walking proved an effort, but I followed to his tent.

Once inside, I watched as a brunette woman lay on a pallet. She breathed in gasps, with pauses in between as if she had to build up the strength. I felt her forehead. A burning fire raged within her. She would die if I didn't do something.

I had done this so many times; I had long since stopped paying attention to my heart. It always said yes. How could it not? "Father, heal this woman, beloved by her husband, from this infirmity."

Nothing happened. "Sometimes, it takes a few moments."

The man glanced at me and back to her. His faith didn't waver, and neither did mine. It would happen. It always did.

Her body shook, and I withdrew my hand. She jerked out of control. Her eyes flung open for one moment and stared at mine. Death and helplessness emanated from them.

Then she fell still. Very still. I felt for her breath on the back of my hand. Nothing. I listened for her heartbeat. Silence. Her open eyes stared at the ceiling.

We all stood there for what must have been several minutes. I couldn't believe it. Every time I had prayed, a miracle happened, except now.

"I'm sorry. I'm afraid she's dead." The words sounded hollow coming from my mouth.

"You killed her." A building rage underlay the tone.

I shook my head. "No, I didn't kill her. I just didn't heal her."

He turned to me. Through clenched jaw it sounded as if a dam would soon burst. "You killed my wife. You'll do miracles for everyone, except for me."

"No, honest. I don't understand what happened."

Helen backed away from me. Jack grabbed me by the arm and pulled me out of the tent. He cupped his free hand and yelled to the camp, "This man killed my wife. He is a murderer. I demand justice."

Justice? What did he have in mind?

A crowd gathered around us. "Where is Sir Edward? I demand justice for my wife's killer."

A man approached clad in mail. A flat-bladed sword protruded from its sheath on his belt—obviously the leader of the caravan.

"Why do you say this one, who is famed to perform miracles, has killed your wife, Jack?" His eyes flashed with a strength I hadn't seen in many.

But what kind of strength?

"I brought him to heal my wife, but when he placed his hands on her and prayed, she died. He must have prayed for her death." His face glowed red.

Sir Edward remained silent for a moment. Then he spoke. "Let's bind him and bring him to the king to be tried in proper courts."

"No!" Jack's face grew redder. "I demand his death. An eye for an eye."

Sir Edward narrowed his eyes. "My decision stands. He will be brought to trial."

Jack shook with anger. "I'll do it myself, then." He grabbed a knife from behind his back, raised it into the air, and drove it toward my chest.

I reached out and caught his arm, but the momentum knocked me off my feet. He fell with me, moving the knife straight for my heart. The ground knocked my breath out. My strength could not hold his off. The knife continued to sink toward its target.

A blade swung over my body, knocking the knife from Jack's hand. It hit the ground with a thud a few feet away.

Sir Edward stood over us, sword in hand. "I said, he will stand trial. Is that clear?"

Jack growled something unintelligible and slammed his fist onto the ground. He released me and stomped into his tent.

I relaxed. I had faced death before, but with God beside me. Now, the calm had vanished with Him. I might as well die. I had broken the vow to God, and now I lay a broken man.

Sir Edward's stern face hadn't flinched. He pulled me to my feet. "You are a prisoner under my protection till we reach Siloth. If anyone harms you, they will face justice as well."

I wanted to say, "Thanks," but didn't think he would appreciate such sarcastic comments. So I held my words inside.

He pulled me till we reached a wagon. He reached inside and threw some blankets on the ground. "We pull out tomorrow. I suggest you get rest and eat to gain your strength. I'll have one of the ladies bring you something."

"You're not going to tie me up?"

"You're not going into the desert in your condition, you wouldn't last long. Besides, then I would have to track you down." He stared at me as if reading my intentions. "And I probably wouldn't bother taking you to the king."

I nodded and sank onto the ground. He was right. It would be foolish to run.

Questions ran through my mind. Why had I failed to trust? Why did I sell myself for food? Better to have died fulfilling His will than as a cursed outcast. What had happened to me? Where did I turn onto a wrong path? I thought I had been doing His will, but I failed.

I stared at the ring on my finger. I wished I had never gone into the steam house, never received this ring and task. I could have lived a normal life like my parents.

I grabbed the ring stuck fast for ten years around my finger. Slowly I applied pressure. It moved. I jerked, and it slid off. The ring appeared dull and dead in my palm. I clamped my hand around it and sunk my head to the ground. Tears fell freely. I had longed to be free. Free to return to Gabrielle. Free to live my life where and how I wanted. But having been freed, I knew I didn't want to lose that gift. Its loss drained my life of meaning. Meaning the steam house had given, and I had squandered for food and water I didn't need.

I sobbed for a long time, and no one bothered the young man who already punished himself for a crime they knew nothing about.

The next morning, the caravan packed up and moved out. Another few days, and we came to the end of the desert. Siloth lay a few hours into the hills, and the time seemed to drip by, but we eventually entered the city's gates.

I had been brought before King Circo and briefly examined. Then they locked me in the prison cells until my fate had been decided. I sat there for many days, eating, sleeping, thinking, praying, and awaiting my judgment.

In one sense, I didn't care. Death had taken hold inside. Might as well make the outside dead too. If they did release me, I didn't know what I would do, where I would go. Would Gabrielle have me back now? Not likely. She loved the boy who could heal and give her security. I had none to offer now.

The clanking of metal broke into my thoughts. Feet shuffled on dusty rock floors. As if in answer to my fears, two people I had never expected to see again stood at the cell's door.

"Gabrielle? Seth?" My heart leaped. I ran to the cell bars and thrust my arms through them. She hugged me back. It had been so long since I'd felt her in my arms; I sobbed. She ignited a spark, and I wanted to care whether I lived again. But would she?

She pulled out of my arms. Her eyes radiated sadness. "Sisko, what happened to you? They announced the judgment on you today. They tell me you are scheduled for death."

Seth patted me on the shoulder.

I held up my hand. "I've lost it. I failed God and you."

Seth gasped. "The ring! Where is it?"

"In my pocket. But it came off because I used it to feed myself when I starved to the point of death in the desert. Now I'm cursed, and they claimed I killed a woman instead of healing her. And maybe I did. I don't know.

"But whether I did or not, the ring came off. I've lost my reason to live."

Gabrielle put her hands on her hips. "Now, that doesn't sound like the Sisko I know." She glared at me. "You've changed, and not for the better. I thought you loved me."

I jerked my head up. "Of course I love you. I wanted to marry you."

She shook her head. "What do you fear losing the most? That is what you love the most."

I opened my mouth, but didn't speak. What almost came out, I didn't want to say aloud.

She leaned against the bars, her face inches from mine. "You loved the prestige, the power, the cheering people who respected you as the mighty healer." She frowned. "That's what you are most afraid to lose—not me."

I turned my face from her. "Are you a mind reader now?"

"No. It's written all over your actions and words."

I dared to gaze upon her face.

Tears trickled down her cheeks. "The first and only thing you've talked about since I've arrived has been the ring. Nothing about us."

I couldn't bear her eyes. I slumped onto the floor; my head buried in my knees. I wanted to say something, but I couldn't. I heard Seth sigh, and then footsteps. Gabrielle's soft crying receded until the metal gate latched shut.

Her words stung. Not because she accused me, but because she spoke the truth. At some point, I had begun caring more about what I could do for people than I cared about the people themselves. The loss of my ability had consumed and mired me in self-pity. I had cursed myself long before the ring did.

The day came at last. I heard the gate opening, and two guards approached my cell. I fingered the ring in my pocket as they unlatched my cell door. It had been on my finger for so long, it might as well be in death. I pulled it out and slipped it back on. A fire glowed on its surface.

The guards tied my hands and led me from the cell. The sunlight blinded me at first, but my eyes adjusted. The square-roofed buildings lined the streets. Floods of people spilled onto the road as they led me to the city's courts. Some people jeered, others cried. I wondered whether they cared, or if they mourned for their son or daughter who would not receive healings.

Stop it, stupid. That kind of thinking put you in this mess.

Then my eyes caught Gabrielle working her way through the crowd. She burst through the lines of people and enveloped me. Tears streamed down her face.

"Sisko, maybe your love for me has died over the years, but mine for you hasn't. I love you." Her reddened eyes told me she had cried all night.

I grabbed her hands, and her thoughts flooded my mind. Shocked that I could still feel them, the intensity of her emotion crashed through my pride. "I love you too. My selfishness had buried it."

"I know." She kissed my cheek before a guard pulled her away. I stared at her receding form; our faces locked onto each other until the crowd swallowed her from sight.

As we entered the courts, rocks pelted me. I could feel the warm flow of blood on my neck, and welts ached under my clothes.

They led me to a platform. On one end, a wall had been erected. From the wall, the floor expanded out in the shape of a bell. Opposite the wall, five archers waited, arrows already strung in the bows.

They placed me against the wall and tied me to hooks protruding from it. The small arena of the court held a full crowd. Many also stood on the ground by the stage. I spotted Gabrielle and Seth. Then I saw Jack and Helen. Jack's eyes locked onto mine, and he smiled. I smiled back, and he scowled.

"Attention, all hail the king!" Silence covered the crowd like a blanket. Eyes turned to the king's throne on one end of the arena.

He stood and scanned the crowd before landing his gaze upon me. "We are all gathered here, in the sight of God and man, to administer justice, as is my duty to perform from time to time. We have before us one who has performed many miracles, and for that many are grateful. But he placed his hand to one and killed her instead. He committed an abuse of power. As God's dealer of justice, I have sentenced him to death before a squad of archers."

At this the crowd roared, but the king held out his hand, and they silenced once more.

"Sisko, do you have any last words before we execute your sentence?"

All eyes turned to me. Eyes that would have been turned in hope of healing now stared at me with disdain and judgment. I didn't know what to say, but as I opened my mouth, words poured from my heart.

"Honorable King of Siloth and its citizens, I stand before you a condemned man. I condemned myself through selfishness and allowing my love to turn from God and people to my gift. So God departed from me. Whether I killed the woman, or fate laid its hands on her the same time I did, I cannot say. But I did not pray for her death. If this is God's will, then so be it. I am ready to release my life if it be His desire. May God have mercy on me, a sinner."

The crowd mumbled for a few seconds until the king gave the order. "You may proceed with the execution." He sat down.

A man I could not see barked out orders. "Check your bows. Rise. Aim. Pull…"

The man let two or three seconds pass by—an eternity when arrows are ready to shoot.

"Release!"

My body slammed against the wall with the impact. My chest burned. Overwhelming pain grew until numbness overtook it. Screams and gasps filled the air. I examined my chest; five arrows protruded from it. My body seemed distant, and my vision dimmed. My life disappeared into a black void.

Oddly enough, my sight returned, yet now I floated over the scene of my death. I watched Gabrielle leap onto the platform and fall upon my body. She sobbed and wailed. My heart, though no longer physical, broke at the sight. If I could have cried, I would have.

Then I felt a pull. It grew stronger and stronger until the scene I watched receded. A force pulled me into the heavens. The world accelerated away from me into a little ball until the blackness dotted with stars swallowed it whole.

Still, I flew among the stars until they blurred, and time crawled to a halt. Then as I focused in the direction I raced toward, a light grew. Though brighter than any I had ever seen, I could stare at it without harm.

The closer I came to this light, the more I felt myself expand. No longer confined to the five senses—worlds, people, and the vastness of creation awakened to my soul. Like releasing a coiled toy, my senses increased a hundredfold.

Another feeling dominated as I approached. Joy. Pure, unadulterated, joy. Not a giddy happiness, but a sense of complete belonging, perfectly content in my existence. The perfect joy didn't flow from within me, but a sense of infinite love enveloped me, united with me.

The light grew until I raced into its circle. I shot onto this strange world. A few feet over land, I slowed until I rested on a grassy knoll in the midst of a forest.

I had never seen a forest like this one. The colors flowed rich and vivid, as if each contained its own fire radiating within. No, reflecting a fire permeating everything, radiating from seemingly nowhere. No sun lit the sky, but the very air throbbed with its energy.

"Welcome, Sisko."

I turned to see a man, clothed in garb reminiscent of old Rome. "Who are you?"

He spread his hands. "St. Valentine. Surely you've seen my pictures?"

"Yes." I studied his face.

"Well, they aren't exact duplicates of how I look anyway." He grinned as if this pleased him.

"Where am I? This place is beautiful beyond description."

He sat cross-legged on the grass beside me. "Many names for it, but essentially, it's Paradise. A taste of Heaven."

"A taste? If this is a taste, I can't imagine what Heaven is like."

"No man hath seen nor heard." He laughed.

"But I failed. Why I am here instead of Hades?"

"You confessed and held repentance in your heart." He touched my spiritual chest.

"But I'm cursed. I broke the vow of the ring."

He shook his head. "Dear Sisko, are you so unaware of God's mercy? Yes, you will have to deal with the consequences of your sins, just like King David, and yes, myself as well. But God forgives those humble of heart."

"Shouldn't St. Peter have been here to meet me?"

He waved his hand. "St. Peter's busy. Besides, God assigned me to you specifically."

"Me?" I felt confused and joyful at the same time.

"Yes. You have a decision to make."

I furrowed my brow. "A decision? Here?"

He pointed to a spot against a tree, and a window grew until the scene I had left in my former life appeared within it. Gabrielle hugged my dead body now lying on the platform. Seth consoled her and cried himself. Guards stood around, giving them time.

I caught his eye. "Why are you showing me her? Aren't you the patron saint of love?"

He laughed again. "Yes, I sort of ended up with the title. Not sure what I did to deserve it, but I'm honored. Though many in your old life have perverted it something awful. Still, a nice holiday, to let people know you love them by showing affection in some way." He grinned. "Not every saint gets his own holiday celebrated by Christians and non-Christians alike."

I scrunched my eyebrows. "What are you talking about?"

"Oh, I forgot, that all happens many years after your time. Ignore it."

I focused on Gabrielle. "Then, why show me lost love? Am I to be punished even in Paradise? Eternally reminded of my failure with this window?"

"Oh, of course not. You see, you are getting special treatment. You've tasted heaven, but do you love her?"

I saw her hugging my dead body. I recalled her last touch, and what I felt. "Yes, I do love her."

"Enough to give up all this you now taste and return to her?"

"Give up?"

"I don't mean permanently, but for now."

"You mean, go back?" Something inside me didn't want to, and yet it did.

My eyes soaked in the surrounding perfection and then landed back to her in the window. "My decision, then, is to give up perfect peace and joy for pain, suffering, dealing with evil people, to lose my expanded senses, and be crammed back into my physical body in order to be with her?"

He slowly nodded. "Yes, that about sums it up. What you are feeling now is greater than any physical sensation you could ever have of pleasure. It is a spiritual pleasure of union with God. There is nothing to compare with it in the corrupt world you lived in."

He spoke the truth. I wouldn't go back for mere physical pleasure. Nothing in the old life came close to what I felt now, a mere taste of what would follow. I could go deeper into this bliss and experience full union with God.

Gabrielle had stood. Seth held her in his arms; both still sobbed. Selfishness had perverted my love. Love isn't about what I want, but about meeting the other person's needs. I knew that. The steam house had revealed that in me. But somewhere along the line, that had changed and my love had grown introverted.

"If I can go back, I must return. I'm not done with what God called me to do. I didn't finish it the right way."

"So, you'll give up Heaven for now to be with her?" He raised an eyebrow.

Doubt raced into my mind, but I chased it out. "A fire burns within me. What joy and peace is truly perfect when marred by failure to love as I should? I must go back."

I saw his face glowing with radiance. I felt his satisfaction with my decision internally.

"Now that, my dear Sisko, is true love. To release what you most desire, to bring a little of this joy to another who needs it. You have chosen well."

"But what about God? Shouldn't we love Him above all others?" I scratched my head.

He smiled. "When you love another, you are loving God first."

"But I can't do miracles any more. How can I help people?" Strange to feel sadness with pure joy.

"The ring was a sign, a vow, a calling for you. God uses all sorts of things to accomplish miracles, from dead men's bones to a handkerchief or a donkey." He drew closer. "Your ring didn't bring forth the miracles. Your hope, faith, and love in God did. You will still yet do miracles. Maybe not ones people will flock to you for, but miracles nonetheless. The miracles Heaven will notice, but not men."

I nodded. It made sense, and how I had missed it till now seemed senseless. I checked the scene back in the old life. A guard shoved the arrow shafts through the body and pulled them out the back.

I took in the scenery, the vivid colors, the pure peace, contentment, and joy; I purposed to store it away in my soul so I could share it with others.

"Okay, I'm ready. Thanks for helping me."

He embraced me and a pure, brilliant light ignited in a burst of joy, diminishing what I had experienced thus far.

"The honor, Sisko, has been all mine."

A yank on my soul lifted me off the ground. A resistance to leaving flooded my mind. It said stay, but my heart said go.

St. Valentine cupped his hands as I ascended into the sky of Paradise. "And don't forget, share the miracle of true love."

Now the light of Paradise shrank into the distance as I raced faster and faster into the depths of space. Along with it shrank the feeling of pure peace and joy. I ached for it, and the desire to return burned within me. Newly acquired senses dulled as I hurled through time and space, like someone shutting down and disassembling parts of me so I could fit back into my body.

Everything blurred into streaks. Whole galaxies flew by at astounding speeds. Then a blue, green, and white-capped ball grew in size. I flew down into it, though clouds, and toward the city in the hills. I shot straight for my body without slowing down, until I slammed into it like sunlight into a flower.

I felt half dead, like some force crammed me back into my broken shell. I jerked as sparks shot through me and my heart pumped. I felt the wounds seal and strength returning to my body. I opened my eyes and sat up.

Guards with mouths open wide stood before me and backed away. Some women screamed and fainted in the crowd. Gabrielle and Seth stared at me wide-eyed. Shock turned to joy. Then they sprinted to me. Gabrielle flung her arms around me and held me tightly.

I smiled. I felt a little taste of Paradise in her love. "Why so surprised? I said I would come back for you."

"Sisko…" Seth stood over me with a giant grin on his face. "This has got to be the most amazing miracle I've seen you do yet."

I chuckled. "I didn't do it. But even if I had, it is nothing compared to the miracle you two have done for me." I squeezed her tighter. "You've literally redeemed me with your love. With God's love."

As I hugged her, I saw the ring on my finger, sparkling in the sunlight. I released her and pulled at the ring. It didn't budge. "Looks like God's not done with me yet."

She frowned.

I shook my head. "Oh no, this time what God has for me involves you. Will you marry me?"

Her face lit up. She flung herself onto me. "Oh yes, yes I will marry you!"

I knew nothing in this world could compare with the love I experienced in Paradise, but hers was amazingly close. Very close, indeed.

I couldn't wait to discover what God had planned for us next.

After serving as a minister in two churches, marrying a life-long partner in 1982, helping to give birth and raise three wonderful children, and work his way up to an experienced bookkeeper and now financial officer for a Texas city, what would be the next challenge for R. L. Copple? He discovered in 2005 a passion for writing fantasy and space opera. Since October of 2005, R. L. Copple has published numerous short stories and flash fictions at magazines such as Dragons, Knights, and Angels, Everyday Fiction, Digital Dragon, and Resident Aliens—a complete list can be discovered at his website: www.rlcopple.com/published.php.

He has written more than seven novels and saw a novella and novel published by Double-Edged Publishing, and now *Reality's Dawn* and *Reality's Ascent* are being published at Splashdown Books, to be followed by the third and final book, *Reality's Glory*. Be sure to follow blog.rlcopple.com for the latest updates.

The Reality Chronicles
by R.L. Copple

Reality's Dawn
Reality's Ascent
Reality's Glory

Coming in April 2011
from Splashdown Books:

The Crystal Portal
by Travis Perry and Mike Lynch

And Yeshua said,
"His ears will be a sign to you."

A time-travelling warrior elf on a
manhunt for an evil genius.
A state-of-the-art robot from New
Los Angeles. And a carpenter's son
from first-century Israel.
Entering the Portal to the Crystal
World, they join forces with a
princess of Sapphire City to defy
their power-mad adversary.

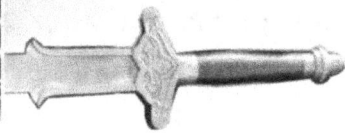

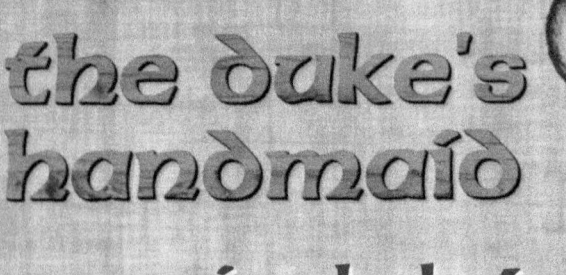

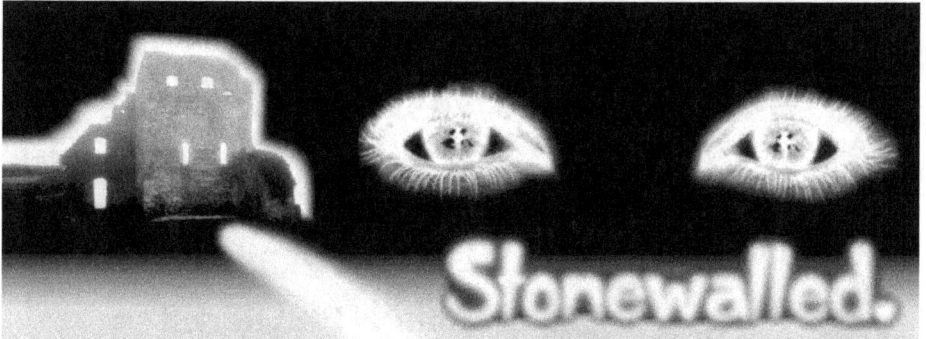

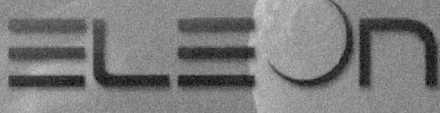